PENGUIN BOOKS
THE HOUSE WITH A THOUSAND STORIES

Aruni Kashyap is a writer and translator. He is the author of the novel *The House with a Thousand Stories* (Penguin Books, 2013). Aruni is also a translator from the Assamese, and wrote the introduction for celebrated writer Indira Goswami's last work of fiction, *The Bronze Sword of Thengphakhri Tehsildar*, for Zubaan Books (2013). He won the Charles Wallace India Trust Scholarship for Creative Writing, the University of Edinburgh, in 2009, and his unpublished poetry collection, *There Is No Good Time for Bad News*, was a finalist for the Marsh Hawk Press Poetry Prize and the Four Way Books Levis Award in Poetry, both in 2018. His short stories, poems and essays have appeared or are forthcoming in various journals and anthologies, including *The Oxford Anthology of Writings from North-East India*, the *Kenyon Review*, the *New York Times*, the *Guardian*, *The Hindu*, *Joyland Magazine*, *Evergreen Review* and others. He is an assistant professor of creative writing at the University of Georgia, Athens.

PRAISE FOR THE BOOK

'Aruni Kashyap's narrative prose has the compulsive assurance of a master storyteller'—Namita Gokhale

'Unflinching and tender'—LiveMint

'Evocative and somewhat surreal'—*DNA India*

'One of the most original and honest voices from contemporary India'—CNN-News18

'An achievement for a first novel'—*Indian Express*

'Every work of literature asks one question: How do "stories" originate? This young writer sets out to answer this question by putting question marks instead of full stops to punctuate the history of his people'—*India Today*

'A haunting and poignant story'—Women's Web

'[An] abiding sense of hurt and separateness from the Indian state permeates *The House with a Thousand Stories* . . . [Kashyap's] tactile prose, beautifully flawed characters . . . brings to life and empathy a little-known corner of the region'—*Elle*

'It is remarkable that Kashyap has been able to weave the theme of the insurgency and the consequent extrajudicial killings in Assam in the 1990s deftly into the everyday lives of his protagonists'—*Frontline*

'*The House with a Thousand Stories* leaves one with the feeling that something is irretrievably lost, and yet, as the entrancing, languorous love scene at the end suggests, there is much beauty, more rarefied for being so transient, strained out in the process'—*New Indian Express*

'Kashyap brings home the reality of the terror that his characters live with'—*Daily News & Analysis*

The House with a Thousand Stories

Aruni Kashyap

PENGUIN BOOKS

An imprint of Penguin Random House

PENGUIN BOOKS

USA | Canada | UK | Ireland | Australia
New Zealand | India | South Africa | China | Singapore

Penguin Books is part of the Penguin Random House group of companies
whose addresses can be found at global.penguinrandomhouse.com

Published by Penguin Random House India Pvt. Ltd
4th Floor, Capital Tower 1, MG Road,
Gurugram 122 002, Haryana, India

Penguin
Random House
India

First published in Viking by Penguin Books India 2013

10 9 8 7 6 5 4 3 2

ISBN 9780143450016

For sale in South Asia only

Typeset in Dante MT by R. Ajith Kumar, New Delhi

Printed at Repro India Limited

www.penguin.co.in

MIX
Paper from
responsible sources
FSC® C047271

This is a legitimate digitally printed version of the book and therefore might not
have certain extra finishing on the cover.

For
Ma and Pita

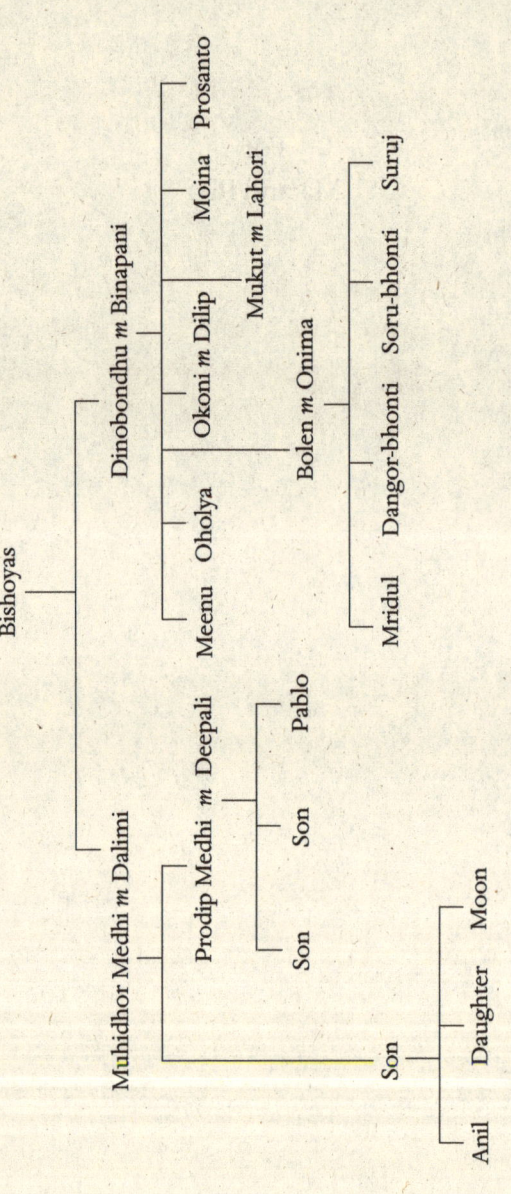

One

When my cousin Anil-da started telling us what he'd heard at the market about the groom's family, at my aunt Moina-pehi's wedding in January 2002, his eyes shone like inky marbles reflecting sunlight. Nonetheless, he made a sad face, pouting and hanging his head. An expression I expected him to conjure up when he started saying, 'Should I say this at all? I don't want more drama because of me . . .'

Rumours arrive at a wedding like unwanted guests. Sometimes old, hoary, hunchbacked women who enjoy spreading bad news bring them. Sometimes old men who have nothing better to do, and sometimes even young men or women, who love to pull the strings and watch a new scene in the large wedding drama, usher them in.

So there was nothing to be scared of. But as usual—as it happens with every rumour involving the groom's family—people were scared. The women were the most animated. 'My God, what will happen to poor Moina now?' They sucked their teeth and listed various horrible things that could happen to her.

A while later, as Anil-da narrated the story, he froze at least seven people who were busy doing different things for the wedding, busy playing their small roles in the larger drama—

peeling off a large heap of betel nuts and slicing them; cutting the pointed cone-like tips and tails of the heart-shaped, dark-green betel leaves; mixing water with limestone, to be served with the betel nuts. The maids were mopping the courtyard and the veranda with algae-green cow dung mixed with white soil brought from the bank of Pokoria River.

Oholya-jethai—my father's maternal cousin and the bride's elder sister—was forever ready for gossip. She was the first one to react. She stopped pounding betel nuts and leaves with the dark-brown iron pestle and craned her neck towards him. 'Why wouldn't you tell us? Tell us what you've heard,' she demanded in her loud, booming voice.

Surprisingly, I was glad to see her usual curious and domineering self back at least for the moment. And sitting beside Anamika on the veranda, a little away from Oholya-jethai, I realized—against my wishes—that I loved, indeed preferred, the scary, petty, prying Oholya-jethai. Not the quiet, secluded one we had been seeing for the past few days. She had been depressed—a recluse for the last few days after what happened while her brother Mukut-khura was digging the earth one night after dinner. After that episode, the bitter, forever-prying, annoying, questioning, unpopular Oholya-jethai all of us were familiar with had suddenly vanished. It was as if her earlier avatar took it for granted that just as the clock would chime thrice when it was three, and leaves would fall when the wind would rise, it was natural for rumours to intrude into a wedding.

Anil-da's story was one such rumour. You couldn't avoid it, though you knew that such rumours should be avoided. They shouldn't be discussed and dissected, brooded and cried over.

Anil-da had created this tense situation with his ability to inspire curiosity. He wanted people to ask him questions. He wanted them to be afraid, to think that the wedding might not take place at all.

He'd returned from the market with coloured papers to decorate the wedding tent, which was made of thick, green-and-red cloth. It had a tall, fat banana plant in the middle as the main pillar. The entrance was made of the trunks of two large banana plants near a bamboo gate. Long, golden-yellow marigold garlands hung from them—some of them had red centres. Both the banana plants drooped towards each other like two people exchanging greetings, bowing. Their soft, thick, leafy vines were tied with a coir rope in the middle to form an arch.

It was afternoon on the day of the *juron*—the day before the wedding. The women from the groom's family had just left after anointing the bride with a paste made of turmeric and pulses and dressing her up in the new clothes sent by the groom. They had given her five silk dresses, a set of gold ornaments, a make-up kit, two large packs of Pond's face powder, Charmis cold cream, two lipsticks—one red, like the stains of betel nut on old women's lips, and the other soft pink, like a cow's salt-hungry tongue (Anamika had said to me the previous night that a lipstick looks like a dog's penis, and we had laughed so much)—one large bottle of fragrant coconut oil, footwear, bras (some of them had lace), panties, soap, toothbrush, toothpaste and handkerchiefs.

After the juron, she would not wear anything given to her by her own family. She could not take anything to her husband's house either.

Some of the girls were still singing juron songs:

Ram-Ram, take off the ornaments from our mother's house,
Ram-Ram, wear the ones from your husband's house.

Ram-Ram, take off the clothes your father gave,
Ram-Ram, wear the ones your father-in-law gave.

Ram-Ram, depend no more on your father's earnings,
Ram-Ram, like starflowers are your mother-in-law's earrings.

Onima-borma, Moina-pehi's elder sister-in-law, was scaling the large borali fish by moving it left–right, left–right as she warned the curious children not to come too near lest they stain their clothes with fish blood. Okoni-pehi sat beside her, disembowelling the massive heap of medium-sized, peepul-leaf-shaped puthi fish for dinner. Okoni-pehi was as sharp-tongued as her elder sister Oholya, but she wasn't the kind of person who sniffed around for gossip to raise a mountain out of a molehill. A few years ago, she was married to a lower-primary school teacher in the village, who lived just a few houses down the road. She visited almost every day and that was why, though she was married off, no one missed her. She was always there to take care of many things in the household she was supposed to have left for good after her wedding.

From the veranda, I could still hear the sudden squeals of laughter from the room where all the young girls had gathered. Someone was perhaps teasing someone—that soon she will be also married off—and the girl who was being teased must have blushed, encouraging the other girls to burst out laughing. Or someone must have pinched the bride's breast. She must have screamed and they must have asked what she would do when the groom would bite her nipples on the wedding night, darkening the already dark tips. I wondered if they were Moina-pehi's friends who had arrived a few days ago.

Mukut-khura had sent Anil-da to buy coloured papers from the market. He put them down with a huff on the table that stood on the veranda. The table was covered with a green, embroidered cloth, woven in the handloom by one of the many women of the house. He said, 'Ah, please give me a glass of water. I think my head is spinning. I heard some terrible things.'

Seven figures froze.

~

Oholya-jethai was always the first one to react. She loved gossip and I wondered if that was because she was the subject of the biggest gossip in Hatimura Village, Mayong, many years ago. And I was glad—in spite of the restlessness inside me, in spite of the rage and loneliness inside me—that she was once again on the verge of switching back to her unpopular self.

I had developed this strange sorrow that morning, and it was gnawing at my heart. But Oholya-jethai had acquired her sadness many years ago, when she was young—the perfect beauty with puffy eyes, large buttocks and long, black hair, fit to be the subject of the biggest gossip in Hatimura Village.

'I wasn't born then,' Papa says when Mom asks him what happened with Oholya-jethai. But, apparently, my grandmother, who I called Aaita, never agreed with him. 'You were born by then. I remember carrying you on my back for six miles to reach Mayong. We walked to your mamee's house that year. In those days, the only way to reach Mayong was by foot. People used to refer to Mayong as Kalapaani.' After saying this in a decisive tone, she would stand up and say 'OK' and Papa would know that the conversation was over because whenever my grandmother stood up and said 'OK', at the end of a sentence after a little pause, it meant she didn't want to discuss the topic any further. No one risked riling her up.

These conversations used to take place when Aaita was alive. Many years ago. She was always ready to go to her youngest brother's house in Hatimura, Mayong. Shortly before she died, her yearning for her mother's village, Hatimura, had turned into a compulsion. During her last days, she kept saying, 'Please take me back to Mayong. I want to bathe in the Pokoria River.' She was obsessed with Mayong and we used to laugh at her obsession.

Hatimura was less accessible than the village my grandmother was married into—Teteliguri, which was around forty-four kilometres away from Guwahati. Hatimura was my father's maternal uncles' village. Mridul was my father's first cousin's son. It was the death of Mridul's father, in 1998, that had brought us together for the first time, when the road from Guwahati to Mayong via Chandrapur wasn't even conceptualized in the dusty, prehistoric offices of the Assam Secretariat. Mayong was still a 'remote' place, though it wasn't too far away from the big city, Guwahati. In order to reach Mayong, you needed various means of transport. From Guwahati, you had to take the bus to Kolongpar, from where you would take a bicycle and ride for miles, and then walk for hours because most of the *kuchcha* road didn't allow even two-wheelers to ply on it. During summer, when the monsoon winds brought incessant rain, people went to Mayong in boats from Kolongpar. But still, I loved going there. So did my father. But when we visited Mayong in the winter of '98, we drove our car through meandering paths that took us much longer. Papa didn't want to use public transport. He wanted to take his car. 'Thankfully, the roads are just potholed, not broken,' he murmured several times.

My father, a strong and proud man who would not express his love even to his children, cried when he heard that Mridul's father, Bolen-bortta, had died. 'They were very close. They were not cousins; they were best friends,' Mom whispered to me in the dining room, while I sipped tea silently that evening. Papa was in his bedroom. I could sense an unnatural silence had descended on the house.

On the way to Mridul's house, while he drove us in the new Maruti Esteem, which had just come into the market, Papa told Mom and me about Bolen-bortta, who had died after years of alcoholism. His liver gave way. He vomited blood one day and died on the way to the hospital, Papa was telling Mom. And I knew she knew all of it, but he still told her. In a deadpan tone, as if he were reading the news on a government TV channel. As if he were a newsreader telling us how militants came and massacred hundreds who had taken shelter in a camp after prolonged ethnic riots.

In fact, he was telling *me*. He told me through Mom. Mom always said, since I was a child, 'You must listen to your papa. Without your papa you wouldn't have been born this way.' I never understood what 'this way' meant. I never asked. I was too embarrassed to do so. At the time Bolen-bortta died, I used to think 'this way' meant having too many pimples. Later, during Moina-pehi's wedding in 2002, I thought it meant that I was five feet seven inches tall, had thick, black, shiny hair like Papa, which I found difficult to run combs through, and had a large, fat, ugly toe just like his. I never tried to decode Mom's mysterious 'this way' after that.

Papa was telling the story of how they used to play. And how Bolen-bortta had proclaimed, after looking at the photograph of Mom with prominent curved sideburns and stretched eyes, 'This should be my *nobou*.' Mom added with a faint smile, her body reclining against the backseat of the car, 'Maybe your papa wouldn't have married me if I had not been approved by his best friend.' Outside the trees were running away from us. Inside the car, it was warm and the atmosphere solemn.

Papa's best friend. What did that mean? Was their friendship like what I shared with Probal? Did they watch porn together? Did they even get porn during those days? Did they have wet dreams at night that made them want to go to the doctor? Who must have laughed then? In my case, it was Probal who had laughed. He knew so much more than me.

'You don't *see* anything?'

'Good boys shouldn't watch porn.'

'Everybody watches porn. Even your father did. Otherwise you wouldn't have been born.' He rolled his eyes. According to him, watching pornography was an indispensable step in the process of producing children.

'Was it Sabina you saw in your dream?' he asked. I laughed and thought of the large buttocks of our classmate Sabina. She didn't walk. She danced. Her buttocks swaying left and right, left and right. Like Onima-borma scaling the large borali fish brought by the groom's relatives on the day of the juron.

'Was it Sabina you saw in your dream?' Did Bolen-bortta ask Papa something like that as well? Same question, but with a different name. In Assamese, not English. Did they speak about who they saw themselves having sex with in their dreams? He didn't tell me. He couldn't have told me. Of course. I felt my cheeks burning. And I knew my ears were red too. Not because he was my father but because I was already embarrassed that he was speaking about how he selected Mom from a range of photographs due to her prominent sword-like sideburns and stretched eyes. 'That was the fashion in those days. Zeenat Aman had just arrived like a fresh breeze blazing the silver screen, you know? But we didn't copy her. We were good girls.' Mom added, 'I went to watch *Bobby* with your papa, and guess what? He wanted to take Bolen-kai too! At last he sent Bolen-kai with his wife for the next show because I had refused to go.' Mom was not happy telling us all this. She was speaking in a deadpan tone. Husky. There was no excitement in her voice. Though she spoke, reminisced, I thought she was actually silent. That it was all a slow dream. 'It was hilarious. She almost died blushing. She wouldn't speak to your papa after coming back, for sending her to watch such a "shameless" film!' *Bobby* was a film that many parents didn't let their children watch when it was released in 1973.

Why wouldn't a rural housewife who never took off her veil in front of Papa be ashamed if sent to watch *Bobby*? Apparently she didn't watch the film and had a prolonged fight with Bolen-bortta for watching the whole film in the hall from which she pleaded throughout to be allowed to escape. No wonder she lectured on the 'corrupting influence' of Hindi films so much, and didn't ever allow a television in the house. At least till Moina-pehi's wedding. Even on the day of the wedding, the family members (extended and immediate) who wanted to 'have a little fun' with back-to-back screening of Hindi and Assamese films had to bring a Philips VCD player on rent from the market. Borrow the Onida twelve-inch colour television from Bolen-bortta's youngest brother Prosanto's colleague Manob, who worked in the local Mayong College. Certain excesses were allowed, even at the cost of 'corrupting influences'. After all, it was a wedding. A wedding was taking place after a long time in the family. A wedding interrupted by the news that Anil-da brought in with the coloured papers.

The year Bolen-bortta died was also the year when we bought the Maruti Esteem (though our driver had said the car would be discontinued very soon) just because Papa fell in love with it. Like wine bottles, Papa loved cars too and changed them whimsically. A few weeks before Bolen-bortta died, Papa had called him up and told him he might visit him during Magh Bihu—mid-January—in his new car, and had asked him to keep a 'fat duck' ready for him. Bolen-bortta didn't know what a Maruti Esteem looked like, though he had seen Ambassadors, since the local MLA, Bikas Gogoi, who was also his brother Mukut's friend, always moved around in the village in one. So Papa explained: 'Do you remember Hiren's car? That's a Maruti 800. Our car is made by the same company, but it's flat and dark green in colour and has a longer nose. And it's almost black.'

In Hatimura, only Hiren needed and could afford a Maruti since he was a SULFA member. The SULFA were surrendered ULFA rebels. The ULFA wanted a separate country called Asom and wanted to free Assam from what they called Indian imperialism, so they fought with Indian forces with guns, bombs, AK-47 rifles, kidnappings, op-eds, books published under pseudonyms and jingoistic music albums released abruptly that had words like 'sun', 'blood' and 'sacrifice' in their titles. The SULFA owned a lot of the business enterprises in the state, since they got large bundles of notes from the generous Assam government as compensation when they surrendered arms and went back to the 'mainstream'. Everyone in our village was scared of the SULFA since they carried carbines and AK-47s with them all the time and roamed around everywhere at will; apparently they needed these to protect themselves. People also said that they were allowed to do so by the government, since the ULFA were jealous of the SULFA's nouveau-riche status. While the

ULFA suffered from jaundice, malaria, mokhlong fever, hunger, rain, sun and malnutrition, fighting for the cause of Assam's independence from India, the SULFA basked in their wealth. No wonder the ULFA wanted to kill them.

All the papers wrote about the ULFA. What they did; how they killed people; how they were killed themselves; how they set up schools and libraries; how they didn't drink alcohol and punished alcoholics in villages; how they respected women; how they prepared young students in remote villages for their matriculation exams because there were no government schools in those places; how they set up hospitals in remote villages where the jeeps, guns, bombs or even the army of the Indian government couldn't reach, since there were no roads.

But everyone only spoke about the SULFA, didn't write about them. How they roamed around carrying guns. How they married whomever they wanted to, since the girl's family didn't have the courage to refuse them (even if they did, the SULFA would take the girl away by force). How they started new business enterprises and generated employment for the local youth. How friendly they were with the political leaders. How they gave out information about the ULFA and conspired to kill them or to force them to surrender and take large bundles of notes from the government to become rich businessmen. How some of them were so respectful to women that no goons and roadside Romeos from nearby villages dared to even whistle at the girls in that area. No one wrote about the SULFA except in a few short stories that Mom read out to me where they were referred to as 'surrendered rebels'. She suggested that I must start reading Assamese fiction too.

I had met Mridul only once until Bolen-bortta's death. He had come to attend my grandmother's funeral in Teteliguri in 1993.

On the day of the fish-touching feast—*matsya-sporsho*—we were so bored of the chanting of *montros* and people praying that Aaita be happy up there that we went to the village stream and sat there with our legs dipped in the flowing water. We were startled by tiny fish nibbling at our legs. I shivered when the water sped past between my toes. It was winter.

'What if the snakes get us?'

'They don't come near human beings. And they are all hibernating now.'

Mridul was the first person who told me that snakes didn't chase human beings but attacked only if someone disturbed them. 'I have passed by many snakes. They didn't do a thing to me. You'll just have to go on your way without disturbing them and you'll be safe.' I thought he was the bravest guy in the world. I wanted to ask him if he would be my 'best friend' but didn't, since, from the first day of school, it was Probal who I sat with, shared my tiffin with, and one day we had made our best-friendship official by shaking hands while sitting on the last bench of the class. 'We are best friends from today,' we had told each other. Probal would be offended if I asked another person to become my best friend.

Back home, everyone was looking for us. Oholya-jethai, who had come all the way from Hatimura, as soon as she had heard about Aaita's illness, scolded us. As usual, she had taken it upon herself to scream at all the wrongs, create panic and terror and be at the centre of attention. When she saw us, she yelled, 'What if a tiger had come?'

I didn't know whether tigers chased human beings—though I saw in films that they did, but so did snakes—so I kept quiet.

Mridul had muddled up all my ideas about the animal kingdom. Even bees recognized their owners and wouldn't sting them. If you left a beehive facing east all day, the bees would sting anyone. They become a very angry group of bees then, and people say their honey turns thicker and sweeter. Mridul told me all this while we let our toes be inspected by shoals of fish, which I found so funny. Compared to that, my father's tonsured head on the occasion of Aaita's funeral was less funny.

Anyway, when Papa, with his tonsured head, asked me where I had been, I said, 'I was sitting with Mridul. He was telling me something about snakes.'

To my surprise, and much to Oholya-jethai's astonishment, Papa just said, 'Let it be. My children should know the place where I grew up. No tiger chased me and ate me up. My son will be safe too. Is he the only child who is roaming about?'

I saw Oholya-jethai's lips curling like a bow. She was looking at me. She kept looking at me. I thought she'd poison my tea. I imagined myself retching blood and Mom crying over my dead body. I sunk into a depression instantly.

'Prodip.' She looked sternly at Papa.

There were very few people who could look at Papa like that. Or would use his first name. Even his childhood friends called him 'Sir'. He would scold them, ask them not to, but they wouldn't listen. Whenever we stayed in Teteliguri for a long time at Aaita's place during festivals, I would find Papa sitting with his boyhood friends, a *gamusa* wrapped around his waist not longer than his knees, eating coconut. They chatted about tribals in Teteliguri selling land to city-businessmen. He urged them to try and put an end to such a trend. 'Where will *our* people go?' he said. And I liked the way he said 'our people', though we were not tribals. 'The times have changed. You can't go and settle in any place now without buying land. Everything is owned either by the government or the people. We must avert the invasion of Guwahati City! We must preserve our natural beauty! Don't sell your land!' I would find them calling him by his first name then. 'Prodip, you are right!' They used '*toi*' to address him then, the informal pronoun used only between intimate friends, unlike the '*apuni*' used to address elders, or people one is not close to. But each time he went back to his ancestral village in a new car, Papa would have to go back to trying to get them to call him '*Hei* Prodip' instead of 'Sir'.

Oholya-jethai was one of the very few people who could tell Papa to his face, 'Prodip, you'd better stop gossiping with them and come and eat your lunch'—that sort of thing.

Papa turned back towards the woman who I thought would poison my tea if she got half a chance. His glance meant, 'Yes?'

'It was my duty to point out. Keeping children in rein is always a good thing. Don't blame me later that I didn't warn you.'

He smiled warmly. It erased all tension and the creases on my uncles' foreheads that were perhaps the result of the apprehension of an impending verbal war between Oholya-jethai and Papa.

Oholya-jethai was not someone who liked to be contradicted. She was used to being listened to. She was used to nodding heads.

'No, I won't, Oholya-bai,' Papa told her. But I still thought she'd poison my rice, if not my tea, which she boiled with aromatic bay leaves, ginger and lots of milk. Everyone praised her tea.

~

The trees were running away from us as we entered Hatimura.

Papa had stopped telling Mom about Bolen-bortta, *Bobby* and how it was suggested that he should marry Mom because she had nice, prominent, sword-like sideburns and was 'MA passed'.

The trees were running away from us, but not the dust. It stuck to our car like dewdrops on leaves and left a white film over it.

Later in the afternoon, under the slanting rays of the yellow winter sun, I would write my name on the back of the car: Pablo. Prachurjya Medhi. Mridul would cross it out, smiling. I would think he wanted to write his name too. He, too, wanted to feel a car. It was not often that people saw cars in Hatimura. I would find naked, half-naked, and milky-mucus-dripping-mucus-congealing children whispering 'gadi, gadi'. Car, car.

I would feel ashamed of myself for feeling superior for having a car. Not only could I write my name in the film of dust covering it, but also sit inside the car, put on the cassette player if I wanted to. I was stricken to identify Mridul's quivering eagerness to feel the car, to touch it, to sit inside it, to cross out my name written in the dust that covered its body.

Later, when I would go with Mridul to cover the car with a large sheet of tarpaulin before going to bed, I would see many names inscribed in the film of dust. Palm impressions. So many that they'd look like the lines on a palm: indecipherable. Lines that you couldn't follow. I'd feel confused and recall the map of Assam, criss-crossed by so many blue lines that I could never count how many rivers flowed like blue veins through my state.

That Papa wanted Mridul and I to be friends, even if not the closest of friends, was evident the next day, when Mridul wouldn't let me leave Mayong. Oholya-jethai screamed at him, saying that was not the right way to behave—he might not study, he might roam around all day, and since he did not have his father any more to force him to study, he'd soon ruin his own life. But he should allow his cousin to go back to Guwahati in the green Maruti car, almost black.

My mother took her aside. 'Oholya-bai, be kind to the poor fatherless boy!' We could hear her whisper.

Mridul looked distraught. I felt that if I said that I preferred to go back, that I had my vacation homework to complete, he'd give back everything he had hidden. My watch, my bag, my shoes. He'd let me go with a heavy heart.

But Papa gave the final verdict. 'He will stay.'

He looked at me and said in English—at which Oholya-jethai commented dismissively, 'Who knows what the father–son are saying in *Engrazee*'—'You should stay.'

I tried to sound calm and answered back in English, 'I have a lot to do. I've got all those Agatha Christies to read and the books you got me from Panbozar. And I'm halfway through . . .'

'I think you can read them later. What you will learn here, you won't learn anywhere else, ever.'

'And my clothes? I just have a pyjama and two pairs of jeans and two T-shirts.' I was embarrassed to say that I had only two briefs. I think Mridul understood those English sentences. '*Arrey, mur kapur pindhi lobi?*' He offered his spare clothes.

'I will leave some money with your uncle Mukut. He will buy you new clothes from the market here.' And then he smiled very strangely. 'But they won't be branded clothes. Well, I never wore them either.'

I was surprised. Seeing Papa so happy and friendly was beyond my expectations. Papas don't smile like that at their sons. Papas don't behave like friends with their sons. Papas aren't dramatic. Papas don't cry.

Two

In 2002, when Moina-pehi's wedding took place, I was old enough to go to Mayong alone. When I heard Mridul would be coming to invite us and we would go for the wedding, I jumped with joy at the thought of going there after so long. The last time I had gone there was in 1998, when Mridul's father had passed away. But though I had stayed back, I had to leave abruptly after a few weeks because of certain developments in the village that worried my parents.

When Mridul arrived with a bunch of invitation cards to distribute among relatives in the city just before the winter vacation, I didn't want to think about what happened the last time I was in Mayong. I didn't want to think about the smell of shit and blood, the cries, the heart-piercing wails. I sealed them away from my thoughts as a mother hides memories of her lost child in a secret chamber of her mind. I wanted to think about the wedding of 2002, not the funeral of 1998.

Mridul offered betel nuts and leaves with each invite. Like a responsible representative of the family, he bowed before each invitee and it was difficult for me not to laugh out loud when he did the same to Papa—who frowned at me. I couldn't tell why it was funny. Maybe I wasn't prepared to see Mridul behaving like a grown-up. I knew the Mridul who could sing songs. I knew the dimpled Mridul on whom girls had crushes, who played the *dhool* in the village school for me, who wanted to make sure I got the best of village life even though I had gone there to attend a funeral. But that Mridul wasn't serious like this Mridul. That Mridul was affectionate, playful, naughty, boastful of the female attention he got.

He reached our house in Guwahati on a windy day when the coconut trees around our house were swaying, as if saying 'no, no'. The red-rose bush that was blooming near our large iron gate was nearly ripped apart by the wind; the red petals were strewn in front of the gate when he stepped on to our compound. He must have felt bad trampling over them. There was something forlorn about that windy day though he had come to invite us to a wedding. He didn't look very excited either. The air smelled of dust.

Mridul and I had not been in touch all these years.

The last time we met was when his father had passed away, when I had met most of my extended family for the first time, observed them and judged them like a primary-school teacher frowning upon the uncut nails of children. I couldn't understand their strange behaviour. It was only with Mridul I felt an unconditional bond of friendship. During the mourning period following his father's death, Mridul and I would sit down together and sing songs. I found it absurd in the beginning—that we were singing in a house that was grieving. He'd proceed, twanging his guitar, to produce a soft melody. '*I can't be darkness, and I don't want to erase; the open-winged past, then how do I forget?*' He'd hum these lines from a popular Zubeen Garg song.

Though Mridul and I hadn't been in touch, I felt we still shared the same strong bond the moment I saw him. We couldn't stop smiling when we saw each other. I didn't hug him. I thought that would be too dramatic. I thought *I* might want to hug him, but what if *he* didn't feel the same way?

He smiled more than he was supposed to as he said, 'Moina-pehi's wedding has been fixed *at last.*' I had to think for a while when he mentioned her name. I tried to remember who she was. I thought deeply and a light-skinned broad face that always had a smile on the lips, a voice that peppered every sentence with nasal sounds like 'eeesh' and 'eeeh', came to my mind. She was cheerful. But there was something dejected and distant about her. Although she was much older, she didn't belong to the world of aunts bound by rules of propriety. Rather, she belonged to our world of guitars, love letters, Zubeen Garg and A.R. Rahman.

When Mom started talking to Mridul, the reason why Mridul had such a serious expression on his face became clear to me.

I was noticing how Mridul had changed: he had the air of old men who thought girls were burdens that increased in size and weight as time passed. Even the guard didn't ask him any questions, or call our landline to ask if he should let someone called Mridul, from Hatimura, enter the house. Mridul had changed: badly tanned from working in the fields, he had lost the fair, bright complexion I used to be so envious of. Over the course of the day, I would observe that the eagerness in him to groom himself with regular shaving, after which he rubbed a small piece of alum over his face, had vanished like camphor exposed to air. He had passed the second year of his undergraduate degree and was in the third year now. But his marks were not good enough; he didn't have an honours degree since he had no time to study for one. He had started going to the fields along with Mukut-khura, who taught at the village school. Last year, Mridul had applied for a post in the school his father worked at, on compensatory grounds, but nothing was working out, and he had already spent around fifty thousand rupees bribing various officers in Guwahati, and also the local MLA, who always spoke to Mukut-khura when he visited Hatimura, since they used to go to watch *jaatra* plays together during Lakshmi Puja and also run away from school together to eat sour green mangoes. Mukut-khura spoke proudly of those shared memories with Bikas Gogoi. So, when Bikas Gogoi said they would have to spend some money, Mukut-khura was really surprised; but he soon said that after all there were people above Bikas as well who had to be mollified.

Mridul told Mom, 'Ma was very anxious until everything was fixed.' He sat on the sofa and continued without waiting for anyone to speak, 'Okoni-pehi had exhausted all her resources in getting a match for her. Finally, Dorongi-aaita found a match for her.'

Mom asked immediately, 'Dorongi-aaita?'

'My maternal grandmother. She never went back after Deuta passed away. She has lived with us since 1998. My mother is her only daughter-*je* . . .'

Mom said, 'I'm so glad to hear that Moina is getting married finally! *Our* Moina is a pretty and talented girl. Please don't be offended Mridul—but your uncles took too long to fix her wedding. Pablo's father would often worry if she too would turn out to be an old maid in that house. Okoni was married almost at forty. Oholya-bai never married. I will never believe it if they tell me that there are no matches to be found for a girl from the Bishoya family and though Oholya-bai was the subject of gossip, she has a very respectable position in the village now. Your grandfather Dinobondhu Bishoya was a freedom fighter, Mridul—yes, he didn't follow the ideals of Gandhi and resorted to violence, but, still, it ensures respect from seven villages around for your family for another two generations at least.'

She took a breath and went on before a silent Mridul, 'I don't know how both your uncles, Mukut and Prosanto, had the heart to wait for this long, to not bother at all about the youngest daughter of the house when a living example such as their elder sister has always stood in front of them. Oholya-bai was more beautiful than Moina, and much more talented. Pablo's father says, Mridul, there was no one like her in seven villages around.'

'Well, Prosanto-da is too preoccupied with his own world. He has no time to think about his unmarried elder sister,' he said hesitantly, in a sarcastic tone.

'What happened? He is a responsible boy, Mridul, isn't he? I hope he is not planning to join some militant organization, is he? There are too many around the state.' Mom raised her voice—'I just can't understand what's wrong with all the highly educated young men in this place! Once upon a time, there used to be only the ULFA. People used to feel proud of them. Relatives used to whisper to their jealous neighbours that their son or daughter had joined the ULFA, pride gleaming in their eyes. But what happened? The army came and broke everyone's spine. And now we have so many organizations: ulfa-sulfa-malta-santa-kanta-and-whatnot!' Mom sounded worried and irritated and impatient and shrill. 'Tell me, Mridul, instead of looking away.'

I thanked God Papa wasn't around. He would have said that her middle-class upbringing wouldn't help her understand these things. That she wouldn't be able to understand (he would lay stress on 'understand') why a bunch of young men in their teens and early twenties had left their bright careers to go to the forests of Burma with nothing but the dream of overthrowing Indian rule in Assam. They died like flies, he would go on, until

Mom would make a face, looking as if she were holding a large amount of water in her mouth—her cheeks forming two rotund mini domes.

Prosanto was my father's first cousin, Mukut-khura's younger brother. He was the youngest, tallest and fairest among Papa's cousins. When he kept aside the knee-length dhoti on the wooden clothes horse in his room and wore jeans and formal shirts to go to Guwahati or to his college to teach, he reminded me of Hindi and Assamese film heroes from black-and-white films who sported finely combed and carefully trimmed moustaches. Familiar with the songs of Zubeen Garg and A.R. Rahman, he belonged more to our world—Mridul's and mine. Of guitars, of the latest Hindi films, of the latest compositions by A.R. Rahman and that was why I called him 'Prosanto-da' instead of 'Prosanto-khura'. How could I address someone as young as him as 'khura'? He didn't even have a pot belly like Mukut-khura! Prosanto-da usually stayed away from Mridul, trying to keep some distance as his 'uncle'. But sometimes, when I was there last, for instance, he would sit down with me for a chat when Mridul wasn't around. I was much younger when he used to visit us during his student days in Guwahati. He'd always bring me chocolates. Maybe that was why I could relate to him a lot. Since he had studied in Guwahati, I felt an affinity with him; we had common things to talk about. But he surprised me often by saying things like 'It's good that you can speak English so well, so many things become easier in this country if you know that language. I wish I could speak English as well. I wouldn't be stuck here then.'

Did Mom notice his frustration? That though he was highly educated, he was stuck in a village that was so close to Guwahati where nothing happened in terms of progress. Not even the roads were good enough to get out of the village.

One evening, when we were having tea, he told me not to stay on in Assam. He said that I should go to America or London for higher studies as soon as I could and never come back. Things were becoming worse each day, a lot of his former classmates had joined the ULFA, and more people were joining every day. The army killed a few; both the government and the rebels were just killing people. His voice became slightly louder and he asked, 'Is this a revolution? Will it help Assam secede from India?' Keeping aside my cup of tea, I asked him why he hadn't joined the organization, why he didn't dream of a free Assam, and he said he would have loved to, that sometimes he felt frustrated since, for the last five years, he had been trying to get Mayong College—the college he founded with some of his friends—nationalized, but their file would just not move through the labyrinths of bureaucracy. At every stage, they needed to pay the concerned officer. He said, sooner or later, I would face a similar predicament as well if I chose to stay on in India, work in India and grow old in India. Sooner or later, if I loved my state, I would discover why Assam was rich in natural resources but one of the poorest states in the country; why Assam was the richest province in British India and one of the poorest states in independent India. He said all this before walking away. I looked at his straight, glistening back and puzzled about many things. But I remember, though he was unhappy, though he was complaining, Prosanto-da hadn't walked with a slouch. He told me all these things in a nonchalant tone. He wasn't agitated. In a way, he had accepted his plight as a way of life and perhaps that was why he could live with it.

What was wrong with Prosanto-da now? Was he planning to join the ULFA? Mom's suspicions couldn't be unfounded.

But Mridul wasn't replying. It was as if he was embarrassed

about something. As if, he wanted to tell us, and yet, he wasn't sure if we should know it. Mridul fixed his gaze on the floor, on the intricate design of the carpet.

Mom was still looking at him, anticipating a reply.

He took some time to speak up. 'Maybe he would listen to you.' He said slowly, 'Speak to him when you come for the wedding. He wants to marry a divorcee. She teaches in Mayong College.'

Mom tilted her head and sighed. Mridul must have thought she was empathizing with him. But I knew *why* Mom had sighed. I looked at her. She didn't have an expression on her face. I knew she didn't want to argue with him. She knew there was nothing wrong with Prosanto-da's wish but she also knew it was not something easy to do in a village. She didn't reply, but started walking towards the kitchen. 'I'll get some tea and snacks.'

I told Mridul, I would be there for the wedding. I would go to Hatimura with him a week before the wedding to participate in all the festivities—wedding preparations, inviting guests in the village (that is often done last), going to the Bangladeshi migrants village nearby to get buffalo milk for all the curd that would be served with flattened rice made from manikimodhuri grains. I smiled too much. I felt foolish. Clownish. I was really happy to see him.

Outside, the coconut trees kept saying 'no, no, no'.

Mom screamed from the kitchen when she heard my plans. 'Oh, I thought you had your SATs to study for? This is not done! You will not be allowed to go two weeks before the wedding. You will just hop around and disturb them!'

There was something cheerful about Mom's complaining voice. So I said bravely, nearly laughing, 'Oh, they will be happy to see me, I know. And I need a break anyway.'

'Borma,' Mridul looked at Mom and pleaded, 'please let him come?'

'No, Mridul, no. He has a lot to study. His father won't allow him to go to the wedding so many days in advance. You know his grades have fallen so much! They are abysmal!'

She said 'abysmal' in English and later, after Mridul had gone to bed at night, I told her that she shouldn't use words like 'abysmal' in front of Mridul. He couldn't understand English very well.

'You are always pointing fingers at me, Pablo! You aren't going, that's it!' She said 'going' loudly, with a lot of emphasis. 'How will I show my face if you flunk your SATs? Mrs Barua's daughter has gotten through California State University. Aren't you ashamed? Don't you feel like doing well in life too? I am so sure you are going to ashen my face. I would have to find a mask to roam around the neighbourhood after your SAT and board exams. Maybe Rehanna will lend me her burqa.'

'Rehanna-pehi doesn't have a burqa by the way.' Mom gave me a stern look because she didn't mean that she would literally borrow a burqa. I said, 'There are other ways of doing well in life, Mom. You don't understand how good I feel in the village. I won't turn into a loser—unless you treat me like one—if I didn't make it to California State University or Harvard for that matter, but the way you are panicking, I think I might flunk simply worrying about your health.'

Had I really said that? What was it that was pulling me to Mayong that year?

Mom stared at me for a long time. 'I don't know what variety of itchy yam I ate while carrying you that your tongue has turned out to be as sharp as a razor. What a shame! What a pity!'

For the last two short, crisp sentences, which had come like whiplashes, she had switched to English.

I calmed down. 'Don't you keep telling me yourself to go to the village, spend time there, get to know our culture? Then why stop me now?'

'Of course you must know where you belong and where your father comes from but that doesn't mean you must waste precious time needed for preparing for these tests and go to the wedding. Haven't you seen how I have embraced village life? How many professors of Cotton College go to spend their Bihus and Pujas in their husbands' villages? How many of them go to touch the feet of every elderly person on the first of Bohag every spring? You should be proud that you have a mother like me.'

'I am very proud of you,' I said with feeling.

Perhaps she was amused by my theatrical tone.

She calmed down. 'Do you know how much I had to pay to register you for SATs? I was fleeced, and I won't let you throw it away. I won't let my children waste money like that even if we can afford to. Your parents have worked hard to reach where they have in life.'

I sat down beside her on the bed, legs folded. I must have looked arrogant since the annoyed expression on her face hadn't changed though her voice had calmed down. 'The only thing I can promise you is that I will do well. I won't *ashen* your fair and lovely and beautiful face.'

'You really know how to flatter and mock at the same time,' she said, breaking into a reluctant smile, keeping aside the red plastic comb on the bedside table and picking up the night cream that she would massage with her fingertips on her face in circular motions for a while before going to bed. 'We'll see when the time comes. You better study hard until Mridul comes back to pick you up from here—two weeks before the wedding. If you don't, he would leave this house alone. Don't blame me then. Now leave, your papa will return from the study any minute.'

~

A similar scenario unfolded when Mridul came back a month later. I looked at his eager face and asked Mom how she could disappoint him—it was so difficult to come all the way from Mayong. He had come with so much hope, perhaps even leaving work behind. It would be cruel not to let me go with him, I said. He had come for me, to take me with him to the wedding, to show me around all that would happen until the wedding.

Mom didn't agree until the last minute. When she was battling with the ridiculous argument of sun tanning and dry skin, which would happen once I went there because I wouldn't apply any of the creams and lotions that she would pack for me, Papa interfered.

Papa, who had laid the foundation of our friendship four years ago, allowed me to go.

Mom exclaimed in utter disbelief as if it were raining fishes, 'I can't believe your papa is spoiling you when he speaks about strictness all the time!'

This time, she looked really angry and there was nothing playful about it. I was slightly worried he would change his decision and hoped it was just another instance of mild disagreement between them. One of those days when she didn't like a wedding gift he had bought, would complain about it, go to the wedding with another gift and narrate the whole story to the bride or the groom and alert women of her age that they should never ask their husbands to buy gifts on their way back from office. Papa would remain quiet with a smile on his lips.

'He is more sensible than you, Mom,' I said jubilantly, as if I had won a war, throwing an apple up in the air and then catching it like a cricket ball.

Mridul laughed.

'You will have to be careful. The army is there all the time— apparently they just beat up anyone, Pablo!'

When Mridul heard that, he immediately replied on my behalf, 'Oh Borma, aren't we living there? Aren't others living there? They won't even touch him. When he would speak in fluent, *phai-phai* English, they would think he is some big man's son!' I laughed when he used that superlative expression 'phai-phai' to describe my ability to speak in English.

Mom laughed. 'Well, I guess he knows phai-phai Hindi too, don't you, Pablo?'

'No ya—it's not that phai-phai!'

We all seemed to be suddenly taken over by that phrase.

~

Next morning, when Papa drove us to the interstate bus terminal located in the scum-filled, crowded, Paltan Bozaar market, he played the radio instead of the cassette player in the car.

Mridul sat on the front seat beside Papa. Just behind him, in the back seat, I sat with the window rolled down, the air entering the car unhindered along with the morning sounds that barged in from the streets, lanes, houses, markets and madwomen we left behind. The split ends of Mridul's long hair danced in the wind. Papa asked him why he couldn't go to the barber. He didn't answer. Papa asked if he had ten rupees or not. He didn't answer.

When Papa concentrated on driving, Mridul turned, winked

at me. I raised my eyebrows. I wondered if Papa could see my expression in the mirror that hung over his head. Our luggage was locked up in the trunk. Mridul's tattered red duffel bag (the only one he had) and my large, blue Adidas backpack that I had bought a few months ago much to Mom's displeasure because she thought Papa shouldn't indulge us so much, even though we could afford such things. She firmly insisted there was no point in buying a bag for a couple of thousands of rupees, when we could buy one from Fancy Bozaar for less than three or four hundred rupees. Mom's typical middle-class attitude amused me. But many years later, while I was teaching in a college in Delhi, I would think about her remark and smile to myself as I haggled at a cheap, but good, bag shop in Chandni Chowk, trying to get something that my college teacher's salary allowed.

Even though it was early and there wasn't much traffic on the way, the bus terminus was teeming with people. I thought of the streets of Guwahati swarming with crowds during Durga Puja, of festive evenings in the city when there were so many on the streets that you didn't have to walk, but just stand and let yourself be pushed along the way. You only needed to keep taking the right turns so that you didn't end up in the wrong pandal. Wallets disappeared, girls got their bottoms and boobs pinched, and strange hands felt up men's crotches during those mad evenings.

At the bus station, looking around, I told Mridul that it was the dirtiest bus station in the entire world. He smiled and said that 'your city' is dirty and 'our village' is lovely. I disagreed with him. I argued, trying to protect 'my city'.

Papa asked us (but he was only looking at Mridul) if we would be able buy the tickets on our own and board the right bus. Mridul assured him that we would be fine, since he travelled to the city often, all by himself.

Papa left. I didn't wave at him. I didn't say 'goodbye'. It felt so odd to say 'goodbye' to your strict father. Fathers are meant to be distant.

But that day, he should have stayed back, waited for a while for the news of what had happened the previous night, when the entire city was lost in its morning dreams.

Like many people, we didn't know of the incident, because it happened too early in the morning (or rather, too late at night) to make it to the morning papers.

When we read the papers that morning, we didn't see the news because it had taken place at around four—just before dawn. And it had taken place not very far from our house—we lived in Uzan Bozaar and the incident had taken place in Six Mile.

Papa left after feeling assured that it was just another normal day of busy office goers and school children boarding buses and vendors from faraway places unloading goods from the Assam State Road Transport Corporation buses. He was, of course, wrong.

In the morning, when we were having breakfast (Mridul had rice and I had cornflakes and eggs and orange juice), Mom had scanned the papers—like a kite eyeing lonely preys on the ground—for shutdowns and protests. Papa had called up one of his friends who worked at the All India Radio and asked if any small organization had called for a shutdown. After he had finished the conversation on the landline (people rarely used mobiles in Guwahati back then as they had to pay for incoming calls as well) he told Mom that no big or small organization had called for a shutdown—an Assam bandh. Mom had asked him to cross-check if any Karbi organization was unhappy and protesting because, on the way to Mayong, we had to pass some Karbi dominated areas. Papa had laughed and said that if that were the case we would have been the first ones to know because there were so many Karbi people in our own ancestral village.

Mom hadn't looked too convinced: as if it was abnormal *not* to have a shutdown, some unrest, some killing or an unhappy organization calling for trouble. She had told me that I should get down from the bus and call them immediately if we found out there were a bandh. I had asked how I would do that because a bandh meant complete shutdown—not even PCOs, not even paid urinals, would remain open because no one wanted their shop gutted, no one wanted their restaurant pelted with stones.

Papa had said in an impatient voice that even if there was a bandh we would eventually reach Mayong, and there was no bandh because in the past few days no unfortunate incident had taken place.

I didn't know if he was referring to the killings that were happening around the state. I had lost track of who were killing whom. At first, masked gunmen had targeted the family members of the ULFA. People said it was the government that had employed the mean-eyed, gun-wielding masked gunmen, and one evening, Papa had a huge debate with a guest, who was the ruling party's supporter, about it. The guest said it wasn't the government and Papa was adamant that it was state-sponsored. He said it was 'extrajudicial'. I had to think for a second to recall what 'extrajudicial' meant. The killings had been happening for a while now: severed limbs and heads and upper jaws and thumbs of people who were abducted by masked armed men from their houses were found in expected and unexpected places.

But an 'unfortunate incident' had happened, and bandh was called in the wee hours of the morning. We didn't know about it until we were about to leave Guwahati, when the bandh supporters stopped us.

When the bus named Horo-Gouri with a large picture of Shiva
and Parvati painted on its nose reached the bus terminal, I was
amazed by the way Mridul sprinted towards it beckoning me to
come along with him. He went near a window and threw our
bags on a seat through it, by sliding open the panes. Mridul, just
as he knew the secrets of the animal kingdom, also knew the
unwritten laws in an Assam State Road Transport Corporation
bus that went into the interiors of the villages of Assam. Though
we had tickets on which a seat number was mentioned, the bus,
like a village far away from the Dispur Secretariat and Legislative
Assembly, had its own unwritten rules and nominal head. The
conductor was the Prime Minister and the driver our President
who decided when to get down, when a dying bridge blocked our
way, how many people would travel in that bus that moved like
a fat duck swaying left and right over the uneven potholed roads.
When we sat down in our seats, I admired Mridul's promptness.
I looked at the people standing between the two rows of seats.
They gave us mean looks. That was the rule—you couldn't grab
a seat where someone had already placed a bag, a book, a bottle,
a handkerchief, a folded newspaper. As on any other day, I was
proud of Mridul—whose friendship I liked to flaunt before Mom.

The bus had left the station and moved through the crowded
streets of Paltan Bozaar. The shops had opened by then. I could
see women bargaining with the vendors who sold travel bags,
socks, chains and snacks on both sides of the road. Most of the
shops sold things that one would need before travelling. So there
were no garment shops, but there were shoe shops. Amidst the
small, locally produced wares, the Sreeleathers's showroom stood
regally, looking impressive with glass doors displaying pretty and
ugly shoes. We didn't speak when the bus reached Apsara Cinema
Hall. We didn't speak when the bus reached Ulubari, nor did

we speak when the bus reached Bhangagarh. I wanted to speak but perhaps Mridul didn't want to because he was looking at the shops on both sides and once in a while he would murmur, 'So many shops, so expensive—who buys, who pays so much?' I didn't answer him because I knew those were questions that didn't expect answers. I didn't want to disturb him, his thought process, which was filled with wonder. I didn't want to put a lid on it. We started to speak only when the bus took some momentum near Down Town—not very far from the last stop of the city, not too long before we came to know that something had happened in the city the previous night.

'*Asom bondho neki?*' A man had turned his back and asked us. I could see that he was holding an *Asomiya Pratidin* in his hand. Mridul asked if it was in the papers but the man replied, 'No, but look at Down Town—all the shops are shut! It's scary these days you know. There is a bandh every other day.'

The man sitting beside him who was chewing betel nuts said, 'People in Guwahati don't care. They love bandhs and it is only people like us who suffer because if we don't work for a day we don't get rice.'

'He he,' the Asomiya-Pratidin-man laughed. 'What are you saying, Saikia? People like you?'

Saikia spat out red betel juice through the window. I tilted towards Mridul because I was sitting near the window and was worried that little bits of his spit would fall on my ankle, which I had put up on the window. He said, 'I am a farmer, Dasbabu. If there is a bandh, so much of my goods are wasted. I can't send them to Guwahati and they rot on the trucks. I don't deal with potatoes and grains. My main produce is vegetable. I lose thousands and thousands of rupees.'

Dasbabu sucked his teeth and shook his head again and again

but Saikia didn't look as traumatized, although it was *his* produce that rotted in the warehouse during bandhs. Mridul gave me a strange look, perhaps because he also noted Saikia's odd reaction.

The bus came to a halt just after Down Town Hospital due to a traffic jam. Some people started to show off their knowledge of Guwahati by saying that this wasn't a place where traffic jams happened, so something must be wrong. 'An accident, perhaps!' Dasbabu (the more traumatized one) said and craned his neck towards Saikia. The conductor came in, raised his right hand and assured us that the jam would clear off in a while and we shouldn't panic. He was lying. From the window where I was sitting, I could see a long queue of buses that went on for a long way. I couldn't see the other end of the queue on the road and I realized when I turned around that more and more cars, more and more buses were gathering like a comet's tail behind our bus. We were trapped. It was winter. The sun was warm. A breeze started to blow and the women tightened the wrap of their shawls around their bodies and quelled their children like unruly branches that spank you when you roam around in a dense forest. The men fidgeted more on their seats. Dasbabu stood up, and then sat down. Soon after, Saikia started telling him how people in Guwahati bought videocassettes, meat and drinks the night before a bandh so that they could have fun at their homes. I didn't want to listen to him because I was suddenly filled with embarrassment as this was true. It was true that people complained when bandhs were called on the second Saturdays, saying, what was the use of calling a bandh on a second Saturday? It was then that I suddenly thought of Oholya-jethai. How had she been? Had she changed?

'How is Oholya-jethai, Mridul?' He must have seen the cheerful glitter in my eyes. He smirked, which made his dimples prominent.

'Why? She is fine. She hasn't changed one bit.'

'Does she still scold you for playing the guitar?'

'Scolding is her religion.' Mridul laughed and reclined on the seat. He put his arms around me like he used to when, so many years ago, we used to sit on the banks of the Brahmaputra. I didn't like that. I wanted my shoulder back and didn't like the invasion of my body. I shrugged him off. He looked hurt. I didn't know how to amend that.

Outside, the people from the bus were standing with hands on their hips, craning their necks to have a glimpse of the other end of the queue. No, no one had uttered the words 'Assam Bandh' until then. Bandhs that people in Guwahati celebrated with chicken curry and Hindi films and drinks. Bandhs I didn't want to think about because I was embarrassed by the way the people in Guwahati observed them. So I thought of Oholya-jethai. How we were laughing now, how Mridul could say that scolding was her religion and joke about it. But during those twenty-one days of mourning we couldn't imagine that one day we would be joking about the religion she followed diligently. A religion she had acquired long ago when she was the subject of the biggest gossip in the entire village when even Papa wasn't born.

Three

Although Papa wanted to leave me in Mayong so that I could attend Bolen-bortta's funeral in 1998, Mom wasn't happy about it. I think it was the city-bred girl in her that had stirred her doubts. I think it was the kind of news that invaded our breakfast tables that had made her shudder, wondering how safe I would be if I stayed back. I knew Papa wanted me to be friends with his best friend's son and Mom respected that, though she worried about me too much. Even before she had consented, she started giving me a long list of instructions—not to eat 'anything and everything', not to play with fire (something I loved to do), not to swim in the river or stream (because my horoscope said I should stay away from waterbodies—only Mom could tell what that meant), not to roam around too much, not to . . .

After giving me a list of orders and extracting promises for certain important ones in order of preference, she argued with Papa one last time in the room they were given to spend the night and where our luggage was kept as well. 'The times are not safe—don't you know? How can you leave your son here?' I was standing near the door, eavesdropping. Perhaps Papa was aware that I was standing there but, unlike other days, he didn't ask me to leave.

Papa said, 'Let's see who dares to touch Prodip Kanto Medhi's son! And he is smart enough to deal with any situation. He knows four languages, for God's sake!'

As if proficiency in four languages was equal to knowing wrestling, judo and karate! As if the army would check my CV before shooting; whenever they needed a body to prove to the officials that they had killed an insurgent, they would just shoot anyone at sight, plant grenades or an AK-47 beside it and call the press.

But Mom couldn't argue any further with my father. It was the question of propriety that gagged her. In a village, it was unusual for a woman to talk to her husband during the day inside a room.

Oholya-jethai was already trying to find excuses to go inside the room where they were arguing in hushed tones. She constantly tried to look in through the thin, worn-out green curtains of the room where Papa and Mom were speaking to each other. I knew Oholya-jethai was getting worked up because my parents had broken the village custom by conferring with each other during the day in the privacy of a room. They were violating the propriety that Jethai clung to so jealously, like a hungry dog fiercely guarding its only morsel.

After Mom came out of the 'meeting', I heard Oholya-jethai telling Mom: 'Deepali, I want to tell you something. I hope you wouldn't mind.' They were standing on the veranda.

'Yes, Oholya-bai. What is it? Do *you* want Pablo to leave?' There was a note of sarcasm in Mom's voice.

Oholya-jethai wrapped her right shoulder with the other end of the cotton *sador*, covered her body and said, 'Why would I ask such a thing? There are twenty-four mouths constantly gulping down food in this house—would I not have enough to feed another one? He is the son of this house only. How could you even think like that? I wanted to point out something else. I didn't come to ask Pablo to leave!'

'Then tell me. What is it?' Mom didn't look very pleased.

Probably she had already guessed what Oholya-jethai was about to tell her.

'I think you know this is not your city,' Oholya-jethai said, laying stress on 'city'—as if it were something disdainful, repulsive, like the smell of dried fish that trucks from distant lands carried across the highways in Guwahati, forcing us to hold our noses with the tips of our forefingers and thumbs.

She said, raising her right eyebrow, peering into Mom's face, tilting her face a little, 'I have never raised the issue that you call Pablo's father by his name or that you share a room with him when you visit the village, but at least you should be careful during the day.'

'We were just having a discussion about Pablo. What happened, Oholya-bai?' I think Mom was trying hard to keep her calm. She could stomach Oholya-jethai's nonsense only to a certain extent. This had started happening especially after Jethai had called Papa a 'beggar' in front of many people several years ago when he had bought a flat in Hatigaon, a locality in Guwahati. We hadn't yet built the house where Mridul had gone to invite us for the wedding. I was told later that our plan was to move to the house eventually. As his business would flourish, Papa would build a house and move out of the apartment because none of us liked to live in 'matchboxes'—that was the word Mom used, sarcastically.

Oholya-jethai was invited to the house-warming. She had come with Bolen-bortta. But the moment she had entered the three-bedroom apartment, she had started cursing my father, saying that only beggars live in such houses, smaller than a pigsty.

It had become a matter of great disappointment for her that she wouldn't be able to boast about her cousin back in the village when everyone would ask what the house looked like, what they ate there, and so on. Papa had kept quiet, ignoring her, which had further enraged us. Mom had been very upset. She had fought bitterly with Papa, and for the first time, I had heard her mocking fun at 'your provincial, uneducated relatives'. She had felt sad that an auspicious occasion had been reduced to something so crude.

But those were different days. She had changed a lot and she tackled Oholya-jethai very often with sharp sentences. Probably that was why she could retort, 'What happened?'

'What do you mean by "what happened"?' Oholya-jethai's voice was louder now. 'I know the times have changed and that rituals and customs have eroded along with it, but when we were your age, women used to have some shame. Being a professor in a reputed college doesn't make you one of those modern women who don't care for the veil even before elderly men. Don't you know you shouldn't enter the bedroom during the day? It doesn't look good, and you should know that you must at least bathe if you have entered the bedroom in the day. You may not follow these rules in the city, but at least maintain some decorum in the village.'

Her voice was as sharp as glass, loud, authoritarian. 'So many senior members of the family have gathered from various places to take part in the funeral rituals. What would they say? I know you are from the city, but . . .'

Mom knew her only too well.

Sometimes Mom lost it completely. She lost her cool that day too, while I was busy planning the day with Mridul after it was decided that I was staying back.

Mom said, 'Well, Oholya-bai, if you know that we are from the

city and our habits are different, why are you telling us all this?
You are older than us. It's from you I have learnt that habits are
like lifelong diseases. One carries one's habits to the cremation
ground. And now you are contradicting yourself here—well, we
are uprooted, transplanted human beings, so maybe that means
I don't know what's going on here. I remember you telling me
once that most customs and rituals are no longer followed, they
have undergone great changes, and now suddenly you are asking
me to follow those same obsolete rituals again. What are you
telling me, really? Don't you think it's pointless to keep holding
on to rituals that are no longer relevant? I really don't want to
bathe in this cold for the second time in the day, but if you insist,
get me some Ganga water; I will sprinkle it on myself.'

Mridul and I were standing not very far away from the place
where they were talking. He looked into my eyes and I knew
what that stare meant—the beginning of a storm.

But I knew my mother. She had a knack for terse sentences.
She knew how to snap back and get away with it. She would say
the most bitter things with a bright smile on her face. With her
intense, expressive eyes. And the person those were directed at
would never be able to decide how to react. Oholya-jethai would
also retreat. But, much later, after my parents had left, she'd know
she had been defeated in that verbal duel.

The very next thing Mom said was, 'Aha, who has woven this
sador, Oholya-bai? It's so beautiful!'

She asked this, although she knew that Oholya-jethai would
never wear anything unless woven by herself in her own
handloom. She'd sit there each afternoon till the cows returned
from their grazing. And one of the men or women in the house
would scream, 'Oh Bai, come and control your sweetheart Ronga.
He will soon devour all the flowers in the garden.' Ronga was

Oholya-jethai's pet bull. Every evening, she would go with a handful of salt on a banana leaf to feed him. The ferocious bull would lick her hands. He would poke her softly with his scarily curved horns. Sit down beside her as she picked up some ticks from his head. Only after that would he allow her to tether him in the cowshed. Mridul used to tell me, 'He is always on top of one or the other cow! What a life!'

So Oholya-jethai answered in a mocking tone, 'Your son has almost reached marriageable age. Yet, don't you know that this lady doesn't wear anything woven by others at home? I buy only silk, not cotton. They are all woven with these hands of mine.' She must have displayed her rough hands, work-worn, and said that. We giggled silently—Mridul and I. 'Tell me if you want one. I can weave one for you next Bihu,' she told Mom.

'Oh, so nice of you, Oholya-bai, but let the dust settle down first. Too much has been happening in this house recently.'

'Life's like that, Deepali,' Oholya-jethai said, looking calm and resigned. 'I will weave one for you this coming spring. Why don't you get me some perfume that you city-ladies sprinkle on your bodies? I could flaunt it here during weddings and prayer meets at the *naamghor*! Nowadays, we don't get screw-pine flowers at all to collect their pollen.'

~

The incessant cooing of the doves, the singing crickets and the distant sounds of chattering women and men in and around the house didn't make me feel lonely after Papa and Mom had left at around ten that morning, in the Maruti Esteem (almost black). I couldn't get bored in that house that had seventeen windows but no ventilators. Where someone was always there to talk to, sit with, exchange greetings, reminisce about the sad and happy and funny times.

At lunchtime, I waited for Mridul to come back from his bath; he couldn't eat without taking a bath. Onima-borma prodded me to eat; she said I must be hungry so I should not wait for him. When he arrived, I started eating. The meal was frugal—boiled rice with salt and a sliver of lime. Grilled potatoes mashed with finely chopped ginger and salt. When we started to eat, Onima-borma asked us to eat slowly. She pulled out a large, fat, steaming brinjal from the smoulders and started peeling it. But her pace slackened because she had suddenly started weeping.

'If your bortta was around, he wouldn't have let you eat like this. He would have brought a duck; he would have brought borali fish, tasty yams. He would have asked me to fry bok-phool with gram flour.' She paused to pull the sador and wipe the corners of her eyes. Oholya-jethai was just passing by; she looked in and saw her crying. She came inside the kitchen. Her body was wet and I wondered if that was her twenty-fifth bath because Mridul told me she bathed on every single excuse in order to remain 'pious'. If she stepped out of the compound, she wouldn't enter the house without bathing. If she had some work in the kitchen, she would bathe, enter the kitchen straightaway, and change into her 'kitchen dress'. If she had to enter a bedroom to look for something, she would straightaway go to the pond, before entering any other room, to take a dip. Whenever I found her, her hair would be wet, water dripping from it.

Oholya-jethai looked at Mridul and said sternly, 'Aren't you feeling guilty now? You have forced your brother to eat this frugal meal for the next twenty days!'

Mridul didn't speak. He continued eating. I protested, 'It's all right, Jethai, we are in mourning.'

But no one paid any attention to me. Oholya-jethai continued to scold Mridul, 'All of you are *opodarthos*—singularly devoid of any sense. He must be eating five different delicious dishes at home for every meal. Your father would surely not be happy to see his favourite brother's son eating like this. His family doesn't have to follow any ritual. Pablo didn't have to go through this ordeal.'

I tried to sneak into the conversation but found it impossible to get a word in edgeways. Too many people were speaking; too many sentences were whooshing past my head like lethal arrows. I wondered why Mridul was quiet. It was only much later I came to know that he was truly feeling guilty when we were having lunch that afternoon. Because, just the next day, he would do something that would create a huge ruckus in the household, and as usual, Oholya-jethai would take the lead in admonishing Mridul. But that day, he was quiet. Perhaps he was planning. Perhaps he was regretting his decision to force me to stay back, feeling guilty that I would have to eat the same meals that the family would be eating since they were in mourning.

Onima-borma asked feebly, 'Oholya-bai, don't get angry, but could I ask you something?'

'No, I won't—when do I ever get angry?' she said impatiently, already sounding annoyed.

'Could Pablo have some mustard oil with his potato and brinjal mash. At least it would tickle his taste buds a little bit . . .'

As soon as she uttered 'mustard oil', Oholya-jethai's mouth gaped open and her brows jumped up in horror. I had started protesting even as Onima-borma was speaking, because I didn't want them to make exceptions for me, but my voice was drowned by Oholya-jethai's outburst. 'What are you even saying, Onima?

You can't even *think* of such things. My brother's soul would never get peace if a single drop of oil touches the tongue of anyone staying in this house! But Pablo could eat anything he wants outside this house. Maybe you could tell Okoni to cook something for him in her house—since she is married, she doesn't have to follow any rituals. But don't you dare utter such a sentence again.' Her voice grew louder and louder, more and more impatient.

'All right. But you said you wouldn't be angry.'

'Why wouldn't I be angry? How could I not be angry? Do you know what happens to families who don't follow mourning rituals properly? One by one, the dead drags everyone he loved to his side. Even cows and grass on the courtyard aren't spared.'

Mridul washed his hands on the plate. 'My father won't do anything like that. He was a kind and generous man.' He wasn't eating boiled rice like me, but rotis. Since he was the eldest son, he had to follow the most austere of rituals, which included eating staple just once a day before sunset, wearing no footwear, no underpants, but only one large piece of cloth on his body.

Oholya-jethai hollered, 'Keep quiet! You big fool.' She tilted her head to her right. 'Do you know what's going on in this world? All that you care for is your guitar, your useless music. You are his eldest son—I wonder when you will understand your responsibilities.'

I felt as if the mud walls of the kitchen were rattling. So loud was she. So tall was she. That she-will-poison-my-tea fear was back. I finished my meal quickly. A meal for which I didn't care, but others did. They argued and fought for me though I didn't care what I was getting to eat. I noticed Mridul wasn't looking at her face. He had ignored her and left in a huff. I felt it riled her more that he had ignored her. She wasn't used to being ignored. She was used to being listened to.

~

Some visitors from nearby villages had come around late afternoon with fruits, grams, coconuts and spotted senisompa bananas for us. Most of the people in the house were sitting on the veranda, listening to them. Mukut-khura, dressed in his dhoti, sat there on a chair too, recounting his first reactions, how he feared—after his brother had passed away—for the death of his old mother as well.

'Don't ask me what she did when she learnt that her eldest son had died! I thought—even Mai would *leave us* along with Bolen-kai. He was the one who looked after her almost all the time. Checked if she had taken her medicines, heated water for her, took her out for walks. She was very attached to him. I thought she wouldn't be able to take this stab of destiny.' He sighed.

He was so fat, but also so tall that his body didn't seem disproportionate. Still it didn't stop me from thinking the chair he sat on would break suddenly under his weight. He was so loud too. Aaita must have been in one of the nearby rooms. I wondered if she could hear him.

'I know, I know . . .'—one middle-aged man agreed.

'I think her health deteriorated because of the trauma, not just because of the thick fog this year.'

'For two whole days after his death we sat with her. It was as if she was *leaving* us. She coughed and coughed and was absolutely senseless for those two days. We were almost sure she'd succumb to the grief. When the sun rose on the third day, we brought her out and informed the relatives that she was *leaving* us, and they gathered soon. Some women had already started crying, and someone had poured out Ganga water into a bowl to feed her a drop before she went. But lying there under the sun, she stirred and said, "Could I have some tea, please?"'

'*Nai, nai*, this old woman is not going to die easily. Maybe she'll live on to tell stories to Mridul's children too!' The men started laughing.

Mridul came out of his room and asked me if I was ready. Mukut-khura looked at us when he heard him and Oholya-jethai shot us a stern look. She looked at Mukut-khura's face and, when she sensed no possibility of an intervention, she asked where we were going. Mridul said he wanted to show me around the village—the people, the stream, the temple and the marketplace. Oholya-jethai asked him to stay back; she said there was no need to roam around like that, especially when people were visiting. They would ask for the dead man's son. But Mridul's mother intervened. She asked Oholya-jethai to let him go in her meek voice, wondering aloud for how long a young man like him could lock himself up at home. When we opened the bamboo gate of the compound, we heard Oholya-jethai's loud voice telling someone about how young men might lose the right way if they stayed out of the house for long hours. She said she wouldn't be responsible if the army interrogated Mridul or picked him up. Mukut-khura said something in reply, but by then we had walked farther away from the house, so we didn't hear what he was saying. But I was sure if Oholya-jethai had continued speaking, her words would have pricked us with the sharpness of shards of glass.

Suddenly I was filled with a sense of triumph. It was only a little later, when we had reached the marketplace, I realized I had felt victorious because I had finally figured out that it was possible to do something against Oholya-jethai's wishes in that house.

The market was teeming with people. Among the well-dressed crowd, Mridul looked odd in his dhoti and shawl. He wasn't wearing a shirt. He was barefoot. Among the people buying vegetables, oil and meat from the shops, he looked out of place. With his tonsured head, he looked like a statue, a symbol of sacrifice, a Buddhist monk who had relinquished the pleasures of earthly life.

We had reached a large laburnum tree that stood beside the village road and just on the edge of the road there was an electric pole. I noticed that Mridul stepped out of the road like a meandering stream of water when he reached near the electric pole, to avoid treading on the portion just below and around it. I was behind him and he asked me not to step on the portion of the road that was just under the electric pole. I followed his instructions, wondering why.

'I don't think you should know the reason. You won't be able to digest it.'

I was irritated. 'Is this some kind of a joke? I have digested Oholya-jethai's words; I would be able to digest anything now. Tell me,' I said.

Mridul looked at me, as if he was preparing to tell me something serious and didn't approve of my flippant manner. Without saying anything, he started to walk away; I followed him, asking more questions. He went to a shop where some of his friends were hanging out, chewing betel nuts. He introduced me to them. One of them was called Brikodar, whom he was particularly close to.

'Pabloo wants to know the story of the electric pole,' Mridul told him, with a touch of mockery in his voice.

Brikodar laughed. He was taller than Mridul and plump. He looked like someone who wouldn't weave mysteries the way Mridul loved to. By telling me half stories, by asking me not to walk on a certain portion of the road without explaining why. Mridul laughed, too, at my confused state. I didn't like it. I didn't like it when his friends told me that I would have nightmares if I heard the story and laughed. I didn't like it when they asked me if I would be able to digest it. I felt annoyed because I couldn't tell them I would jolly well be able to, if I could digest whatever Oholya-jethai had been saying all day. I was humiliated because their laughter reminded me that I was younger than them and they had access to worlds I didn't. Worlds that Mridul wouldn't usually think twice before introducing me to.

But now those worlds were suddenly hidden away from me. I was suddenly reminded that I was four years younger than Mridul. I told Mridul politely that I wanted to go home. He was surprised, but didn't protest. He walked with me, said this and that, but I didn't respond. When we reached the electric pole, I saw him avoiding the portion under the pole. I wanted to defy him and walk on it but I felt, whatever the reason was, it wasn't funny; it was serious and he was scared of something, which is why he had walked like a meandering stream that had found an obstacle on its way and changed course. I realized that obstacle was invisible—the obstacle that made him avoid the portion of the ground just under the electric pole that stood just near the road, next to the laburnum tree that hadn't yet bloomed into flakes of gold.

The sun had set by the time we reached home and I thought about how long it took for the sun to set. On our way, I wanted to ask him again what the fuss about the electric pole was all about, but I was too proud. I was offended that he had reminded me of the difference in our age by telling me I would be scared if I knew the real reason behind his peculiar behaviour.

I could smell ghee. I could smell chopped coriander and chopped green chillies. I could smell boiled potatoes and grilled brinjals. Smell of slivers of lime that must be stacked on banana leaves beside a mound of stork-white salt. I knew that smell all too well. The smell of a mourning-house dinner, which we used to have when grandma had passed away in 1993. When I had met Mridul for the first time. When I wasn't old enough to roam around the village alone, wasn't old enough to go to Mayong alone, but Mridul, who, at that point, had disrupted my ideas about the animal kingdom was old enough to represent his family at a funeral. Dressed in a blue shirt and black trousers, he had looked so handsome that I had felt jealous, just as the way I was jealous of his dimples.

'Mridul!'

Oholya-jethai's booming voice invaded the room.

I was sitting quietly on the bed, too proud to tell Mridul that I was offended. He must have been wondering what was wrong with me. So he didn't know what to say or whether he should leave the room. He had started arranging his books on his study table.

Mridul turned towards her.

'I need to tell you something. You will not mind, I hope. You will not pull a long face, I hope.'

He turned his back to her and started rearranging the already-arranged books. He didn't look at her.

'I don't like this habit of yours.'

No one spoke. I looked at Mridul. Oholya-jethai folded her hands and stood there, staring at Mridul. I don't know if he knew that she was staring at him. But her look was piercing and he must have felt it on his back, on his spine, on his neck, on his scalp, and so he had replied after a few uncomfortable moments of silence, 'Which habit?'

'You don't need to roam around like this in the market. There is no need to hang out with those losers like Brikodar and I have always maintained you should stay away from their family. They might feed you some potion and you may end up falling in love with Brikodar's sister. They have been eyeing the men of our family for years now. And what is this carrom fascination? Have you forgotten? Last year, you failed your exams because you spent hours playing carrom and strumming the guitar with them. It's just four days since your father passed away and you are already doing things that would have made him unhappy. You don't deserve to mourn him. Take off your mourning attire and change into jeans and T-shirt!'

She left in a huff.

Mridul leaned on the table. He didn't look at me. How cruel her words were. Just to prove her point, she could say anything. Just to strip down her opponent of dignity, she said anything she could to hurt them. I was suddenly embarrassed for him because she had revealed secrets about him that I wasn't supposed to know. He hadn't told me he had flunked the previous year. Obviously he didn't want me to know. Perhaps he wanted to hide it from me so that I continued to like him, respect him, and didn't look down on him. And when he started crying not long after she had left the room, I didn't quite notice it. I was still sitting on the bed and he had his back towards me. But his back was trembling and his head was bowed.

I went up to him, turned him around and looked at his face. He looked away, wiped his tears with the ends of his fingers. He didn't want me to see that he was crying, that he had lost control. I wondered if he was crying because she had scolded him or whether he suddenly missed his father who wouldn't have scolded him at all, who would have let him hang out with anyone he wanted to.

He wiped his tears and looked at my face. 'You think I can't answer back? You think I can't say anything to her? I just want peace in this house. If you go out, it is the army's fear. If you stay in, it is Oholya-jethai's terror. For a while, the rebels have stopped coming to our house to demand food and shelter. And that was another kind of trauma. Where do I go? Where should I try to find some peace? If I play music, I have to consider what people will think because someone has just died in this house. If I play carrom, I am wasting time and not studying. How can I study? I still miss my father. It isn't going to go away, Pabloo. It will never go away, just like the fear that makes me walk in a curve around the electric pole on that straight road, avoiding the portion of ground just under the electric pole. And not just me, many of my friends do that too because we had seen it first.'

He waited. His Adam's apple moved up, down, up. He wiped the tears with the tips of his fingers. He said it was a nice day. Clear, blue skies. They could even hear the distant bleats of goats. They could see the kites flown by the young boys in the East Bengali village. It was a Sunday. So they had all woken up late but the younger ones had woken up first since they had planned to go fishing, get some crabs, get some pork from the Karbi village, prop up a hut in the middle of the empty fields and have dinner together that night. Eat forbidden food. The fields were bright yellow. The skies looked peaceful. Mridul had first gone to Brikodar's house to tell him about the plan. From there, they had walked down to Binod's house, and then to the market. No one was around. The dogs were barking so loudly.

And since the dogs were barking in the village, dogs from the neighbouring villages had also gathered. But they were scared. They didn't come into the marketplace, into the terrain of the Hatimura dogs. They were barking from a distance. And there were the crows. In a chorus, they had shattered the beautiful silence of that morning.

Mridul said that he had wondered, when he reached Brikodar's house, why the crows and the dogs were making such a racket. Brikodar's mother had said probably *something* was dead. A dog. A crow. A big, fat fox. Something. You know, if you kill a crow, the rest of the crows caw like that. For days, you wouldn't be able to go anywhere near the dead bird because other crows would attack you with their sharp beaks and talons. When Mridul had gone to Binod's house, Binod's grandmother had said the same—why were the crows cawing like mad? Why were the dogs barking so much in the market? Probably something was dead. Something. A dog, a crow, a fox. A buffalo.

'We didn't care,' Mridul continued. 'It was far away—the shops, I mean, are far away from the houses. But we saw him first. I don't remember who informed the police. But we saw the body first. Only in his red underwear. He didn't have legs. They had been chopped off. He didn't have fingers. They had been cut off too. His face was twisted—as if he was repulsed by a bad smell. It was such a horrific sight! Hanging from the electric pole like a dead, electrocuted bat. He was from a nearby village—the brother of an ULFA member. Why did they have to torture him like that? Moina-pehi, who had also seen the body, couldn't eat for three days. She retched and retched. I couldn't sleep for many days as well. Moina-pehi was among the women who cried the most, wondering aloud if the man had loved someone, wanted to marry someone, if he had a sister. His only crime was that he was the elder brother of an ULFA member and the ULFA member, his brother, had refused to surrender to the government and take the money that the government was dishing out so that he could return to society by setting up a business.

'When someone climbed up the pole with a bamboo ladder and cut off the rope that had tied the corpse to the pole by its fingerless wrists, the body had fallen exactly on the portion of the road we avoid stepping on now. It's been almost three months since this happened. More killings are taking place every day. But this was the most horrific spectacle. The East Bengali villagers who use the Pokoria River most of the time say that they have started finding body parts of unknown human beings at regular intervals, almost every fortnight or so. They are so scared that they haven't even informed the police.

'But on that ground where that corpse fell—we still can't walk. Because we saw him first. I will never be able to walk on it. I feel his ghost will enter my soul. It is also a way of respecting the man, you know? His mother had cried so much. We hoped that she would faint and fade away and not have to go through the trauma, but she didn't. His wife did, though. The night before, four masked men had taken him away from his house. He was sleeping after a meal. There were guests. His wife howled, saying how much he loved the turtle curry. When the corpse fell, the blood had splattered around the pole, Pabloo. So much blood.'

~

The next morning was bitterly cold. My teeth chattered when I walked out of my room. The spotted leaves of the yellow and green and brown and red patabahar shrubs in front of the house and the leaves of the sewali-flower tree that leaned against the bamboo gate were drenched with dew. The ends of the long straws from the roofs of the house wept out beads of dew . . . Like rice beer left on a strainer that drips slowly, the dew dribbled like drops of pearl. Sometimes when the sun shone through them, they refracted the light into several colours, creating a halo of rainbow around them.

That was my second day in the house, the fifth day of mourning.

Mridul planned a day full of defiance and delicacies and deliciousness. He hadn't told me about it. He must have been feeling guilty ever since his mother told him at lunch that I would have to eat frugally with the rest of the family. Ever since Oholya-jethai pronounced that even a drop of oil tickling the taste buds of anyone living in that house would deprive Bolen-bortta's soul of peace. The meals that Mridul left behind in the house on banana leaves every evening for the peace of his father's soul wouldn't be enough. The iron sickle that he carried around and the bunch of tightly tied straw he kept in his room wouldn't be enough to help the dead man's soul on the path to heaven. He was the eldest son. He had to do everything diligently. Oholya-jethai said if he didn't do things wholeheartedly, nothing would work. So he followed every ritual meticulously. Sometimes, he bathed several times and Moina-pehi would tease him, 'Are you competing with Oholya-bai? You will never succeed, my dear.'

But this same guy, on the day the leaves dripped drops of dew, planned a deliciously defiant feast for me. Around dinner time, when he took me out of the house, asking me to follow him, I was puzzled. But I followed him nonetheless, wondering where he was taking me.

He took me to Brikodar's house. But as soon as I stepped on their veranda, I felt shy. I was stricken that he took the trouble to arrange this special meal for me stealthily. That he wouldn't be able to eat his favourite forbidden food, while I ate it, sitting in front of him. When they laid out the food before me—rice, fried pork, pork curry with banana flower, a slice of green lime, some salt, a long green chilli—I didn't look at Bridkodar's sassy, chirpy, constantly laughing sister. The sister that Oholya-jethai thought would seduce Mridul and the family would have to bear the shame of one of their sons marrying a Karbi girl. A girl who wouldn't be accepted in that house where something or the other happened every day. Where people fought over small things. Dripping dews, mustard oil, a constantly laughing sister who would seduce one of the men from their family, a guitar, a carrom board.

Brikodar's thin, frail mother had served me. She had bright eyes. She almost laughed whenever she spoke. 'Eat, baba, eat! Your father used to come with Mridul's father to our house to eat pork when Brikodar's father was alive.'

I didn't want to think about Mridul standing there, probably pining to eat what I was eating. I said, 'How can I eat alone? Someone please sit with me. Stop treating me like a guest.'

'But you are a guest!' the giggling sister said.

'Brikodar will have dinner with you, don't worry,' the girl said. The mother introduced us. 'This is Mamoni, Brikodar's sister, my youngest daughter. Baba, what is your name?'

'Pabloo,' Mridul answered on my behalf.

'My mother-in-law, your grandmother and Mridul's grandmother used to have huge fights about who is older than who. Whether it was Bolen-kai, my late husband or your father. Bolen-kai's mother would say Prodip-kai is the eldest, and then came Brikodar's father. But our mother-in-law would scream, saying when Bolen-kai had started to crawl, Brikodar's father was still being suckled and Prodip-kai wasn't even born. Don't ask. The argument would go on for ever. Each wanted her son to be the youngest. That matter was never resolved and they stopped bothering after a point—especially after they became grandmothers. But I still remember; it was really very funny. But the three of them were best friends, a trio, and so were their three sons.'

The mother sat beside me on the mud floor, on her haunches. She peered into my golden-coloured dish made of bell metal that reflected the yellow bulb which shone overhead. I knew it was an affectionate peer. To check if I needed anything. To see if I was eating properly.

'Who got the pork?'

Brikodar replied, 'Mridul paid for it and I bought it.'

'You are here for the first time; you should get a taste of real life of young people here,' Mridul said, smiling brightly. I was moved. So moved that I couldn't thank him there, nor could I thank him later, during the walk back home, when he was telling me not to tell anyone in the family of this meal. When I asked him what I should say if Okoni-pehi or Moina-pehi asked me if I had had dinner, he said I could say that I ate at Brikodar's house but I shouldn't say that we had had pork because Oholya-jethai would then force me to take a bath in the cold and scold us endlessly. He said it was Moina-pehi's idea that he buy some fish or chicken from the market and arrange for a dinner at someone else's house in the village so that I didn't have to eat the bland, boiled meal every day. 'Really?' I looked at him, my eyes large with surprise.

~

Brikodar walked us back after dinner. He joked that I should walk as much as I could in order to digest the pork. The path was dark. There were many fireflies floating in the air like bursting soap bubbles.

Suddenly, Brikodar asked Mridul, 'How is everything with her?'

I couldn't see Mridul's reaction but I was instantly curious to know about this special 'her'. Mridul said, 'I haven't been meeting her. She told Junali that she is sad about whatever has happened and has asked me to meet her once the rituals are over.'

'You are playing with fire, my friend. You know what will happen when people will know about it, right? Your Oholya-jethai doesn't even like our friendship because we are Karbis. But perhaps since your father was a close friend of my father's she doesn't say much,' Brikodar said. He was laughing.

I was getting more and more inquisitive. I thought I would think about Oholya-jethai's prejudices later. I would ask Mridul later what the problem was if someone was friends with a tribal family and ate with them. But who was this girl? Mamoni? The constantly laughing sister? So Oholya-jethai's suspicions weren't baseless? I wasn't pleased that her allegations were turning out to be true. But how could it be Mamoni? If it was Mamoni, Brikodar wouldn't ask Mridul how everything was going on between them. Then who could it be?

'I don't care,' Mridul said, in a resigned voice, slowing down his pace. Somewhere, deep in his heart, he seemed to know that whatever Brikodar was telling him was actually true. That he should listen to him. That Brikodar's cautionary sentences had a foundation made of rock, not soft loamy soil that would wear off easily. But what were they talking about? Who was 'she'? That mysterious 'she', Mridul's girlfriend? We had just eaten forbidden food and now there it was: a forbidden love affair? I wanted to know that forbidden truth. I wanted to be a part of that revolutionary love affair. I was excited. I almost stopped myself from asking if he was dating Mamoni, Brikodar's fair-skinned, slim, sassy, chirpy younger sister who had deliberately served me too much rice when I had asked for a little. Who had said if a young man couldn't eat, who could? Who had said it was just rice, the curd was yet to come. She had taken pleasure at my helplessness. That I was feeling trapped. That I would have to finish everything on the plate now that it was full. We didn't like wasting food. Whatever reaches the plate enters the stomach, even at the risk of overeating.

'What's going on, Mridul? You haven't told me yet!'

'There is no need for you to know. You might blurt it out to someone. You are too free with your mother.'

'Yes, but my mother doesn't know about my girlfriends. She wouldn't know about yours too. That means you don't trust me. And I don't understand why you don't trust me. You were reluctant to tell me about the electric pole too.'

Even in the dark, I could sense that Mridul had turned his face towards me.

'That's because I thought you would be frightened and get nightmares. It's not a story you should have on your mind. If you hear it once, it refuses to leave.'

Around four houses away from Mridul's, there was a large block of stone, under the shade of a tall jackfruit tree. A tiny stream of water as thin as a finger flowed down from underneath the stone. The soil around it was surrounded by grass as fresh as newly bloomed flowers.

We sat there and talked for a while. But it was Brikodar who spoke. Brikodar, who was named after tall, fat, large, powerful Bhima—the second Pandava—from the Mahabharata. But he was so thin. He spoke for most of the time. Telling me things that he thought I should tell Mridul not to do, not to carry on with any further. But why did he say all this to me? Did he believe that Mridul, who was his childhood friend, wouldn't listen to *his* warnings but listen to *me*—who was four years younger than him? Towards whom, at times, Mridul was a little too protective; since he thought I didn't know the ways of the village? That morning, he hadn't let me pull up water from the well when I had gone to bathe. He hadn't said it would be hard work for me. He hadn't said he was worried I might fall into the well because it didn't have a rim. He had just snatched from my hands the bucket that had a long, brown rope tied to it. I had wanted to experience the excitement of drawing water from a rimless deep well. And when I had wanted my bucket back, he hadn't paid any attention to me.

When I had tried to snatch it back from him, Moina-pehi had noticed us and screamed in horror. She had asked why we were fighting over a bucket near that well. She had come running over and asked me to get away from there. When I hadn't moved, she had asked me if I wanted her to inform Oholya-jethai. I had said adamantly that she could do that if she wanted to. She had slapped me lightly on the back of my head. An affectionate slap it was. *'Eeeh!'* she had said in a nasal tone. *'Kotha koise suwa!'* She had joked. 'Pablo, you aren't used to drawing water from wells. This well isn't safe too. We can't let you do it, so no argument, OK? Otherwise, I am really going to tell Oholya-bai.'

Brikodar perhaps didn't know any of this. He thought he could use another authority to warn Mridul that he was walking on fire. That Mridul's relationship could bring such a storm into the house, already shaky after Bolen-bortta's death, that it would blow away its roof, the sheets on the beds, the green tablecloths from its tables, dishevelling the hair of its inhabitants who were not allowed to taste oil and meat at that time. The loss of Bolen-bortta was too much. It meant one less earning member. It meant Mridul's status in the family had come down from 'Son of the Earning Member' to 'Son of a Dependent'. Mukut-khura had married last year. He would soon have a family to look after. Prosanto-da would probably marry his colleague Onulupa who he hung out with all the time. What would Onima-borma do with two daughters and two sons? He had to think, let go the demands of his heart, if he didn't want to etch himself in the memories of the people in that house, in that village, as the 'Selfish Son'. The designation of a 'Dependent's Son' was much better, much nobler. 'Selfish Son' wasn't. 'Offending Lovers' wasn't and nobody anyway cared about 'Revolutionary Lovers'. They died young. They were remembered by the next generation, not the generation in which they lived.

Brikodar told me, 'Maybe he will listen to you. I have been telling him to stay away from her from the day he started hanging out with her. I had sensed the day she had joined our Bihu dance group that Mridul was attracted to her. There are so many girls dying to be with him, so many Assamese girls, but he is interested in that Nepali girl. And whose daughter? Is her father a shopkeeper? Is her mother a teacher at the school? No! She is a wine brewer. Every evening, all the losers in this village gather at her house. Every evening, if you walk past their house that is at the end of the village, you will smell fried chicken and fish and the sweet smell of rice beer.'

I wasn't interested in advising him. I was more interested in the how and the when. Not in the why. Not in what should or shouldn't be done. I couldn't assume Brikodar's self-righteous tone. But I knew why he was saying what he did. I knew that storm would change this house for ever. The house with seventeen windows but no ventilators.

I said, 'You should think about it. This is a village, Mridul. People will not understand.'

Mridul spoke slowly, 'Last year, she had come to join our Bihu group. I was so prejudiced when she had come because I couldn't imagine a Nepali girl as our main dancer. But she was quick to reply that it was just her blood that was Nepali. In her bones, in her marrow, she is Assamese. I was startled. Without saying much I played a beat on the drum, which, as you know, is my habit, when I hold it. I hadn't cared to look at her face, so I looked at the drum and concentrated; but on the floor, I could see her toes dancing, then her heels keeping the beat and in a second, she was there, in front of me, dancing to the dhool. Sounds very filmy, doesn't it? She danced till she was exhausted.'

I made some banal noises such as 'It does sound filmy!' and 'Wow!' but he went on to say that this time no Mango Bite sweets wrapped in a letter came to him, no letter came to him through a little boy playing the courier. There was no messenger. He must have lost faith in his dimples and fair skin and the magic in his small eyes which, he claimed, drove girls crazy. That year it was he who had to look for a messenger, a Morton, a gift, a paper and a pen. Did he get one eventually? I wondered.

'So how did it go? Weren't you scared? After all, the whole village knows that her mother is a wine brewer. What happened to the much-hyped righteousness of our village?'

'People in the village don't know about it yet. We have been careful till now but one day, everyone will get to know. But when it had started, I was very scared, you know. I was very scared and, till now, I haven't told anyone except Brikodar. It would be a huge scandal if someone ever comes to know. Trust me, even when I wanted to put the message across to her, I didn't trust anyone. I used to drop her home after the rehearsals. We had to walk for long distances because her house is at one end of the village and the Bihu Club's office is at the other end. She could have sat on my cycle's carrier at the back but there was an unspoken contract between us that we would walk. That way it was longer, slower, and took us more time. We could chat about every topic under the sun. I want to bring her out of that hell—the daily quarrels between drunk men of the village. Though her mother never lets her serve wine, but every day, when she reaches home, she has to fry fish and chicken. Huge amounts of both. If she were cooking for the household there wouldn't have been anything to complain about. But . . .'

~

That night, home was waiting for us with another surprise—the punishment for tasting forbidden food. I didn't take too long to understand, though when I had entered the compound with Mridul, pushing away the bamboo gate where the sewali-flower tree was leaning lazily, I was startled to see Oholya-jethai coming towards us with the speed of a kite that could scare anyone out of his wits.

Mridul looked at me and murmured, 'Nokobi dei, don't admit that we have eaten pork.' Oholya-jethai wasn't alone. Onima-borma followed her with brisk steps, pulling the end of her sador to cover her head. Okoni-pehi was still around, and it was she who had heard it from her husband and told Oholya-jethai and Onima-borma about it. She followed Onima-borma, looking stern, and when the stream of words came out of Oholya-jethai's mouth, she played the prompter. But at times, she also defended Mridul.

In a sad voice, she said, 'I have always supported you, Mridul, in whatever you have done. Oholya-bai and your mother were totally against your father's decision of buying you the guitar, but this? Today you have started with pork and that too, even before you've reached college?'

Mukut-khura hollered from the background, 'Will he even pass his matric? Will he? College, my foot!'

Mridul looked down. He didn't want to say anything, I knew. But I also knew he wasn't the kind who would listen quietly. He was, after all, an expert at the art of defiance. But perhaps he didn't want to speak his mind to Oholya-jethai.

Onima-borma wailed, pointing towards the many relatives who had gathered there. Anil-da, his sister Moon-baideo (who wasn't married then), Sunjira-jethai, who had come from a nearby village along with her husband, and many more. She said, wailing pitifully, 'You are my only hope after your father's death. You are my eldest son. Why do you chew at the corners of my lungs like this? Why do you stab me in my back like this?'

'Shut up, Onima!' Oholya-jethai screamed, 'Pablo, go to the back of the house and take a bath. Moina is around; she will give you a change of clothes from your bag—but don't enter the house without taking a bath! And use only hot water. I don't want you falling sick. Did you hear me?'

'Yes, Jethai.'

I looked at Mridul for a second and started walking away. He was standing there, in front of a whole lot of people, like a criminal. Facing a crowd, with his aunts and mother occupying the front row and the back rows full of stay-home guests who had come to mourn Bolen-bortta's death, and who would leave only after the funeral was over. They were the audience. Onima-borma was a cameo. Okoni-pehi and Mukut-khura were prompters who completed the lines Oholya-jethai—the protagonist of the play—forgot to utter.

I didn't go near the well at the back of the house. I stood in the middle of the courtyard while Mridul stood at the gate, not allowed to enter his own house, and it was then that I heard Oholya-jethai's loud, booming voice saying that cruel sentence. 'Today you have touched pork—what if you haven't eaten it? *Ghraneng ardha bhojanang!* Smelling is akin to half eating—the shashtras have said that! You have broken your fast. You have broken the rituals. Your father will not forgive you for this. Today, you have bought pork; tomorrow you will buy alcohol, drink it and start sleeping with that wine brewer who was responsible for your father's death, with whom your father had an affair!'

A hum and hush and a wail followed her sentence and I knew, by saying that, she had changed something between Mridul and me forever. She had destroyed the image of his father that he had so painstakingly painted for me. That though he was an alcoholic, he didn't fight in the house. By saying this, Oholya-jethai had only pronounced an open secret. But it was an open secret that I didn't have to know, my father didn't have to know. I could have gone back home without knowing about this embarrassing episode in the family. I saw Onima-borma sit down on the ground as soon as Oholya-jethai uttered that one sentence that totally shook me up, made me wonder how could she, how could she. I was staring at Mridul who had turned back and left the house for the rest of the night. I wanted to follow him and ask him to stop but none of the twenty-odd people who were enjoying that drama had asked him to stop. It was as if they were still relishing the deliciousness of that cruel sentence: 'After all, a drunkard's son would be a drunkard only. Even your father built the steps to death with pork, just at your age.'

Mridul didn't return for the entire night and when he returned the next afternoon, he didn't speak to me for three days. He avoided me. He didn't answer my questions. He didn't return my greetings. He slept in the same room, on his hay mattress, but he came in late when he was sure I would be asleep. Sometimes he replied in monosyllables.

Perhaps he was ashamed that I had suddenly learnt something about his father that he didn't want me to know. Ashamed that he was humiliated in front of me. During that time, I had found a room in the house where I spent those three lonely days. Many years later when I would think back on the house, I would find myself thinking more and more about that one room that no one liked to enter. The room everyone avoided.

Only Bolen-bortta and Papa understood the value of that room, the things kept in it. After all, he was a lover of stories who went to watch *Bobby* with his newly-wed wife, Onima, who despised it. I know it was the story that had kept him glued to the seat. The story of two young star-crossed lovers, who could fight all odds. After all, as Papa says, he was a big-hearted man. He would have allowed Prosanto to marry 'that divorcee'. He would have probably allowed Mridul to marry Manju Mahatu— the daughter of the woman he allegedly had an affair with.

And that's why he was a misfit in the village, in the house, in Oholya-jethai's manual of what should and shouldn't be done. Who should marry whom. Who should bathe when and how many times.

That's why Bolen-bortta had to leave.

Ah no, *leave*.

Four

'Pabloo!'

'Pabloo!'

'What? Have we reached?' I opened my eyes startled, as if someone had woken me from a deep sleep.

'What's wrong with you? Why are you feeling sleepy early in the morning? Stop talking about reaching Mayong, we might have to get off the bus,' Mridul said.

'Get off the bus?' I looked around and found that we were still in Down Town and I had dozed off.

There were very few people left in the bus. When I looked out of the window, I could see that most of the people in the bus were standing outside with irritated faces. I could hear someone talking about the road being blocked by the bandh protestors.

'Bandh? There was no talk of a bandh?' I said, looking at Mridul for support. He looked worried.

'We should go back, Pabloo.'

'How?'

'Call your father?'

'He must have left by now—it's eleven. Mom must have left for college for her classes. No one is in the house. The landline would ring for ever.'

'Doesn't he have a phone in the office?'

'I don't know the number,' I lied. 'I never needed to use it.'

I didn't want to go back. I wanted to go to Mayong. I knew if I returned home that day, Mom wouldn't let me go. She would worry about all sorts of things and chew my brains. She would chew Papa's brains too until he would take back his permission of letting me go.

Dasbabu came and sat in front of us. He spoke loudly, so that everyone could hear him.

'I walked up to the end of the traffic jam. I have found out what is wrong.' He waited, letting the people in the bus, people outside the bus, hear his voice and gather around him. Someone told something to a man who was standing outside. I could only hear, '*Khobor ase*'. The man looked at Dasbabu and started climbing the steps of the tall bus. The people standing outside started trickling in and standing and sitting and leaning around Dasbabu, who seemed to like the attention. Suddenly, the bus became very stuffy. I tried to turn my face towards the window to get some fresh air that was drenched with the coldness of the dew and the fog. 'I have some news,' Dasbabu continued. 'One man has been shot dead.'

'What?'

'Where?'

'When?'

'Today?'

'In Down Town?'

Dasbabu scanned all the faces that asked him questions or the faces that didn't ask him questions or kept quiet looking shocked, staring at him. He seemed to be the kind of person who loved creating such suspense and being at the centre of attention. I don't like such people. But I had to listen to him. I wondered how much oil and masala he would be adding to whatever he had heard. 'Last night. *Eei* just before dawn! So the papers don't have it! A man was shot dead in Down Town! In his house! By the secret killers.' He spoke in a strange way, pausing to note the response of his listeners, see the effect of his story.

'*Guptohotya?*' one man said mockingly, looking bored. 'There is nothing *secret* about the secret killers. Everyone knows who is killing who around the state, who they are working for *secretly*. Two years ago, my uncle's son had gone fishing in the Pagladiya and he ended up having the fishing hook stuck to a man's rotting wrist.'

'Eesh! Eeesh!' Most of the women covered their noses with handkerchiefs as if they could smell the rotting wrist stuck to the fishing hook in faraway Pagladiya River. Some of them shrunk their nostrils while others turned towards that man.

'But aren't the secret killings over after the government fell in May last year? Who is going to kill whom?' a young guy in his late twenties said. He was wearing blue jeans and a yellow shirt, which he hadn't tucked in. He was reading a copy of *Bismoi* magazine that often printed a full-page black-and-white picture of a scantily clad girl on its last page. Whenever a new issue of the monthly magazine reached the market, young men would make a trip and, while pretending to browse magazines, they would pick up a copy of *Bismoi* and turn to the last page. So most shopkeepers had to staple copies of the magazine before hanging them in front of their shops.

Dasbabu didn't look pleased. As if he didn't want to be reminded that the government who was allegedly responsible for the killings was no more in power. As if he wanted the killings to continue.

Drowning out the *Bismoi* reader's voice, Dasbabu said loudly,

'Do you know who has been murdered this time?' Most of the people turned to listen to him now. The rotting-wrist man had lost his momentary popularity. 'He wasn't anyone big. He was just a distant brother of an ULFA member.'

'Distant brother? They have even started targeting distant relatives now?'

'It's been happening for a long time now. Even distant relatives aren't spared,' one woman said. She sounded very annoyed with the interruption. She turned towards Dasbabu and pleaded with him to continue. Dasbabu gave a scene-by-scene description of the event. How the masked gunmen had entered the house before dawn and dragged him out. How his three young children had cried for help, tried to pull their father back. How his wife had fallen on the body of the man and asked them to kill her and not him, told the assassins that he was the only earning member of the family and that he had a small job in a local government school as a bearer. The people sucked their teeth. They remarked how this sort of thing was happening too often and recalled the killing of Mithinga Daimary's entire family one night in 1998 by the secret killers, though I was sure that none of them knew he was also known by his pen name Megan Kachari, who wrote poems about a world that had started behaving like a memsahib.

'Are you sure the secret killings are still going on? The government who started it is no more in power.' *Bismoi*-guy expressed his reservations but no one paid any attention. He looked at the magazine. Perhaps, the last page.

'But don't worry!' Dasbabu said loudly, raising his hands like a politician assuring a large rally. 'Though it's a bandh, it is only Guwahati bandh, not Assam bandh. And they aren't creating any inconvenience for people—why would they, they don't represent any organization, these are just residents of the Down Town area, relatives and friends of the victim's family and members of the Senior Citizens' Club. They will let us go. They are just demonstrating on the main road with the dead body. That's why there is a traffic jam. People will demonstrate in the city today, carrying his body around along the main road. You will be able to see it from your window.'

'Won't it smell by the time it is returned home?' one woman wondered aloud but no one paid attention to her.

Some people looked at the window as if the demonstration was already passing that stretch of the road, while others murmured, 'Oh my God!'

'Won't it smell by the time it is taken around the city? A corpse rots at the speed of a girl's age,' the woman said once again, louder this time, adding some more gory detail so that people responded to her. One or two men turned to look at her.

'Mridul, let's get off?'

'It'd be as soft as a rotten gourd by the time it is taken to the cremation ground,' the woman said very loudly now. But she was speaking to herself. Without looking at anyone. Without scanning the faces of other people as she had done in her previous two attempts.

There was a breeze outside. I stood there and told Mridul I was having a déjà vu moment. He said it must be because I might have been reminded of the horrific incident in Mayong that had taken place while I was there to attend his father's funeral.

I hadn't left Mayong abruptly in the middle of the mourning phase because Mridul had been avoiding me, not speaking to me. I had to leave Mayong because Papa had turned up after that sleepless night of shrieks and blood and guns to take me back. I knew Mom must have fought with him, reprimanded him. I knew she had been too worried to stay at home and wait for me to turn up; and that was why she had also sat in the car and come along with him, wearing a mekhela-sador. But she hadn't spent too much time in the village. About an hour after he had come to pick me up, we had left. Mridul hadn't stopped me. He hadn't hidden my watch, socks and bag, hadn't said that even if I hadn't brought change of clothes, I could wear his spare ones because he wasn't anyway wearing normal clothes.

Five

One important thing I noted during my second visit to Mayong was that everything in the house was crumbling. The roof of the main house had many perforations. The pillars leaned against invisible walls and looked like hunchbacks. Mridul told me that whenever it rained they left those four rooms in the main house and went to the annex that was built after his father's funeral. Bolen-bortta's entire family had shifted to that extension. The walls of that house were made of brick and it had a tin roof, unlike the main house. Only Aaita lived in the main house, with Prosanto-da, whose romantic aspirations were sending ferocious ripples across the entire house, the entire village. Prosanto-da had built two new rooms out of bamboo, wood and mud and also renovated Aaita's room partly.

The room where the books were stored wasn't part of the new house. It wasn't part of the old house that had perforated roofs either. It was actually a storeroom where ploughs made from jackfruit-tree wood were stashed away for the winters. Where old quilts that were beyond repair were spread on the bed as mattresses, forever waiting for quilt makers from Sunapur to arrive, twanging their bow-like machines that cleaned the cotton inside the quilts. The space under the bed wasn't spared too. Instead of mosquitoes trapped in cobwebs, there was an old harmonium from the days of Oholya-jethai's youth when she was the subject of the biggest gossip in the entire village, a gossip that changed her for life. Beside the harmonium, there were iron trunks and I didn't know what was there in those trunks. There were stools, old bamboo chairs flung under the bed carelessly like leaves swept away by a broom to a corner of the courtyard. The bed was tall, but one of its legs was broken and a few bricks piled on top of each other were used in its place.

Along with the plough, harmonium and old, unused quilts that were spread like mattresses on the bed, the walls of that room were lined with wooden almirahs. Inside them, in shelves, sat books, like rows and rows of soldiers on a battlefield.

It was in that room that Mridul sat with me in 2002, telling me that things were changing in their house, that the house was crumbling just like the almirahs, the books, the walls of that abandoned room. There was growing tension between Prosanto-da and the family. There were growing fissures between his mother and Mukut-khura—who listened only to Oholya-jethai and not to his mother. There he had told me that they were just waiting for the wedding to get over. His mother had decided to have a different kitchen, her own set-up in which she didn't have to bathe twenty-five times a day. Where she didn't have to work under the hawk eye of Oholya-jethai who had such a long list of what should and shouldn't be done.

When I came out of the room, I thought of the perforated roof. I saw that the house had tilted to the left, like the Leaning Tower of Pisa I had seen in my high-school G.K. books. It was crumbling and that was the other important thing I had noticed during my second visit.

But on the day I had entered that compound to attend the

wedding, I had no idea that the house was *crumbling*. I thought everything was normal. As usual, Oholya-jethai looked angry. She was older and thinner.

She greeted me with a sarcastic statement: 'At last you remembered us! Otherwise who remembers this godforsaken village?' A smile was stuck on her face.

She didn't wait for my 'That's not true, Jethai!' protest but started abusing one of the maids. '*Moroti!*' she cursed. 'I asked you to sweep this courtyard long ago, didn't I? Now our Guwahatia guest has come and stepped on this rubbish! You all are good for nothing. None of you can do the simplest job properly, and yet never feel ashamed to take up to four helpings during meals.'

Sayamoni, the maid she had been cursing, entered the stage with a large broom, her eyes almost watering and her breasts the same size, large and round, as I had seen last time I was there. 'Sayamoni is still here? I thought she was married off.'

'We wanted to get her married. She doesn't want to get married! Don't know what she has planned for herself. She loves us too much—or so it seems.'

Onima-borma came out of the house, a pink-bordered white sador wrapped around her body, a white mekhela around her waist, and I was shocked to see her emaciated figure. She had large dark patches all over her face and almost opaque dark circles around her eyes. She looked at me and complained about the dust all over my skin.

Mridul's younger brother, Suruj, came running and took my luggage away. I laughed. 'Borma, this is Mayong's dust. I don't mind it.'

She started to weep. 'Could you not visit us some day? Your father has stopped coming too. Earlier, he used to come every month when Mridul's father was alive. You have all forgotten us.

Just come and ask, "How are you?" and we shall be happy. We don't want anything else except a few kind words.'

I felt awkward, and suddenly Anil-da came to my rescue. 'Eh eh . . . tsk tsk. This is not the time to cry, Khuridou! Let the boy rest for a while.' He pulled me closer to him firmly, pressed me to the right side of his body and cuddled me with one of his arms. 'My God! You have become so tall! I saw you last at Moon's wedding, right?' I looked around for Prosanto-da, but didn't see him. I asked Anil-da where he was, but he kept saying other insignificant things about the wedding.

Moon-baideo was his youngest sister, who was married off to an autorickshaw driver in Rojakhat, another village nearby, but a slightly developed one, with a highway cutting it into two halves, six kilometres away from Teteliguri. Moon-baideo was standing a little away, and beside her was another girl, with long hair, dressed in a blue salwar kameez.

The other girl was standing with her back to me, so I couldn't see her face. The afternoon sun had sat on her hair, giving it a reddish, golden halo. I wondered who could be the owner of such beautiful hair and such an attractive back with a deep valley where the spinal cord ran straight. Through her light cotton kurta, I could see the faint outline of her white bra. I shivered. It was as if an ant had run through my entire body at great speed across my spine, my chest, my legs. I couldn't decide if her back felt so attractive because of the hair or because of the way she had left it open. I wanted to know who that girl was. I couldn't take my eyes off her. I wanted to see her face but she wouldn't turn. I thought of asking Mridul about the girl. Later, I decided, when we would get some time to have a private chat.

Anil-da was a popular guy. I didn't know how many girls threw love letters at him wrapped around Amul milk chocolates. But he was a guy in demand among the girls eligible for marriage, and also among all men and women due to his helpful nature. He was present at all weddings, all funerals, and worked from the first day to the last for every household. He didn't have a job. When he was in need, he'd borrow money from anyone in the village and they didn't mind lending him since each family in the village—and not only the affluent ones—had sought his help in some way or the other many times. So he never had to hear a 'no' from anyone. As a child, I remembered Anil-da as the nicest cousin. He was the only one among the elder guys who'd be nice to my two elder brothers and me. The others didn't have time. They either felt shy or treated us like guests. They stayed away. He was the one who roamed around with us, made us sit on his lap even though we were old and big enough to break his leg, bought us salted peanuts. He had three younger sisters. They would all get married in the subsequent years, but he wouldn't. He would go ahead to file nomination for the local panchayat elections, almost become the head of the panchayat at a young age, but would die unfortunately as a result of a political conspiracy years later. A few days later, it would be he who would bring in a rumour that would change the mood of the wedding radically. People said, 'Anil behaves like a woman: loves gossip, loves to create it, and takes part in all the women's activities. Don't trust what he says.' But no one bothered to worry about his unreliability, that he liked to exaggerate things, that he was a compulsive storyteller.

At Moina-pehi's wedding, he had a moustache. He had developed a paunch and his skin had darkened. He chewed betel nuts all the time that lent a repulsive red tint to his face. I couldn't believe that this was the man who had such fair skin once upon a time that he was made to play Draupadi in the one-act plays during Janmastami. When he wailed during the disrobing scene, real tears flowed down his cheeks and most women in the village couldn't stop themselves from sobbing into their handkerchiefs. But still, he was the nicest man around, the most helpful and the most reliable in terms of lending a helping hand at social gatherings. He saved me from that awkward moment when Onima-borma started to cry. 'Eh eh . . . tsk tsk. This is not the time to cry, Khuri. Let the boy rest.' But he continued to say something that was far from sending me to a place conducive to rest. 'Come and see the bride, come! In a wedding house, you should see the bride first.'

~

Okoni-pehi was standing near Moina-pehi, when I went inside the room. Anil-da stood beside me when I spoke to her. Some of her hair had greyed and she had developed wrinkles on her face. Her teeth had more gaps between them and were stained brown and red with the betel nuts that she chewed with limestone constantly. I was surprised, because she looked older than Oholya-jethai when it should have been the other way round.

'O aai! It's Pablo!' Okoni-pehi screamed immediately.

Moina-pehi said in her usual style, 'Eeeh! At last you remembered me?' There were other people in the room—Sunjira-jethai, Moon-baideo, Dorongi-aaita, Moina-pehi's friends and young kids I couldn't identify. Moina-pehi hadn't changed. Her skin looked bright, smooth like porcelain. On the bed, there were many white polythene packets and clothes strewn around that Moon-baideo was folding.

'Of course, Moina-pehi. Nobody has forgotten you! And you didn't keep dropping in at our house eight times a week either, no?'

Both of us laughed. 'Eeeh, I really would have liked to go on my own to invite you all. But that big gate, the security guard! I feel really scared to go to your house. Feels as if I am entering the house of some *minister-sinister*. Eeeh!'

Minister-sinister. I was amused. I said, 'Oh, is that so? I will tell Papa.'

'No, don't, don't!' she screamed, while Okoni-pehi was telling Mridul that I had grown so big in such a short time that soon they'd be invited to my wedding. She was beaming, her broad face full of compassion.

I liked Okoni-pehi. Like Moina-pehi, she was married very late. She used to visit us in winters when the roads were dry and the travel to Guwahati wasn't difficult. She wore a blue blazer with her mekhela-sadors and saris. Later, Ma and I would laugh at the blue, yellow, green, pink blazers that women in Mayong wore. They grew so popular after the Sunday market started selling them that a blazer became the ultimate fashion symbol in the entire region of Mayong; on any special occasion, in a festival, we would witness thousands of women of all ages in blazers. Young girls fought with their parents for a blazer and didn't eat rice for days until it was bought for them.

Moina-pehi said, 'No, don't, don't! I just felt very awkward going and inviting your father to my own wedding.'

'What is there to feel awkward about?'

Okoni-pehi explained: 'She is not like your townia girls, Pablo. Our village girls would definitely feel shy to talk about such matters.' Dorongi-aaita looked at me and nodded at everything Okoni-pehi was saying. Moon-baideo had no reaction on her face. She often looked unhappy and annoyed by something.

More and more people started pouring into the room. Moon-baideo wanted to know when Mom was coming. Sunjira-jethai wanted to know if I was going abroad for further studies after my higher secondary exams. Meenu-jethai asked when I would get married and Anil-da expressed his desire to feast at my wedding.

After a while, I walked out of Moina-pehi's room. Mridul followed me. 'Let's go and sit on the banks of the Brahmaputra?' he suggested.

It was usual for me to agree with him. We loved those walks. It lent us privacy, to be out in the open, under the sky, that allowed personal matters to be discussed, after which I invariably told him that these matters were not really personal after all, but all related to his house and its various members, including him.

The forever-intruding Oholya-jethai met us on the way— 'Where are you going? When will you come back? Why do you have to go to the Brahmaputra? Have you not seen a river before? Don't you know that Mrigen's son drowned in the river last summer? So what if it's not summer now and there are no rains? Don't you know there is always enough water in the Brahmaputra to drown two elephants even at the height of winter, though the river looks calm, it's also short-tempered? You shouldn't test its patience. You have come all the way from Guwahati—I want you to go back safely. And don't listen to this guy who doesn't study but roams around all the time, lives in his dreamworld all the time, twanging his guitar. Don't give me more worries, more tension, please! How much more will I carry in this old worn-out head all alone? If I don't monitor anything, nothing in this house happens in the desired way. And now this wedding! If something happens to you all? What will happen then? What will happen to the wedding? What will I tell Prodip?'

Oholya-jethai had not changed. She was still devoted to her 'religion'—scolding.

I knew what was to be done. We had to just ignore her. But you couldn't ignore her in an obvious way. You had to be subtle.

'We will come back soon.'

'We won't take long.'

'We won't go to the Brahmaputra.'

'We'll just sit on the rocks, far away from the river . . .'

We left.

He had picked up some guavas with red centres from the kitchen when he had come to take me away from Moina-pehi's room.

'She looked so happy, Mridul,' I said with feeling.

'She is eager to get married. But she is old. Nearly thirty-two. Which young man will marry her now?' He chewed the red insides of a guava as he spoke to me. 'Who else will marry her other than a forty-five-year-old frustrated man? I don't know why that bastard has not married till now.'

A breeze brought in the mild fragrance of wild gulonch flowers. It had mixed, as easily as salt in water, with the smell of dry cow dung from the East Bengali village nearby. Mridul told me that the village, sprawled around the foothills of the Kasosila Hill, was in the middle of the Brahmaputra once upon a time, back when his father was a baby, suckled by Aaita. At that time, the Brahmaputra flowed far away from where we were sitting now.

I felt I had wanted to ask Mridul something, but had forgotten what it was. I tried to remember it, but found myself thinking about that village and the river instead.

Many years ago, when Bolen-bortta must have started taking his first wobbly steps, the Brahmaputra fell in love with the lush, green youthfulness of Borongabari—the village of the East Bengali refugees—and started inching towards her. In the process, the son of Brahma—Brahmaputra—twitched, and moved away from his earlier love Hatimura, relieving the people there, but increasing the tears of the people of Borongabari during seasons when the sky wept for days, weeks and months. Slowly, it engulfed the entire village. Like leaves falling around the trunk of a deciduous tree in autumn, the villagers gathered around the Kasosila Hill, hoping that the simple-minded God Shiva would save them from the lunatic love of Brahmaputra.

The Brahmaputra had embraced Borongabari, their village, whose earth they had tilled like earthworms to grow a golden harvest of paddy. Since then, the river has been moving more and more towards Hatimura. People prayed for his destructive love to be diverted to some other village. Villagers from other villages hoped and prayed that he wouldn't love them too much. 'Stay away, Son of Brahma, who are born from the navel of Narayana,' they pleaded, 'stay away.'

I thought back on the times when Bolen-bortta had been suckled by Aaita. Where we sat that day, we would have found a lush, green, crowded, rich village with granaries full with golden seeds sprawled in front of us. But the river took away the village chunk by chunk, tree by tree, house by house, leaving an endless expanse of water before our eyes.

I thought about the eroding banks of Hatimura. Would this village remain when I grow older, when the children of my children would suck at the breasts of their mothers?

I felt strange.

I felt small.

Time felt immense.

I didn't want to think about all this any more, though the image of the disintegrating books in that abandoned room of the house came to my mind and Mridul's remark that his house was crumbling started crawling all over my thoughts like ants on skin.

I felt annoyed that I had now forgotten all about something important that I had decided to ask Mridul. Like a distant song that comes floating in on quiet afternoons, the question kept niggling at my mind but refused to reveal itself. It stayed trapped in my mind's web—like a fly entangled in the silky threads of a spider web.

So I asked him about Moina-pehi. 'Then why are you letting her marry this man?'

'She doesn't want to. Pehi is so beautiful . . . but for a long time no one took any note of her.' He lamented slowly.

I knew what he meant. Such neglect befell most youngest daughters. Hence, in many families, the mother and the elders never allowed the brothers to marry before doing their 'duties' by their younger sisters.

Moina-pehi was too young when her brother Bolen-bortta married—so he didn't bother about her marriage at that time. And perhaps nobody noticed when the tiny girl who cried for milk all the time grew up into a young woman with large breasts, a black mane of hair, a tall figure and such fair complexion that each year after dancing Bihu with Mridul's group, she would get the largest number of gifts from the guys. She refused to accept those gifts, and then one day, like the gifts, she even refused to take part in the Bihu dance. Perhaps no one noticed that the guys who she used to dance with had got married; and most importantly, all the girls with whom she danced, spoke of men with the broadest shoulders, shared sour fruits sprinkled with black salt and green chillies, had been married off in nearby villages and had given birth to their first or second child.

No one noticed these things. But everyone noticed that she had acquired the art of weaving in the loom from Oholya-jethai.

People didn't see why she had chosen to learn this skill. People didn't see that she was no more of that age when a young girl would sit at the loom not to weave but to look at the road facing the house—most looms were in front of the house on the veranda—to check out her man, whether the man she dreamt of was cycling past. And so, the weaving would go for a toss and the poor girl would end up with a mess, with all the threads entangled. Moina-pehi was no more of that thread-entangling age. When she wove, no one heard her complain that it was the skylark that had swooped down on the loom and got all the threads mixed up, or that a neighbour, jealous of her beautiful designs, had jinxed the threads.

Three years after Bolen-bortta's death, it was Okoni-pehi who first realized that Moina couldn't spend her entire life weaving at the loom. Dorongi-aaita agreed with her, mentioned possible contacts who could find a groom for her.

'When Okoni-pehi broached the topic, Dorongi-aaita said she knew someone in Sonapur but who was much older. Moina-pehi immediately left the place. She didn't want to be a part of the conversation,' Mridul was telling me. 'She was shy. Just shy.'

I slowly repeated his word 'shy', as if rolling a chewable cough drop under my tongue. And I laughed. Mridul asked me why I had laughed and I didn't want to tell him that she *had to be* shy. There was no other option. Otherwise people would pierce her with questions, bitch about her behind her back, saying she was a shameless girl, and would make it out to be the reason for her remaining unmarried till then. There was no place for unabashed girls in our society just as there was no respectable place for an old maid. Moina-pehi didn't want to marry the person chosen by the family. But she had to.

'Had Okoni-pehi not mentioned the topic, we would have had

another Oholya-jethai in our house,' Mridul continued.

They weren't just marrying her off. They were shedding a huge burden off their shoulders. I wondered how a family that was trying so hard to rid itself of a burden couldn't understand the kind of burden Onulupa's father was carrying in his heart when he had requested Prosanto to 'look after' her. Didn't they know the history of the pledge Prasanto-da had made holding the dying man's reed-like hands? Didn't they know she was the first love of the son they were trying to protect with all their might?

And yet, they couldn't accept her. Couldn't shift around a chair, a bed, a table, a glass, to make some space for her in that L-shaped house with seventeen windows.

They talked about her protruding jaw, her flat chest, her 'already-touched' body. Behind her back, they mocked her as a 'sucked sugarcane'.

Yes, Onulupa: Prasanto-da's girlfriend.

'The divorcee' he was once dating and had now decided to marry.

Of whom Mridul was ashamed as well and wanted my mother to chat with Prosanto-da, hoping that he would listen to her and not marry his first love from his university days—back from a time when he used to write long letters to Bolen-bortta.

People in the house were scared of Bolen-bortta. He wasn't a hard man. He was generous, kind. But he was the sort who didn't want to hear thank yous from people he had been generous to. Whenever someone wanted to express gratitude—the poor farmer from the East Bengali village or the distant relative who had lost her husband—he brushed it away. When that distant relative would come in her white clothes, he would say, 'Go away, and don't show me your tears. Keep your children well fed.' When the poor farmer wanted to thank him by touching his feet, he would jump back like a person confronting a snake sprawled on his way. He would say, 'It's all right, it's all right. Instead of touching my feet, stop drinking and work hard.'

I didn't hear these things from Papa. It was Mridul who told me about him during those days of mourning when he used to pull out the guitar (that his father had gifted him despite Oholya-jethai's protests that money must not be 'thrown into the water this way') from his room and sing that he couldn't be darkness, he couldn't forget the winged past. In between that Zubeen Garg song and the stories he used to narrate, he told me about his father. Clearly, he was proud of him. He wanted to make sure that I had a high opinion of him. That my father's best friend and first cousin may not have studied at Cotton College, the best college in Assam, may not have cleared the civil service examinations or built a two-storey house in Guwahati, but he was in no way inferior to my father. If my father made it 'big' in the city, his father was widely respected by people in the village of Hatimura as also by people from all the seven villages that surrounded Hatimura, and maybe beyond. If my father was friendly and spoke with his son in English forming a bond that the people in the village thought was too strong, his father bought him a guitar by 'throwing money into the water'. I listened to him carefully, nodding my head, agreeing; because I knew, somewhere in the large tracts of fields of his heart, a storm was raging. A storm which was breaking down the branches of the trees that grew on it. A storm that was bending the long stalks of reeds that thrived on its fertile soil.

And that storm was his awareness that I could learn, just like the whole village knew, that his father had died an alcoholic, because of a liver malfunction, that he had an affair with Anjali Mahatu. It was deeply embarrassing. Something that would never escape village talk for years to come, a knowledge he would have to live with, like a permanent scar on his forehead, like a stain of blackberries on white clothes. But he didn't want me to remember just the salacious gossip. He wanted me to know that there was more to his father than the beer he bought from the Nepali brewer who lived at the other end of the village. How kind he was, how lovely he was. How he took care of his wife and never ever scolded her, never raised his hand on her like most other men in the village, for which he had even faced general criticism of being 'uxorious'. How, unlike many other men in the village, he cared too visibly for his own mother. He woke up early in the morning to pick fragrant wild paans for his old mother from the hilltop. Ensured personally her clothes were clean, she had eaten well, dressed properly; he would also regularly check the amount of cough syrup left in the bottles. After that night—when Oholya-jethai had mercilessly predicted that a drunkard's son would be a drunkard—Mridul had started talking about his father even more, as if trying to undo the damage she had done. He didn't know that he was trying to stop the cold from coming in through the cracks by pasting coloured posters on mud walls?

Though I was bored, I listened patiently. I wanted to tell Mridul that he didn't have to tell me more about his father. I would remember him as Papa's best friend, not an alcoholic who woke up one morning and fell down while having a glass of Horlicks and didn't survive until the next day in the hospital because his liver was totally damaged; because, though he was asked by the doctors not to drink even a drop of alcohol if he wanted to live, he was drinking every morning, secretly mixing Horlicks with vodka. It didn't matter to me. What mattered to me was that he didn't have fights at home after he drank—didn't hit anyone, didn't raise his voice, didn't mumble or scream abuses at people he didn't like once he was inebriated.

But I let Mridul mould his father's image for me, as he wished. Bolen-bortta: who everyone in the village, despite the way he died, respected. Bolen-bortta: who spoke less, so less, that even his wife Onima-borma thought twice before speaking to him. Bolen-bortta: whose presence in the house ensured silence and order. Except for Oholya-jethai, no one spoke loudly when he was in the house. And even she respected him. She made sure he got the largest portion of fish, the biggest share of every curry and fry, and the tallest stool to sit on while eating, because he was the head of the house: 'The Highest Earning Member'.

It was only his youngest brother, Prosanto-da, who could talk freely with Bolen-bortta. Crack a joke with him. Pick up a biscuit from his plate while he was eating. Mridul was around eighteen when Bolen-bortta passed away, and Prosanto-da was around twenty-seven. From his university hostel, he wrote long letters to Bolen-bortta, told him about the awards he had won in the college festival: best scriptwriter, best actor, best director. Did they speak about girls?

~

We had finished eating the guavas with red centres and Mridul said that he should have brought some more. I said that it was enough—how much could we eat anyway?

'Prosanto-da and Onulupa have been going out since they met in college,' Mridul said, throwing a flat stone into the river that broke out into delicate ripples.

'Then why aren't you supporting him—at least you should! They work together in the same college and they have even set up the college together. They have done so much for this village. Is this the way to repay their kindness and commitment?' I asked him impatiently.

'Well, earlier it was different,' Mridul said. 'She dumped him and got married to an army officer her father had chosen for her. If she loved Prosanto-da, why did she marry another guy? The family had accepted her as a prospective daughter-in-law already, but then, one evening, suddenly she turns up with a wedding invitation and a ring on her finger. We were stunned. But in a way, both Ma and Okoni-pehi were kind of happy because they thought she wasn't suitable for him. He is so handsome. And she is ugly.'

He curled his lips when he mentioned she wasn't pretty. I thought about her face. I had met her once when she had come to our house while Prosanto-da was studying in the university. She had also come over a couple of times after Bolen-bortta's death. No, I couldn't remember her face. I couldn't remember how she looked like. But I remembered she had sat with Papa and discussed medieval Assamese literature. Madhob Kondoli's Assamese Ramayana. The Borgeets. Later, Papa had said she was 'intelligent'. And Papa rarely praised anyone.

I teased Mridul. 'It's his choice—who are you to call her ugly? I will see what kind of a fairy you would end up marrying.'

He blushed and said, 'You will see. You will see soon.'

At that time, I didn't know he had major plans for marrying a girl as beautiful as a wing-clipped fairy. Plans that could create a furore in the wedding. He was yet to tell me, yet to ask me to be complicit in what he was scheming to do. He wouldn't tell me about it for a long time. I wanted to ask him, but I was too proud. We were friends, why wouldn't he tell me on his own? I thought.

'What do you mean? What are you talking about?'

With a naughty smile on his face, he repeated, 'You will get to know soon.'

Even then, I wanted to ask him about Manju Mahatu but I wanted him to speak on his own. Did I also want him not to marry her? The wine brewer Anjali Mahatu's daughter who he was in love with when I had come here last time? The girl he had told me about the night I had pork at Brikodar's house.

Mridul changed the subject. 'There is so much tension in the family these days because of Prosanto-da. My mother has tried to talk him out of this mess but he is adamant. You know, her father blackmailed him emotionally.' Mridul raised his voice, as if he was angry that an old man who had never been to his house could disrupt peace in his family from afar with his reed-like hands, with his slowly dying soul.

'What do you mean? Prosanto-da isn't a kid, Mridul. How could he be emotionally blackmailed?'

A little ahead, some fishermen were returning. They wore short, green gamusas that revealed their legs glistening in the river's water. To our right, on a large block of stone a woman was washing clothes, wearing a petticoat that was pulled up to cover her large, drooping breasts that hung like huge jackfruits. I wondered if the men had fish slithering inside their pot-shaped bamboo creels. I wondered if the woman had a lover and a child and a husband. What she would be cooking that night after washing the clothes. The sun was golden now. Behind us, the Kasosila Hill stood, as if protecting us, looking at us, listening to us. We could hear the chirping of birds that were perched on the trees of that hill. Trees that were covered with yellow parasitic creepers.

'Prosanto-da and Onulupa-baideo were two of the founding members of the college,' Mridul began again.

He took a deep breath, as if preparing to tell me something long. He stared at the horizon where the birds could be seen flying away from us, and from the sands that we were sitting on, it seemed as if the birds were plunging into the river, committing suicide. The wind came and left waves on the river.

Mridul started telling me about Prosanto-da and Onulupa. 'Pabloo, Prosanto-da's life's work is the college he started with a few others. But the college isn't nationalized even after so many years. It will eventually happen. We are hopeful. After working in the college for two years, Onulupa had married that army officer who lived in Delhi. She had to give up her job since she was leaving Assam forever. Prosanto-da had lost contact with her, had stopped speaking to her, and one of his colleagues, who he started going out with after a few months, helped him get out of his emotional crisis. She nurtured him like a plant that had lost its roots. But one fine day, after one and a half years, Onulupa turned up at our doorstep. She had lost weight and seemed as if she had been ill for a long time. She told us she couldn't live with the army officer. Though he had grown up in Guwahati in his uncle's house, his family who lived in Delhi was totally north Indian. She looked so ill. Oholya-jethai thinks it was not because of the tension and physical strain she had to endure after her father was diagnosed with cancer, but because she had gone through an abortion at an advanced stage. You know, Oholya-jethai can get all these things very easily. She can read people. Prosanto-da was very much in love with that other girl by then. They were often spotted together long after the classes in the college got over. She would come with him to our house and take care of everyone. She had won our hearts, including Oholya-jethai's, and you know how difficult it is to impress her. She was pretty, loved by everyone. Not that Onulupa-baideo wasn't popular, but everyone thought the other girl was the perfect match for Prosanto-da and she too, just like him, taught political science. So they were working in the same department. But we don't know what happened after Onulupa returned. They stopped hanging out together. Old passions were perhaps ignited.' There was a note of sarcasm in the way he said the last sentence.

'And Prosanto-da started hanging out with Onulupa. One day, Okoni-pehi confronted him, asking what was going on, and he said he would let us know. The next day, he went to Tezpur to drop Onulupa-baideo at her house because her father's condition had worsened after a chemotherapy session. He was in a terrible state. Apparently, he held Prosanto-da's hands and requested him to "sort out her life, look after her" and sought forgiveness for not letting them marry before. Prosanto-da promised him, holding his reed-like hands, that he will marry Onulupa because he had always loved her. We of course don't know how exactly he had made this promise but we heard it from his friends. Things don't remain a secret in the village. He is planning to marry her soon—just a small court marriage, right after this wedding. Ma cries all the time to Aaita. Oholya-jethai keeps asking Aaita to tell him not to marry her. It's such a mess in the family. And since no one in the house has given him consent, he has been staying away. He comes sometimes, but never spends the night in the house. He stays over at his friends', with our cousins. Since the day before, he hasn't come back even once. He had a huge argument with Oholya-jethai and she was, as usual, very harsh on him. It is as if Prosanto-da is trying to tell us that he will leave the house forever if we don't welcome Onulupa into the family, if we don't give him our consent to marry her.'

I was trying to decide what exactly to say. Prosanto-da was a rebellious lover according to the standards of the village. And I was surprised at Mridul's judgemental tone because he, too, like his father's favourite brother, was a 'rebel lover'. Someone who would perhaps become the subject of Bihu songs in the years to come, who would inspire intense couplets about lovers who broke away from traditions and became a part of history in spite of the disapproval of their family, the village council, in spite of offending the sense of propriety of people like Aaita.

But back then, I was only thinking about Mridul's judgemental tone, a boy who himself was breaking the rules by committing the crime of loving a Nepali, a wine brewer's daughter, and wondered why he didn't realize the irony. Was he proud that he was marrying a young virgin? Was he proud that he was marrying a girl who hadn't worn the red mark on her head before, who hadn't sat beside the sacrificial fire for hours, listening to Sanskrit chants? What was making him miss the point, the fact that he wasn't much different from Prosanto-da in terms of romantic aspirations?

No, I didn't ask him to think about all this because I knew he wouldn't understand. He hadn't been conditioned to understand things this way.

Behind us, I heard the sound of a jeep passing by. I turned to find that a large cloud of dust, instead of the usual children shouting 'car, car, car', trailing the jeep. It was full of soldiers. Standing and sitting soldiers. Brightly smiling soldiers. Mean-eyed soldiers. Tall and muscular soldiers. Some of them were laughing, while the others looked around, as if mesmerized by the most beautiful river in the world. I wondered if they had seen such a big river before. If they had seen such a beautiful sunset before. I wondered what they must be thinking about our river, our sunset, our skies, our village, our songs, our chatter, our walls, the sound of our looms, our birds, our dust.

A little farther down the grass-covered road, the jeep stopped, two men got off to pee and that was another important thing I noted—not the peeing soldiers in green clothes, but that so many soldiers were roaming around the place even during the day. The last time I had come, they spent most of the time in the camp, didn't make rounds in the jeep during the day, but emerged like bats, mosquitoes and owls only in the depths of the night.

When I had gotten off the bus (three hours late because of the Guwahati bandh and the procession), they were the first and the only human beings I had seen because the marketplace where the bus had stopped was deserted. It looked like there was a Mayong bandh. Standing by the road, they didn't ask me anything, but had just stared, throwing raven-mean glances at me. I realized, suddenly, that was why there weren't many people out on the streets of the village that day, although it was a lovely afternoon washed with golden sunlight.

Six

Back in 1998, three days after Oholya-jethai had called him a drunkard's son, Mridul was seething in anger in that abandoned storeroom. 'You think I can't answer her back? Do you think I couldn't come up with a suitable reply although she insulted me in front of so many people? People have come to mourn here, and when you mourn someone, you talk about how great that person was. You don't soil his image. Chee!'

Mridul had avoided me for three days and to relieve myself of the boredom, I had taken refuge in that roomful of books and abandoned objects. It was on the third day of his absence from the house that I had decided to leave. I wanted to call Papa and thought of seeking Prosanto-da's or Moina-pehi's help. I knew they wouldn't like to hear that I was leaving but would surely help. Just as I was about to express my wish to leave to one of the two, Mridul had barged into that room. Seizing the horror novel from my hand, he put it inside one of the wooden almirahs and shut its door. Quickly, he also picked up a novel of the Dosyurani Bijuli series that had pictures of a busty woman on its cover, in dark, tight-fitting clothes.

I was looking away from him, annoyed with him for seizing the books from me. He asked me again, 'Do you think I am not capable of giving her a suitable reply?' He still looked angry.

I knew Mridul was the kind of person who wouldn't apologize for avoiding me for the last few days. He had expected, hoped, that I would understand that he was apologetic. And that annoyed me even more. That he didn't apologize, didn't furnish an explanation for his strange behaviour, and there he was, sitting in front of me, expressing his anger as if nothing had happened, as if it was only last night that Oholya-jethai had said that a drunkard's son would only turn out to be a drunkard.

So I snapped, 'Why tell me, Mridul? I am here for just a few days. I am only a guest. If you are capable of saying something, you should go and say it now, instead of telling me you can answer her back.'

Mridul stood up. He looked straight into my face. 'You really think I can't give a good reply to Oholya-jethai? You are very much a part of this family, Pabloo.'

I started walking away. 'I don't see the point of this discussion.'

'You wait and watch the next time she tries to insult my father or me.'

'All right.' I shrugged.

The sarcasm wasn't in that tone; it was in that shrug.

Did he want to go out of the house with me to meet Brikodar? Brikodar and his always-laughing sister and forever-happy mother. I wanted to avoid Mridul as well. Just as he had avoided me. I wanted him to feel what it felt like to be avoided.

That night, he tried to rope me into a conversation. Probably to make up for the last three days of rudeness. But I was silent. I replied only in monosyllables. Sometimes in brief sentences, when they were absolutely unavoidable. He tried talking about girls in order to get me into a conversation. Not getting any response, he shifted the topic to the tension in the village but that night I didn't express any interest in it either. He said he had met people from the new colony of the village this evening, that some masked gunmen had come to Hiren's house and asked him to persuade his former comrades—the ones who were still underground—to surrender. I was looking at the cobwebs again, trying to think whose faces those cobwebs resembled. I didn't turn my face towards him or pay any attention to what he was saying.

He pulled up the quilt and wondered aloud who would want them to surrender except for the government or the army. I remained silent but he continued, feigning enthusiasm. He said it had been happening for a while: the former insurgents who were now into business were regularly threatened by their former comrades who were still underground. The ULFA warned them to stop playing into the hands of the government, but they didn't have an option. They couldn't refuse the government that had helped them get back into the 'mainstream'.

I maintained my resolution to keep quiet and that angered him more. I wondered if he knew his conversation was boring me. What was he trying to do? Patch up by sounding like a weekly political review? For a while, he spoke on his own. Outside, a dog was barking impatiently, as if something really serious was afoot. Mridul said slowly, 'I get really worried when dogs bark like that . . .' I shut my eyes and pretended I was asleep. After a while, I felt the light in the room was switched off. 'Reminds me of the man who was hanging upside down from that electric pole like a bat,' Mridul murmured and I shuddered although I was quiet.

~

The next afternoon, we were sitting under the sun—almost all of us. Dangor-bhonti, Mridul's sister, sat beside me and laughed at

the smallest and the most unexpected of 'jokes'. Onima-borma
sat on the ground over a betel-nut leaf that had curled under the
sun like fried prawn. Meenu-jethai, Oholya-jethai's elder sister
who was married off in Bordubi, was lamenting to a group of
women how her second son had married a low-caste girl against
the family's wishes and didn't live with them any more in the
same house.

Some of the men (Mukut-khura, Meenu-jethai's husband,
Okoni-pehi's husband, Dilip-peha and others) were taking a
walk near the bamboo gate, chewing betel nuts. Bits of Meenu-
jethai's lament must have reached them like drops of summer
rain stealing into the house through an open window. They
spoke dismissively: how women spent time repeating worthless
stories. Someone must have laughed. But yet they listened and
filed away somewhere, in the depths of their minds, the image
of that hapless mother who had wept when her son married
against the family's wishes. The event won't be forgotten. When
their own sons, or young men they knew, would come home
late at night, they would remind themselves, their wives or their
mothers, '*Remember* Meenu-bai's son? Even he behaved this way.
We know what's happening.'

Then lunch was served. People ate. Small quantities of
unstrained rice, served with chopped green chillies and salt. Long
slivers of lime jostled for space beside them.

Mridul was in a good mood that day.

I had started speaking to him normally that morning. Pleased,
he had even made my bed. Walked with me to the well and drew
water for me. Gave me a new bar of soap because he thought
the one that was already there had sand stuck to it after someone
had dropped it.

At noon, Brikodar had brought him a letter from Manju

Mahatu, which he had read lying on his back on his bed that was spread on the ground. He had dangled the letter in front of my eyes like a proud fisherman dangling his prize catch. I was curious to know what was written in it. I had never read a love letter before. I had heard love letters being read out in Hindi films: where the face of the letter writer appears on the letter, with the script serving as a watermark of that speaking image.

I had noticed Manju's letter was written in beautiful Assamese handwriting. The colour of the ink was red. She had drawn small roses on the margins. From a distance, the letter had looked like the Assamese traditional gamusa because of the red roses and the red script on the white page. I had tried to snatch it away from him but he didn't give it to me. We had giggled. He had blushed. When I had told him if he didn't give me the letter I would inform the High Court (Oholya-jethai) about Manju, he had said, 'Yes, yes, go and tell her right now! Go, why are you waiting?' We had laughed. He had laughed more than me. He had blushed again.

So, after lunch, he took out his guitar and started playing a song on it. A Hindi love song sung in a terrible Assamese accent where 'chahe' became 'sahe', 'pehla nasha' became 'pehla nosa'. I was amused by his Hindi pronunciation.

While he played it, he kept calling me to come to his room since I was sitting outside in the sun. 'Pabloo, Pabloo,' he cried every once in a while. I was chatting with some of the relatives; they were asking me about Papa: how he was doing, was his blood sugar in control, did he still have that temper he was so well known for. So I didn't get a chance to reply. I stopped paying attention to Mridul and everyone kept talking until we heard Oholya-jethai's loud voice.

Oholya-jethai was standing in front of his room. 'Stop the

music! Do you think this is a wedding going on? Now that your father's dead, you have gotten a Free India!'

But Mridul was ready to shock that day. 'Of course not, Jethai—what do you want me to do? Sit and cry? So that people believe that I am really sad?' He didn't keep the guitar aside. He kept holding it carefully on his lap. Three of his fingers continued strumming its strings lightly.

She was startled for a moment but Oholya-jethai was not someone who would give up easily. Her mouth opened in a silent 'aa' but she soon asked, raising her eyebrows, rolling her eyes, pointing her finger at him, 'How dare you! Do you know who you are speaking to? Your dead father didn't dare look at my eyes while speaking, Mridul, and you were born just yesterday! How dare you! Do I need to remind you who you are speaking to?'

'Yes, I know. I'm speaking to Oholya Bishoya, my father's elder sister who has nothing better to do but fight with each and every one in the house, who doesn't care for what's going on in the hearts of the family members and how they are trying their best to cope with their emotions. Why are you so worried what people would think, Jethai? Do you really believe these people are here to sympathize with us? They have come to see us cry. Do you get that? They want free entertainment. They are all here to enjoy the drama.'

'What did you say?' She was trembling in anger.

I wanted to pull Mridul away. I thought, if she could, she would have killed him then and there. She had heard him clearly. He was distinct. Hers was not a question, but more of a condemnation. A challenge. A warning.

'What did you say?'

He continued, his voice growing louder each passing moment, 'They have come to gloat over our misfortunes and like fools you think that they are sympathizing with us, that they have come to help us. Since Deuta is not here, they won't even come to shit in this house after the mourning period is over, as they have nothing to gain from us any more. No gifts to go back with. Wait and watch. What do you want me to do? Go and cry in front of them? No, I won't. If you ask me to stop trying to keep myself distracted again, I'll go and ask them to leave and say, "Look, there is no drama here, no story to gloat over, the dead man's son is not crying, and since he is not crying, neither is his mother."'

She covered her ears with both her hands and ran out of the room screaming at the top of her voice, her sador trailing behind her. '*Raiz!*' she addressed the crowd sitting outside. 'Listen! Listen to this disrespectful kid! He has insulted the whole village! He has insulted your love! Oh dear! Nobody has spoken to me like this before!'

Oholya-jethai rushed into the courtyard continuing to scream, collapsed on to the ground near the chattering women who were agreeing that when someone died, they usually left signs to people they loved the most; hence, Okoni-pehi's milk had attracted a mosquito soon after Bolen-bortta had passed away.

She covered her forehead with her palms and started to yell. 'Not a month has gone by since my brother's death and his children are treating this unmarried woman like garbage. What will happen to me! Such injustice! Aha!' She ran to Meenu-jethai, held her hand and said, 'Meenu, take me away from here. I am sure there will be some place in your cowshed. I will pack my bags and go away with you.' She didn't wait for Meenu-jethai's response and now ran towards their neighbour. 'Gulapi, will you ask your husband to make me a hut at the back of your house near the toilet or near the garbage dump? We have known each other for so long, wouldn't you give me a few yards of ground to stand on, to protect my head from rain and hail in my old age?' No one spoke; they were perhaps stunned by the way she was screaming. Now Oholya-jethai raised her hands to the sky and looked up as if calling out to the gods. 'I devoted my life to this house, to these children, this family, but I should have hung myself with a jute rope from the jackfruit tree behind our house than listen to such abuses from my own brother's children. My brother, who came out of the same womb I came from! And his children! His children are treating this helpless old woman like this! Where are you, Bolen? Why did you leave me? Where are you, Bolen?'

Within minutes, people from the neighbouring families started coming out with their friends, foes, spouses, children and emissaries to see what was happening. Not a single moment could be missed.

~

But the intense discussion of the drama, in which the old, helpless, hapless, unmarried sister of Bolen Bishoya was insulted and oppressed by his son a few days after his death, came to a pause only at night, when three masked gunmen came to Hatimura and gunned down Hiren's entire family.

Hiren—nearly six feet tall, brave, outspoken, kind and generous—was a surrendered militant and was doing very well in the Assamese-silk business that he had started. All the unemployed guys of the village worked at his silk farm, which looked like a forest of mulberry bushes on which the caterpillars fed all the time. A lot of people were required to run the large, multi-acre farm. I had never seen it but had heard about it from several people by then.

After dinner, I was sitting with Mridul and telling him that he shouldn't have behaved with Oholya-jethai the way he did that afternoon, when we heard a commotion outside the house.

There were around fifteen men and women sitting around the fire in the courtyard talking about how great Bolen Bishoya was when suddenly they started to run towards the main road.

'Killed! Killed all of them!'

Even we joined them.

'Who killed whom?'

'How did they kill? How many people were there?'

'They came with guns!'

Mridul was ahead of me. I ran after him past that large block of stone where we had sat the other day, past Brikodar's house, past the laburnum-flower tree in front of his house that stood like a nude woman with her hands raised towards the sky, past the large paddy fields stretched along the right side of the long, white path that divided the village into two halves, past the village market, the electric pole and the small bridge near the house where Aaimon, who threw a chocolate wrapped in a love letter to Mridul at a wedding last year, lived.

Hiren Das's house was in a different part of the village. It was a new colony that had developed around Mayong College and the higher secondary school. The cost of land was higher there and people who lived there were mostly those who worked in the government higher secondary school or the college. Hiren was perhaps the only one who had bought land there after his silk business flourished.

There was a sea of people around Hiren's large house that night. The whole village had congregated there. At that time, I didn't wonder why the atmosphere there was so still, why nobody was crying, why all that I heard were the heavy breaths of people who had come running, leaving meals, beds, dreams and their lovemaking behind.

It was foggy and very cold. I had left the endi shawl that I had wrapped around my body to beat the chill and, on reaching Hiren's house, I felt a cold sweat gradually drenching me.

It was a double-storeyed house, made of concrete, the only such building in the whole village. The sea of people just stood around, watching. I couldn't see anything. I pushed in to have a better view, without even thinking that the images could haunt me for years. The smell of sweating bodies of people who probably hadn't bathed for several days in that chilly winter hit me. It made me queasy. I continued my attempt to have a better view. But Mridul didn't let me through the thick curtain of people gathered around the house's entrance. He had elbowed in earlier and had come out of the crowd by the time I reached there.

I saw the horror writ on his face when he came out. Everyone in the family had been killed. Hiren, his wife, their two sons who were in primary school, his eighty-year-old grandmother, his mother, his father and the maid who came to help them with the household chores from the nearby hamlet.

Someone in the crowd asked, 'What about his grandfather? Eh eh, is he killed as well?'

One man hissed, '*Ou Ram-Ram!* He is still on the bed. He can't speak, he is paralysed.'

'Yes, yes, he was paralysed seven years ago and his son used to massage his body every day and bathe him. Why did the killers leave him to witness all this? What sins the old man must have committed in the last birth!'

'Yes, yes, he can see everything, he understands everything, but he can't speak, can't move! Oh oh, poor man. Why didn't they kill him? He should have been killed as well!'

I had never encountered such an eerie silence in my life until then. Even the large group that had gathered was whispering. There was no one to cry for them. The whole family had been gunned down. And people were so scared that they couldn't cry. Did they think if they cried someone would come and gun them down too?

Mridul didn't let me go in. 'It's too bloody. There is blood on the walls, on the chairs, on the courtyard, on the bed, on the bodies, on the faces, on their bellies, on their chests . . .'

'Mridul! Mridul! Are you all right?'

I screamed, looking at his dazed face. I had started weeping and I didn't know that until he looked at me, concerned, until I felt the warmth of my tears on my cold, very cold cheeks.

'Hey! What happened? Don't be afraid. We will send you home tomorrow.'

I couldn't say anything though I wanted to say that I wasn't afraid and didn't want to go home the next day. I was thinking about the paralytic grandfather. I just kept shaking my head left–right, left–right, unable to say anything.

That night, a drizzle sprinkled a light film of water over the roofs, leaves, firewood, the dead bodies, softening the clotted blood, washing down the white dust off the roofs, grasses, trees and flowers. Aaita wrapped two endi shawls around herself, sat huddled in one corner on a mat and complained of the cold. She burned a fire in an old, black iron cauldron that was no longer used and told people that it was raining in the height of winter because of the killings. I thought the sky was crying for the paralysed grandfather since I couldn't cry enough for him. I slept late that night. I could hear Mridul twitching all night on his bed. A little before the rooster's call, he asked me, 'Did you manage to sleep?'

I didn't reply.
'Even I couldn't.'
He said and turned again.

~

Papa and Mom came soon after in an Ambassador car to take me home. I wanted to ask Papa what about the people living in the village. Where would they go? I could go to Guwahati, even to Delhi if I wanted to, or to London. What about the people here, his own people? But I didn't say a word. Maybe because no one was asking me to stay back. Maybe because Mridul hadn't hidden my things that day. I just put my bag in the car's trunk and got into the back. Mom touched my head, tousled my hair lovingly, and started weeping. 'I was so worried, oh God!'

Seven

We left the banks of the river after the soldiers finished peeing and drove away because Mridul was scared they would notice us and come to question us. I wondered if this was the same batch of soldiers who had swarmed like bees on the lanes of the village after Hiren's family was gunned down in 1998. I wondered if they were from Punjab or Chandigarh or Darjeeling; if they liked living in Assam. But there was no time to sit and wonder. Through a path that cut through people's courtyards and backyards, we went to visit Brikodar. When we were standing in their veranda, I stole glances at the patch of golden laburnum flowers in front of his bamboo gate. Bright yellow. The tree near the gate had faint strokes of green. It was covered with a rebellious yellow, bursting with youthful energy.

I was still wondering what was it that I had wanted to ask Mridul but couldn't remember. Was it something about Prosanto-da? When I had asked Anil-da, he had evaded the question but a while ago, on the riverbank, Mridul had already told me what was up with Prosanto-da, why he wasn't seen in the house. I felt annoyed and irritated with myself. I had forgotten the question like the old prayer we sung in school in our childhood. I knew its tune, the twists and turns of the hymn, but had forgotten the lyrics. I didn't tell Mridul about it.

Brikodar's mother had come out with diced betel nuts dried in the sun, yellow, dry betel leaves and molten limestone on a *bota*. She must have noticed that I was looking at the flowers. 'We sweep it away twice a day but within minutes we have that yellow carpet ready! Who can fight with nature? How are you, baba? Do you want to come and eat pork one of these days?'

'Yes, we must!' Mridul said.

But I was thinking about the laburnums. 'They look lovely. It seems as though they are made of gold.'

She didn't respond to my compliment. Instead she apologized for not being able to serve green betel leaves. 'We sold most of it in the market. That's how some money flows into the house now.'

There were two other women, who were perhaps not Brikodar's family members, pounding rice into a fine powder in the wooden foot-grinder, *dheki*. They laughed at my compliment. One of them spoke. 'Oi, the townia boy is very amazed at the beauty of the village. Baba, we are used to these things here. I have never been to the city. Perhaps I too will be amazed by ordinary things in the city that you will not associate with "beauty" at all. But I have heard the city air is full of smoke from the cars. I feel like throwing up whenever I board a bus to go to the market in Sonapur. I don't know how people live in the city.' I looked around for the always-laughing Mamoni but she wasn't around. I thought of asking about her, but didn't.

The other woman, who was sitting on her haunches, sieving the pounded rice, collecting the fine powder in a large bamboo plate—*dola*—added, 'They don't get to see all this, after all. Why are you laughing?'

Binod came with some other guys. I knew some of them by their faces, but I only knew Binod and Brikodar well because I had eaten at their house the last time, and Binod had visited us in Guwahati with Prosanto-da once.

Both Binod and Brikodar showered me with questions. 'When did you reach, Pabloo? How is Guwahati? Is this film released in Guwahati yet? For how long are you staying? Have you come for Moina's wedding?'

The army jeep came when Binod was telling us about Diganta and Tapan, SULFA members who had fled, leaving their milk and vegetable business for good. Several masked gunmen had come twice already to ask where they were. By then, I could take part in those discussions. When I had gone back home in 1998, I had started reading the two local Assamese newspapers regularly and had realized the great disparity between news published in the English papers and the Assamese ones. There was no space for hard news in the English papers. I was talking to Gogon, who was telling me excitedly how the peace of the village was lost since the army camp was built in Mayong.

'It is quite certain that it is the government that is doing all this.' I almost dropped a bomb. It exploded and spread a thick blanket of silence for some time.

Brikodar's mother raised her voice. 'What are you saying, baba? Please don't say such things. There are ears everywhere in this village nowadays. You will be in trouble. It's not the same village where we grew up fearlessly.'

I was startled. 'Why are you feeling so scared? I'm not saying the government *is doing* this, but that it is a very strong possibility.'

Mridul patted my shoulder with his right hand and said, 'Hey, let's not talk about these things.'

'Why? Why shouldn't I? Don't you think it's the government that will benefit the most if the SULFAs and the ULFAs keep fighting among themselves? I'm almost certain *they* started the killings. *They* sparked off this fratricidal conflict. There is not much difference between the colonial British and our own government, which is no more than an agent of the Delhi government. Their policy is to divide and rule.'

Only Mridul, Binod and Brikodar understood what I was saying, perhaps. But it was evident they didn't want to take part in the conversation. They looked petrified. And it was then that the army jeep stopped in front of the bamboo gate. Crushing the laburnum flowers with their boots, the soldiers walked in. Flowers bright like gold smeared with dust.

'*Kya ho raha hai?* Meeting?' All of them were tall. Suntanned. Broad shouldered. Like men who were stripped naked in Moina-pehi's imagination when she used to go to dance Bihu with her girlfriends.

Immediately there was a sense of urgency among the women. They stood up, as if ready to run. But they were too scared to run. They must have thought if they ran, they would be shot down. They stood near the dheki. Brikodar's mother stood up and kept standing and staring. And it was only then that I noticed Mamoni, crouching on the floor, in a corner of the veranda. She didn't stand up. I looked at her and thought her eyes would fall out right then. I had never seen so much terror in anyone's eyes before.

'*Kya meeting ho raha hai?*'

What kind of meeting is going on here?

The men were scared as well, and tongue-tied. I felt Mridul's hand on my right shoulder. He was trying to push me behind the human curtain. It puzzled me. I resisted his mild moves to shield me since I didn't know from what he was trying to protect me. Perhaps I was too busy trying to figure out what had made the young men standing there feel so guilty. So frightened. All of them were looking at the ground as if the answer that they had forgotten was written on it.

'*Batao! Batao!*' Tell us! Tell us!

The army officer got down from the jeep and demanded. Roared. Threatened. He had a moustache and looked like a high-ranking officer. I tried to read his name. Count the number of stars. But I couldn't. '*Kya kar rahe ho?* So many men here?' His sonorous voice boomed in the yard. I could see another handful of laburnum-flower petals falling down. *Jhup-jhup.* I listened to the sound of the flowers falling. But I couldn't stop wondering if it was the booming, sonorous voice of the army officer that had broken down the churning of nostalgia, had startled us like children caught by their mother while stealing sweets. It was then that I noticed. There were twelve of us.

I knew that none of them could speak Hindi well. Where would they learn it? Hindi came to them through Doordarshan or through Hindi films played on videocassettes during weddings when television sets were permitted into the house. And after all, in that village, inundated by laburnum flowers and dust during winters, there was only one TV set.

I assumed the army officer would know English. 'I'm here after a very long time. They just came over to meet me.' Mridul was alarmed, I knew; but he could do nothing. In front of the army, he couldn't stop me, he couldn't make it obvious that he didn't want me to talk to them, that he thought it was his duty to protect me from becoming a second Dhoroni—the young man who was shot dead because he had started to run after seeing soldiers one morning. 'What will I tell Prodip-bortta?' He must have thought like Oholya-jethai, who hadn't let us leave the house, and he must have thought he should have listened to her. 'Don't you know Mrigen's son drowned in the Brahmaputra River? How much anxiety can this old woman take?'

The army officer was examining me. I was wondering if he spoke English or not. I knew Hindi, but not as well as English or Bengali. I had a very funny accent at which all my north Indian classmates laughed. And most of the time I confused the gender since in Hindi everything has a gender as in most European languages.

'Then why can't they speak up? It's all too suspicious, young man,' the officer responded.

I smiled, knowing it sent tense ripples among the people who couldn't speak English, who didn't have a television set in their houses. 'That's because they can't speak either Hindi or English. They are petrified of you all.' I had moved closer, and later, Mridul would tell me that I shouldn't have, since they didn't like men acting cocky. Paritosh Shome. A Bengali. *Aapni ki Bangali?* I smiled warmly. He smiled back at me. I knew I had impressed him even more, though he was already impressed by the fact that I spoke a British-accented English—with a deliberate slur—which I hated doing. When I spoke English elsewhere, I spoke without a Western accent, but I knew a pretentious British or American accent would help me impress him easily. Perhaps he'd be scared to touch me then, thinking I was too educated and since I was *too educated* I could have important connections.

'What are you doing in an Assami village?' He asked me in Bengali and I replied in Bengali saying, 'It's Asomiya, not Assami. In our language, Assami means criminal.'

I switched to my pretentious, accented English to imply that he shouldn't try to harm me. If he did, my laboured, accented English that sounded so funny to my own ears would go a long way in harming him back. 'And I'm not a Bengali. I have a lot of

Bengali friends. I'm here to attend a wedding after four years. My father grew up here.'

He shook hands with me and left, leaving twelve pairs of eyes admiring me. It was then we heard the scream. Mamoni had stepped down from the veranda, sat in the courtyard and started to scream. She wouldn't stop, she kept screaming like a lunatic until she fainted. I saw the whites of her eyes; the irises of her eyes had disappeared. She was still sitting. I saw the pale yellow trail of urine sliding down on the courtyard. I had never seen anyone so scared. 'What happened to her?' I asked Brikodar, but he didn't say anything. I asked Binod, but he kept quiet as well.

Later, on the way home, Mridul told me she had been raped by four military men when she had gone to wash clothes in the Pokoria River last year. I didn't want to think about those white eyes, and tried to focus on those golden laburnum flowers that I loved so much. But the more I tried to think about the golden flowers, the more they reminded me of the yellow urine. As the army jeep was speeding away, the image of the dry leaves chasing the car came again and again to my mind. I thought about the white of always-laughing Mamoni's eyes and I thought if those leaves were like the dust that chased our Maruti Esteem when we came to visit Mridul's family after Bolen-bortta died. But I decided those leaves were not like angry bees, and they chased the jeep like little children running after a car in a village.

'Mridul! Mridul!' I could not sleep. I sat up on the bed suddenly at midnight and started shaking him vigorously, trying to wake him up. He must have thought something terrible must have happened but I asked him where exactly had Mamoni been raped and he kept staring at me. I wanted to slap him for being so dull. I wanted to slap him hard.

～

A little later, Mridul went back to sleep. Most of the guests who had come for the wedding were also deep asleep by then. I slipped on my black jacket and went outside. I moved stealthily, like a cat, so as not to wake up Mridul again, like I had about an hour ago thinking about Mamoni. I wanted to step out of the house, but perhaps it wasn't safe. The army must be on patrol now, out in the thickness of the night like bats looking for rodents. They were suspicious of anyone out on the road at night. They remained forever alert, like crows.

I knew I wouldn't be able to sleep that night. I wanted to talk to someone. Someone who wouldn't speak in a judgemental tone about 'that divorcee'. Someone who knew there was a different world outside the village. The village that had remained cut off from the rest of the modern world for so many decades because there wasn't a good road connecting it to Guwahati. Mayong wasn't too far from Guwahati. Talks about a road via Noonmanti, Loonmati, Bonda and Chondropur had been on for a long time. The previous day Okoni-pehi had said that the constructions had started and she would be able to visit us 'tireek-tireek' after the construction of the road was completed. Her phrase had amused me. When was the last time I had heard that phrase? When was the last time I had used that phrase? I couldn't remember.

Outside, it was as cold as a snake's skin, I was shivering. The dog woke up when it saw me and came to sniff at my legs, wagging its tail. Slowly, I walked to the room where Prosanto-da slept. After he had started working, though he didn't get enough money—seven hundred and fifty rupees only, per month, from the panchayat fund—he had built an annex to the main house and joined two rooms to it. The first room was used as a study. It had chairs. When friends visited, they sat there for long hours and chatted about the development of the village—about the road that was being built and would be soon done, and how tireek-tireek they would be able to go to Guwahati. In the other room he slept. There were books in that room too. The room where he wanted to bring the woman he loved.

I wanted to talk to Prosanto-da. I hadn't seen him around ever since I came and that was the other important thing I had noticed: his conspicuous absence. Softly, I tapped on his door, but after a while, it was Anil-da who opened the door, instead of Prosanto-da.

'Pablo? Why aren't you asleep?'

'It's too early to sleep, Anil-da. What time is it? I sleep at eleven.'

'This is a village; by eleven, people are fast asleep. It's eight thirty.'

I looked around and was surprised to find how early it was but how late it felt.

'Come in, come in.'

In the first room (where the wooden chairs were, where the books were kept) three other men were sleeping on a large mattress spread on the floor. Bamboo bookshelves stacked with Assamese and English books leaned against the walls. Books that Prosanto-da taught in the college. Books that weren't abandoned like the pulp fiction novels in the other room, books that he had bought in second-hand shops of Guwahati when he was a student.

Clearly, Prosanto-da wasn't around. I hadn't seen him last evening. He wasn't in the courtyard chopping bamboos. He wasn't in the kitchen eating dinner. I hadn't seen him ever since I had arrived. I wanted to meet him, talk to him. After all, he was the only one in that house with whom I could talk about things I was familiar with: films, songs, albums, Guwahati, Panbozar. After all, he was the only one who looked like a hero from films of the Eastman-colour days. His problem must be really acute. It was true he wasn't spending time at home to suggest a warning that he would leave the house if they didn't let him marry Onulupa.

But we needed someone like him in this house, just as we needed a rebel lover like him in the village. A radical love story is the only device that makes the time-chariot of a village, a city, a country, gallop faster. Such a love story pulls the wheels of that chariot from a murky, regressive past towards a spotlessly clean road under autumn-blue skies. And for that chariot to move forward, to bring change in the village, you don't have to be conscious of being a radical. You just have to fall in love. Head over heels in love. We needed someone like Prosanto-da in a wedding because I had seen what changes he could bring to a wedding. Just the way we needed storytellers and singers in a wedding to make people laugh and cry and giggle, we needed Prosanto-da too. In December 1995, when my father's younger brother had married, he was a college student in Guwahati. People in the village wanted to watch old Hindi films from the eighties—*Tezaab*, *Dil*, *Karma*—and I had laughed, he had laughed (Mridul hadn't come). I had told him, 'Prosanto-da, if you get such films, I am surely not going to spend the night watching them.' It was fun to watch films in the courtyard, under the open sky, huddled on mats, on bed sheets that were spread on layers of hay, but it wasn't worth it if the films were old, familiar ones. Teteliguri had only one TV then and that, too, was black and white. So the colour, fourteen-inch BPL TV set, the videocassettes and the sound box were rented from a shop in Sonapur that was about half an hour away by bus. It was Prosanto-da who had brought *Dilwale Dulhaniya Le Jayenge*—which people hadn't heard of till then, since the radio hadn't yet played its songs. It was a fresh love story about an adamant young man who wouldn't marry the girl he loved without the permission of her father, and who hatches a plot to impress his prospective in-laws by pretending to be a friend of the man his beloved was being forced to marry, and thus managing to spend much of his time in her company under the same roof. And I knew that this year if he didn't participate in this wedding, there would be no love story, no fresh breeze, no enthusiasm for a new release. People would watch jingoistic anti-Pakistan films like *Gadar: Ek Prem Katha* and weep for the Partition victims and separated lovers from two different countries and two different religions. *Dil Chahta Hai* wouldn't be the big hit among the village crowd, a film in which a young man falls in love with a woman much older to him, and another one changes girlfriends like summer vests. Even Mridul couldn't be so imaginative. We needed people like Prosanto-da for that extra jolt of energy, for the time-chariot to move ahead.

Anil-da tightened his green-striped white gamusa around his waist and sat down. He told me I would have to get used to sleeping early for the next one week or so. 'Are your parents coming?'

'They might. But where is Prosanto-da? I haven't seen him around at all.'

'Uh, don't ask about him in this house. He isn't a good name to take in this house right now.' Anil-da spoke in his roundabout way, kindling curiosity. 'Even I wondered where he was when I came. I went to our High Court,' this he said with a smirk on his face, 'and asked her. She wouldn't answer. I went to Khurideo, Onima-borma—she snapped, don't ask me. I sensed something was wrong.'

'But what *is* wrong?' I pretended I didn't know much. I wanted him to tell me what he knew. 'Is he too busy with the wedding chores?'

'Busy with the wedding chores? Are you mad? All the villagers have lent their hands! Everyone loves Moina, has high regard for this family. People in this house are blessed. Of course, the residents of Hatimura are also wonderful people. Not unlike our Teteligurians,' he said, moving his face up a little. 'So, there's help from everywhere. He has nothing much to do. He just needs to play the host.'

'But where is he now?'

'Eh, you are too young to know all these things. You should go sleep. Otherwise we will wake them up.' He referred to the people sleeping in the other room, on the floor.

'Who are they?'

'Montu and all?' he said, as though I should have known who they were. But I didn't know who 'Montu and all' were. I think one of the 'all' was Roton, who was helping around with the wedding pandal, digging up holes for hearths in the backyard where the feast would be cooked. The tent wasn't erected in the courtyard yet. Roton would be doing that very soon. Only his face was visible because it was outside the quilt. The other two guys had covered their faces.

'Anil-da, tell me where Prosanto-da is. Has he left the house for good so that he can marry *that divorcee*?' To extract the story from him, I had to speak in his language. I pronounced the word 'divorcee' in such a tone that it sounded reprehensible.

Anil-da's face brightened up. 'Yes, you know!' He patted my shoulder gently, as though praising me for doing well in an exam, just like my mother would. 'I never believed he would be so irresponsible. Such a shame. If Aaita dies, it would be because of him. She has seen so much in this life. The death of her eldest son, an unmarried daughter who grew old in this house. And now, if her youngest son marries a divorcee—how will she survive it? She has taken ill and we are now worried, she wouldn't make it through the wedding. Mukut-khura has already bought some *mokordhwoj*, so that if something happens she could be kept alive until the wedding is over. *If something happens* during the wedding, the wedding would have to be cancelled and stalled for another year; God knows what will happen to poor Moina then! She would have no option but to hang herself or jump into the river with a brass pot tied to her neck. I told Moina yesterday to pray but she started crying. She is so unfortunate.'

Of course she would start weeping, thanks to his graphic, sensational imagination, I thought. He was speaking as if Aaita were already dead. That was one of the reasons I couldn't stand this guy. He was the one who would make matters worse—a rotten potato infects the rest in the creel.

'All right, all right, nothing like that is going to happen,' I said firmly.

'What do you know, ha? Have you seen Aaita's condition? She isn't one who likes to lie around in bed. Even though she is eighty, she used to be so active. But ever since Prosanto-da said he would marry that girl, she has taken ill. She has already stopped eating. Just takes vegetable soup during the day and eats one or two grains of rice.'

Oh Anil-da, I thought. There is a joke in our house: if Anil says the snake that entered his room was ten feet long and as fat as the trunk of an elephant, we should take it to be a puny little snake. If Anil says someone has been crying all day, all night, rolling on the floor, we should understand that the person concerned must have wept for a few seconds, shedding just a few tears.

'That's very selfish of Prosanto-da. But where is he spending his nights?'

'In different houses of the village! Do you think there is a shortage of houses? This is his village. His first cousins are around.

His aunts and uncles are around. His friends are around, but who knows?' He brought his face closer to mine and whispered, dilating his eyes. 'But who knows where he is sleeping. I am pretty sure, though he says he spends the nights with his friends, he must be spending nights with her too. If you look around his room, none of his important belongings are here. His clothes, his books, his notebooks, he has packed everything. I went to Jitendro's house yesterday, just to find out if he had been using their spare bed. But I didn't see any of his stuff there. There was nothing, except for a pen he had forgotten. You know—that girl has *given* him everything and gives him every night, that's why he is so mad about her.'

'Oh, I should go sleep now,' I said.

'Don't mention our conversation to anyone, okay?'

'No, I won't.'

He must have said that to so many people and asked them to keep everything to themselves!

~

When I had stepped out of that room that night, and walked on to the courtyard, I don't think I had made any noise. Because, just about an hour ago, when I had left the room carefully without waking up Mridul, who was sleeping on the other bed in the same room, I had worn the quietness of a cat's paws on my feet. Because, thinking back, if I had made any noise, the female figure with her hair all open, who was sitting like a three-headed old woman on the veranda opposite Prosanto-da's room, would have moved.

The house was L-shaped. Mridul's room, which we shared, was in the vertical bar's tip of the 'L' and the room before which the

girl was sitting was on the tip of the horizontal bar of that 'L'. If
I had made a sound, she would have moved a little. She would
have stopped sobbing, looked up at me. She would have stood
up and walked away, embarrassed. But she didn't do anything
of that sort. I don't remember if Anil-da had seen her. Perhaps
he hadn't. He was too eager to return to the cosy warmth of the
room from the chill outside. So he left without looking around.

What would have happened if Anil-da had hung around? He
would have looked at that figure and screamed, 'Who is that?
Who is that sitting out there? Are you crying?' It was dark but
there was a dim bulb glowing far away in front of Mridul's room.
It must have been a low-voltage bulb because the light that was
reaching her wasn't enough. And because the light that lit her up
was so faint that whatever fell on her hair was immediately sucked
in by the blackness of her tresses. A mane of dark, cascading hair
that she held like a black kitten on her lap, like a bamboo creel full
of ripe blackberries, which stained the tongue. She was wearing
only a full-sleeved, dark-coloured chemise. The chemise covered
the upper portion of her body. On her exposed thighs, the yellow
light slipped down, like oil on the freshly bathed, slippery skin
of a baby. The lights slipped like the resolves of ascetics when
they see a nude fairy in front of them. Her thighs, white and
glowing like peeled banana trunks, glistened in that little light.
On the veranda, she, with her open hair, her bamboo creel full
of blackberries—all were part of the night's darkness.

Was she a ghost? A *jokhini*? I first thought. But her glistening
thighs, her sobbing, pulled me to her like a puppet. 'Is something
wrong?' I asked, sitting beside her on the cold veranda. So cold
that my body shook when my butt touched it. She turned, looked
at me, but kept quiet. 'I don't know who you are, but I am Pablo.'
She wiped her tears with her palms, where the story of her life

was written, the story that she was refusing to tell me. Where the reason why she was crying was inscribed in a language of criss-crossed lines that I wouldn't have been able to decipher. Did it mention that a young guy would sit beside her one night with the intense desire of touching her fair, exposed thighs? If there was enough light, I could have even seen her breasts better. Years later, when I was more severely judgemental about my younger self, I wondered if it was the exposed skin that had tempted me to gravitate towards the girl. Slowly, taking his time to sit, stopping himself from touching the light-kissed part of her body that was glowing in the dark, the younger me had been held in a spell.

She didn't answer me. She must have fought with someone. She must be one of the wedding guests. 'I am fine,' she said and started walking towards the tip of the vertical side of the 'L', and when I saw her back, her half-exposed back, I couldn't breathe. She was walking with her long hair pulled towards her chest but even in the dark, I suddenly realized that I had seen that back before. That back belonged to the same girl whom I had seen the day before, when everyone was tormenting me with questions, about the dust, about not coming too often, and so on. And there she had been, standing with her back to me, talking to someone, nodding her head. She had looked beautiful. *She* was the question I had forgotten to ask Mridul when we were sitting on the banks of the river, and the soldiers had come just then, peed and driven off. I was annoyed I had forgotten to ask Mridul who that girl in that blue salwar kameez was.

'Hey!' I called out.

She stopped, and turned.

'Are you here to attend the wedding?'

She kept staring at me. Then she started walking once again. I quickly followed her.

'Why were you crying?'

She gave a smirk. She tried to pull her chemise to hide her fleshy thighs from me in vain. As if she had suddenly become too conscious of the exposed parts of her body. She was closer to the light and I could see them better now.

'Because I am here to attend a funeral,' she said.

A sarcastic smirk played on her face.

~

Aaita's room was very close to Prosanto-da's room. There, to please her, he would play Borgeets and other devotional songs in Assamese—I had seen how much he cared for her, just like Mridul did. To make her happy, he would play chants of Sanskrit verses that you could buy from the market in cheap cassettes. But the next morning, I hadn't gone and stood inside his room because I wanted to see those cassettes, because I wanted to check out the cheap music system for which two large earthen pots served as sound boxes. I had just returned to the house after bathing near the well that was in the backyard of the house. In the courtyard, I saw many people wearing tense looks, with crinkled eyebrows. Outside, Meenu-jethai was standing beside Okoni-pehi and talking about something very seriously. Mukut-khura was nodding at what the doctor was saying and when I went nearer, they both started walking towards Aaita's room. I followed them but Oholya-jethai looked at the procession of people trailing them and asked us all to back off. She said she didn't want a crowd in her mother's room. The wall between Prosanto-da's room and Aaita's room was a thin mud wall; I went in, trying to listen. Okoni-pehi soon entered the room too. 'Let me also listen,' she whispered pressing her ear against the wall. I didn't say anything.

There were no voices for a long time.

'The doctor must be examining,' she told me, whispering.

'What happened, Pehi?'

'Mai has become senseless. But she is breathing fine. Mukut wanted to give her sulphur of mercury, but he wanted to talk to the doctor before giving her anything.' She kept whispering.

'What is that?'

'Mokordhwoj? It saves life.'

'Is it a medicine?'

'No, it just extends the life of a person.' She wiped her tears. 'We need to keep Mai alive till the end of the wedding.'

I shuddered at the thought. What would have Bolen-bortta said to this? And Prosanto-da? To keep a person on ventilation despite knowing it was inhuman torture for him?

'Has someone told Prosanto-da?'

'Does he care? Does he care?' She started hissing. 'No one cares, Pablo. If the people in this house had paid attention to the storm raging in his heart, we would have had the son of the house in the house itself, looking after his mother. After Bolen-kai, Mridul and he are the only two people to whom Mai speaks her heart out. Both take care of her. All these years it was Oholya-bai, but after Bolen-kai's death, she has been gradually leaving her and depending more on these men. Look at Mridul—he is in another world. He rarely stays home these days. I don't know if he too is dating some girl.' I smiled at her worries. 'And what is there to hide from you?' She sighed. 'You know what Prosanto has done, don't you?'

'Will you let him marry that girl? I mean Onulupa-baideo?'

'It's so difficult to get a person who you can share your heart's torments with. He has found someone, and we have no right to stop him from marrying her. Oholya-bai is opposing this marriage in such a way as if she is going to share her bed with Onulupa for life. But the village won't understand, baba. You are too young to understand these things. The panchayat will make life hell for him. Hush, is the doctor saying something?'

We tried to listen, but couldn't understand anything. The whisper was like the distant mournful song of a cowherd. You could hear the tune, but never quite get the lyrics.

After the doctor left, I waited for the people to leave Aaita's room. Outside, Dorongi-aaita was sitting on the veranda and wiping her tears. Okoni-pehi sat down beside her sadly. Leaning on one of the pillars of the veranda was Lahori-khuri, Mukut-khura's wife. Where was Moina-pehi? Was she also crying? I went inside Aaita's room. I heard Mukut-khura say, 'There's nothing left to do but pray. I hope somehow she lives through the wedding. She showed similar symptoms after Bolen-kai had passed away but pulled through.' I heard the sound of someone's sobs from a room soon after he finished speaking. I could hear Oholya-jethai grumbling loudly, 'The old woman hasn't left us yet and people have already started planning the menu of the fish-touching ceremony!'

In the windowless room, Aaita was lying on a thick mattress. There were coloured pictures of ten-handed, four-handed, blue-bodied, many-headed gods around her. In one corner of the room, incense was burning, just beside a mustard-oil lamp, in front of a picture of Lord Krishna. A professional reader had been called to read sections from the Bhagwat that night. Aaita loved listening to those but, more than anything, she also loved the company of Mridul, who had suddenly become aloof. (I would come to know the reason behind his aloofness soon.) She loved the company of Prosanto-da, who was away, somewhere far from this house. Would he know that she was *leaving* us? Would someone inform him that he needed to see her one last time? What kind of silent protest was this that tortured his mother so much? I decided I would go find him and request him to come back. But where would I look for him?

I felt someone's presence in the room and looked up. It was then that I saw her again, standing there, with a bowl in her hand. What was she carrying?

'How's she?'

'How are you?'

'That doesn't matter.'

I stood up and looked at her for a few moments. 'You didn't tell me your name.'

'My name doesn't matter. I don't have a name.'

I shook my head. Not in disbelief, but in amusement. 'Will you help me find Prosanto-da?'

Her eyebrows jumped up. 'What?' She fixed me with her stare.

'Yes, will you help me find Prosanto-da? If he comes and says a few words to her, she might pull through.'

'Prosanto-kai isn't a young boy that we need to find him—you make it sound as if he is lost, kidnapped . . .' Ah, that sly, sarcastic smile. That piercing look, full of mockery. But strangely, they weren't offensive. They were entertaining. They were prodding me to say something further, to challenge her.

I looked at her properly. She had long hair, black like charcoal, which glistened like the shiny body of a cobra crawling on grass at noon. She could very well become a Sunsilk shampoo model, I thought. The light had brightened up her face and I saw there was nothing special about her face. But her body was toned, slim and tight. Her breasts mature like taut, green coconuts; the silhouette of their sharp tips visible through her cotton sador. Her fair skin was bright, fresh, just like new leaves that have recently sprouted from a mango seed after the first rains. She had tied her hair into a long braid that day and I wondered if it was long enough to tether a goat.

'Jitendro, my cousin, should know where he is. Please help me. No one in this house is keen to inform him about his mother. As if they want to punish him by not informing him.'

'News travels fast in a village,' she said, placing the bowl of soup near Aaita. She looked at her for a while and said that there was no point trying to feed her or force-feed her. We should wait until she gained consciousness. She didn't leave the room.

'All right, if you don't want to go. I think this news needs to reach him quicker than the speed at which news travels in a village.'

When I turned to go, she said, 'My name is Anamika.'

Was this her way of saying that she would come with me?

Anamika: the woman without a name.

I thought, and smiled at her and when we ambled down the village road that morning in search of Prosanta-da, I felt as if we were on a grand mission. I didn't know that when I would think back on that sun-smeared morning. Years later, I would be surprised to find that I would faintly remember the shape of Onulupa who I had a glimpse of when we knocked on her door. Our guess was correct. He was there. Not in Jitendro's house, where he had left behind a pen by mistake. It was Prosanto-da who had opened the door after our knock. Dressed in his navy-blue trousers and white formal shirt, he was getting ready for the day's lectures. I was disappointed to find him there because, if storytellers like Anil-da, who loved to create suspense and panic and send sinister ripples through a wedding, had found this out by some chance, they would have felt vindicated. They would have gloated over the fact that Onulupa 'had given everything' to Prosanto-da. People like him would go around telling others that Prosanto-da was found holding the divorcee's hands. That he was found there in his shorts, bare bodied. I thought, standing in front of a well-dressed Prosanto-da who was looking at Anamika and asking her how everything was at home, how Anil-da would pause leaving behind an uncomfortable silence after saying 'bare bodied'.

Anil-da wasn't a great storyteller. He didn't know the truth behind great stories, and that was why the story he brought into the wedding on the day of the juron—when Onima-borma was scaling the fish and the girls were singing about the mother-in-law's starlike earrings—only spread panic and suspense. There was no possibility of redemption in his tale. There wasn't an iota of hope in it. But the truth is, life goes on and stories have to end, and yet not end—which is also one of the features of any great story.

And perhaps that was why I told Prosanto-da confidently, sitting on a cane chair, without leaning against the cushions, 'You have to come, Prosanto-da. Aaita is very ill. And no one in the house wants to come and tell you. They think the news will eventually reach you.'

Prosanto-da stood up, his hands folded behind his back. He looked tall. I looked up, observing his face. 'Have you heard?' he looked at the green curtain and said loudly. 'Have you heard? Do I need enemies if I have such family members?'

I could sense the presence of a human figure behind the curtain. I could see the feet of a woman who was wearing slippers with a blue stripe. 'Well, they are upset with you.'

'But still, Ma is so ill. They could have told me. I have to hear it from guests.' Then he came and sat beside me. 'I am sorry, you aren't a guest. I am sorry.'

'It's all right, Prosanto-da.' Anamika had gone in by then. I could hear murmurings from inside. 'It's fine. How often do I come here? The last time I came here was when Bolen-bortta had passed away.'

'Well, you are here for an auspicious occasion this time,' he smiled and said. 'How is everything at home? How is Prodip-kai?'

'They are all fine. You need to return home, Prosanto-da. You might regret later if something happens.'

He looked at me, smiled and patted my back. He said I had grown up and spoke like an adult. I laughed, and he laughed too. It didn't seem odd to me that I was speaking to Prosanto-da, with Onulupa-baideo, the shadowy presence, hiding behind the curtain. I wanted to see her. But I guessed she didn't want to meet anyone. I wasn't sure why she preferred to stay behind the curtains in her own house. I didn't ask. I thought I might be treading on something delicate if I asked such a question. That I was allowed into the house was a big achievement, that he was speaking to me, letting me tell him what all was going on in his own house, was quite enough for now.

Later, I would hardly remember Prosanto-da's pat on my back. Or the shadowy figure of Onulupa-baideo listening to us, standing behind the curtain without showing her face. Nor would I particularly remember if I had suspected him of spending the nights with her, though it didn't matter to me either way.

I would only remember how Anamika had giggled, how she had looked into my eyes on our way back. How she had suggested we walk slowly because it would be nice if we walked slowly. I hadn't asked her why, but I would remember how wonderful I had felt.

I wanted to sprint across the dusty path. I wanted to jump up where I stood. But I didn't. Because I knew she would think

I was a little boy. Somewhere in my mind I knew I was only seventeen, and yet, at that age, on that sun-smeared morning when the smell of night-jasmine flowers was wafting in the air, I wanted to be twenty-seven. I wanted to think she preferred to walk slowly because she wanted to spend some time with me. She must have read my mind.

'You know how old I am?'

'No. I don't. And I don't think I should ask. Girls don't grow older after sixteen. And after marriage, they don't become older than thirty.'

'I was sixteen five years ago. You are a baby, I know that. You don't even have to say it. Your lips must still carry the taste of breast milk, so young you are! And yet, you were looking at my thighs last night.'

My ears and cheeks were burning. She said they were red and I said she was lying. They couldn't be red. She enjoyed my discomfort.

'I have seen many like you.'

'And I haven't seen anyone so shameless like you.'

'*Shameless?* And me? Who was staring at my chest and thighs last night?' She pursed her lips in such a way that I wasn't offended in spite of her accusation. She spoke as if she was cracking a joke. 'And why did you ask a *shameless* girl to accompany you in this grand mission of finding Prosanto-kai?'

'Wish I had known.'

'*Wish I had known!*' she teased. 'Hey, why did you stop?'

She had walked ahead of me. We had reached the marketplace. We were near the electric pole and there the road had formed a curve.

Last evening, when I had landed in Mayong after being stranded at Down Town, Guwahati, for many hours in the Assam

State Road Transport Corporation bus called Horo-Gouri, I had seen that curve—the curve on the straight road, just under the electric pole, the grass on the part of the road where the body had fallen. That curve was the first thing I had noted when I entered Mayong. I had wondered, only Mridul couldn't have created that meandering, sickle-like curve over the years around the portion under the pole where the body had fallen. Everyone must be walking around that portion all these years, avoiding the imaginary blood-splattered body.

Anamika had walked straight on, stepping on terrains she shouldn't have and that was why I had suddenly stopped, remembering the story Mridul had told me the last time I was there. I was suddenly filled with a strange sense of fear for her and wondered if Mridul and the people in that village felt the same way—scared of an imaginary body. Scared of a body that had fallen with a thud right there, many years ago. Afraid of a portion of the ground which a blood-splattered body had drenched with blood.

'What happened? Why did you stop? Ei, I was just joking,' Anamika said.

Eight

In the village, the hooting of owls near someone's house is considered a bad omen. But the next night, when the owls hooted, none of us could have even imagined it foreshadowed what would happen the night before the wedding. Oholya-jethai promised aloud to her god on that scary night that she'd sacrifice a black male goat at the Kamakhya Temple if the wedding went well, if the evil presaged by the hooting owls lost its effect. The Kamakhya Temple is in Guwahati, on the Nilachal Hill, where human beings used to be sacrificed until the British arrived. It is believed that a man's blood keeps the goddess content for a thousand years.

That something terrible would happen very soon, whether before or after the wedding, was evident the night three owls hooted *niu-niu-niu*, long and hard, so that I woke up from my sleep, startled. Soon, I realized it was not me alone who had been awakened. Mridul, too, lay still on the bed with his eyes wide open.

As if they were singing: 'I will take you away. We shall take you away. Niu-niu-niu.'

It was eerie. I didn't know what bird it was, when I first heard the niu-niu calls. Mridul was home that night, unlike the other days, when he would return very late and slip into bed stealthily. When I asked him what had kept him out so late, he would evade my question. I knew something was brewing and he didn't want to tell me; or maybe he was hesitant.

Mridul sat on the bed and told me while he rubbed his right eye with his left palm, 'Don't be afraid.' He mumbled, 'Those are owls. But it's a bad sign. They hoot like this only before someone dies. They hooted like this the night before Deuta died but we hadn't paid any attention then . . .'

Not long after he said that, I heard Oholya-jethai's voice in the courtyard. 'Oh God, what is it that you are trying to tell us, with an auspicious occasion in the house just days away?'

Then Anil-da's voice. 'This is bad. It's a sign that something terrible is about to happen.'

Other voices. Women ululating in order to ward off the evil effects of the hooting owls.

Mridul didn't stop me when I walked out of the room wrapping the red-and-black striped Naga shawl around my body. He stayed back and walked out only a little later. That was why he missed that wonderful and sinister sight of the three owls playing on the thatched roof of the main house over the room where Aaita slept. Prosanto-da's room was still occupied by Anil-da because, though Anamika and I had informed him of Aaita's health, he hadn't turned up that day.

The sight gave me goosebumps. I was thrilled. I felt guilty that I was taking a perverse delight in that sight, simultaneously mortified and excited, since Moina-pehi was already outside, biting her lips, trying to stop her tears.

Dorongi-aaita sat on the veranda, her hands joined in a silent prayer. In the light of the moon, I couldn't count how many more wrinkles were formed on her old face that night, but I could see her lips moving, murmuring a prayer.

Meenu-jethai gasped, 'Oh God! What is it that you are trying to tell us?'

'This is rare. It never happens. Owls come and land on the roof only before . . .' Anil-da left the sentence incomplete. But I felt everybody knew what he had left unsaid. He didn't say what we all had on our minds, but dreaded to speak out. I didn't like his unfinished sentence. I still think that he had taken great delight in uttering those ominous words . . .

In the commotion, Okoni-pehi had also woken up (she was spending the night in the house since her husband was away in Sonapur for work) and came out of her room tying her bun, using her fingers to push back the unruly night-hair, wrapping a whitish endi shawl around her body. She consoled everyone. 'It is normal for owls to behave like this sometimes. Don't be superstitious.'

Aaita was still ill. But she had regained consciousness that afternoon after Mukut-khura gave her another dose of mokordhwoj. From her room, she was speaking in a faint, breathless whisper. She sounded as though she was suffering from acute asthma. 'What are you all doing, you fools? Go get the conches!'

Anamika ran. She overturned a table on her way. Hurt her leg and let out a shrill scream. Mridul had come out of his room too, tying the knot of the dhoti he slept in, to see what had happened. In minutes, Dangor-bhonti, Dorongi-aaita, Meenu-jethai, Sunjira-jethai, Lahori-khuri and Oholya-jethai were blowing six stork-white conches. Anamika watched them. She didn't blow a conch. When the conches didn't work well, she went in, got a jar of water and poured water into them. Then they shook the conches like thermometers and blew again. The sound was better now, deeper, reverberating. The conches were white like freshly bloomed roses. The choric sound of six conches created an untimely, unwelcomed, suddenly chilling scene in the house in the middle of that winter night. As if the sound of the conches was telling us that we had no control over what was going to happen.

And actually we didn't.

I don't believe it was because of the owls that Moina-pehi drank phenyl the day before the wedding. But the sound of the conches, the anxious reactions of the people and the disturbing but eagerly related stories made her decide that all her troubles would end with a bottle of phenyl.

Everyone started to repeat the name of God. The *'Hori Bol'*, *'Joyo Ramo Bula'* chants became louder and louder; more people joined in. Neighbours soon woke up, jolted out of their deep sleep. Anamika stood in a corner, her lips unmoving, I saw clearly. Somebody was trying to console a weeping Moina-pehi. I thought it was perfectly natural for owls to come and make a racket on the roof. And while the three of them fluttered around, one of them must have broken the rules of their little sport. So they hooted. Looked here, and there, with their bespectacled, pedantic, large eyes, full of curiosity.

At length the women finally stopped blowing the conches. The owls had flown away long before. Frightened, trying to save their lives from these alien sounds. Confused. Grumbling about their friends who had informed them of a large band of fat, juicy rodents scampering through the wedding house. 'We shall never come again'—they must have promised and cursed the house. The house with a thousand stories.

I saw their ash-coloured wings fluttering in the moonlight like suddenly revealed mysteries. Like unexpected twists in stories. The room where the forgotten almirah with old storybooks stood was also the room where rats entered easily through openings in the walls. Yesterday Mukut-khura had gone into that room and put all the food items on the unused broken bed in order to protect them from the rodents. The hungry rodents conspiring to climb up the bed, or to get into the room, must have sent the good news around the 'owl kingdom' in the village.

When the women stopped blowing the conches, the stillness of the night inundated by the smell of the white khorikajai flowers from the nearby house returned once again. Now the only sound was that of Moina-pehi's rhythmic weeping. Attracted by it, the neighbours were crowding the courtyard. As if the women who had been playing the conches were performing an intense musical to which Moina-pehi played the part of a tragic protagonist.

Moina-pehi wept all night: sitting on her bed, lying on her bed, with her mouth pressed against a pillow, leaning against the wall, and with her hair open, her tresses flowing like the waves of a lunatic summer river after many days of rains. Drops of water from that river streamed down her cheeks but most of it covered a larger portion of the wall she was leaning against. It had spread like a peacock's plume on the wall. People took turns to console her.

It was already three o'clock and hence those who had woken up and come to find out what was happening wanted to return to their beds. Only a few did, stretching their arms on the way, yawning, repeatedly looking back to see the people who they were leaving behind in the courtyard.

Anamika lingered around. She kept looking at me and I suddenly felt too awkward to talk to her in front of everyone. I couldn't understand why. If people hadn't been around, I would have been drawn to her like a moth to a flame.

People lit a fire, in the iron cauldron that Aaita used often, sat around it and talked. The fire chased away the fog; the fire chased away the fireflies that came to play in the yard like glowing, winged ghosts when all of us slept. Soft noises could be heard from the cowshed. The muffled mooing of the cows. Cows licking their calves' heads, backs, tails, balls, anuses. Ronga? Oholya-jethai's favourite bull? He must be on top of a cow—I thought. Once Mridul had told me, Ronga was always on top of a cow—what a life, what a life . . .

Outside, Anil-da kept telling stories of what happened to families when owls landed on roofs to sing their odious songs. Okoni-pehi assured Moina-pehi that she'd take a bath early the next morning and take an oath in the prayer room, with flowers, tulsi leaves and a freshly washed one-rupee coin, that she'd fast for twenty-one Thursdays if the wedding went without any incident. She would pray for a happy future for the bride.

In the meantime, Anil-da was telling us the very unfortunate tale of the village headman Maniram's daughter. 'The owls came and landed on top of the wedding pandal. Believe it or not!'

'Destiny!' Okoni-pehi slapped her forehead, not knowing who to blame for the sad plight of Maniram's daughter, even before knowing what had happened, even though she didn't know who Anil-da was speaking about. 'Destiny!' she repeated and slapped her forehead again. Dorongi-aaita didn't utter a word, but she too slapped her forehead.

Oholya-jethai was looking at him with her lips curling like a bow. That 'I-will-poison-your-tea' expression.

'Yes, and all four of them were hooting. The wedding rituals went on. The groom had already arrived and the bride and the groom were sitting near the sacrificial fire. They were just about to exchange garlands when it happened. The priest stood up in absolute horror, and stopped chanting the montros out of shock and bewilderment when he saw the owls.'

'Eeh!'—Oholya-jethai let out a sound of disbelief, her right brow jumping up. Onima-borma looked at him with horror, her face resting on her left hand. 'Why would he do that? How could he do that? If I were there, I would have said, "Pujari, you'd better finish the rituals before you leave this place." I'd have hit him with a cane. What were you doing, you donkey? You are a powerful young man, aren't you?'

He smiled sheepishly at that compliment. 'Eh, *moinu ki korim aru?* Listen. The pujari got up and said, "This marriage will only bring disaster." And even before he said anything else, *it happened*! The bride's dress caught fire. It was up in flames!'

'Flames?'

'Yes, in flames! For a long time she must have been feeling the heat. But it was summer and, anyway, sitting beside the sacrificial fire makes you sweat until you dehydrate. She stood up screaming and we all saw the lower part of her dress was no more cloth, but a large ball of fire burning. She fainted and even before they could pull off her clothes in front of the whole village—it was anyway difficult to remove bridal wear with its many knots and layers—she was half-burned. Didn't survive!'

'Didn't survive?'

'Yes, yes, we had seen it with our own eyes. It's a very bad omen. Please call a Brahmin and do something. In any case, it's not a good sign for owls to hoot near a house and if they come right up to the . . .'

Once again, he stopped, leaving the sentence unfinished. So that the imagination of the listeners could fill in what he left ominously unsaid.

Perhaps everyone loathed him for telling that story. But there was keenness in their eyes, in their quivering lips, in their craned necks, which must have encouraged him to continue. It also suggested that though they didn't want to hear the story, something in them prevented them from asking him to stop speaking. Mukut-khura looked bored. He was sitting on a chair a little away on the veranda. It seemed that it was difficult for the large, fat, tall man to sit even on the largest wooden chair in the house. Anamika sat with the women, but she kept trying to attract my attention—or so I thought. But she did turn and look at me a couple of times. I was sitting on a stool, near the fire. Mridul had returned to his room to sleep.

The sky was gradually removing the veil of darkness with which she covered herself as she made love with the sun, birds and hills all night. She looked bright and resplendent after her lovemaking, filled with a glittering luminous zeal. Perhaps Mukut-khura was thinking just like me—how lovely and refreshed one felt in one's mind and body simply by looking at the sunrise, something that happened every day, without fail, and perhaps that is why we don't quite realize how beautiful and hopeful this world is. Would Prosanto-da return to the house on this new day?

Dangor-bhonti screamed just then and all of us hurried indoors. Aaita was taking deep, slow breaths. It seemed that she was having great difficulty breathing. Prosanto-da's absence was so conspicuous. Onima-borma wiped away her tears looking at her dying mother-in-law and murmured, 'I don't know what's happening to this family. I don't know who has wished such evil on this family.' At the door, Moina-pehi stood. Her eyes were red, the frizzy river hanging behind her, like a horse's beautiful, bushy tail.

Onima-borma walked out of the room and sat down on the soil veranda sadly. She was joined by Soru-bhonti who leaned on to her. The two young daughters of Mukut-khura, who had woken up due to the commotion, came out too and settled next to her. The five maids, including Phulam and Junti who were of the same age as Dangor-bhonti, also came and sat down gloomily. Soon Sayamoni joined them—she had grown up in that house since her childhood when Bolen-bortta had brought her from a remote village, away from a family that didn't have enough to eat and wear. Nahori was the fourth maid. She was old, almost as old as Oholya-jethai, and had spent all her life in that house. Morongi was the fifth domestic help who lived in the same compound, but in a separate hut, with her husband and two children, a boy and a girl. She and her husband worked in the fields with Mukut-khura. Mridul supervised and often lent a hand. At last, another sad face sat beside Dorongi-aaita: she was Mukut-khura's wife, Lahori. You were never left alone in that house, I thought. And something or the other happened there all the time, every day.

~

The morning arrived with the speed of homecoming cows attracted by the irresistible smell of ripe jackfruits: quick, impatient. Prosanto-da's absence and the anticipation of his return hovered over the house.

Lunch was served at around eleven thirty. In the kitchen, I was chewing on a chicken leg that had been specially hunted out of the large cauldron and given to me by Onima-borma, when she broached the sensitive topic of Prosanto-da's absence.

'Does anyone know that one member of this house has not been eating and living in here for a long time now? Don't you think we need to inform him about his mother? We won't be able to show our faces to him if something happens—and anything can happen any time.'

I looked at Mukut-khura, who had the largest bowl, with the

largest portion of the food in it. He had a heap of bones on the side of his plate. His fingers—that were busy mashing the piece of potato he had picked out of the chicken curry cooked with tomatoes—stopped moving.

Mridul, who was sitting beside me, lifted his head and looked straight at her face. Oholya-jethai stood near the door, awaiting a reply from Mukut-khura.

'Can't we discuss this later? We have guests around,' Mukut-khura said.

Onima-borma replied meekly to Mukut-khura—as if she were submitting an application—'Pabloo is not a guest. He is a member of the family. We can still speak. If the whole village is speaking about Prosanto and Onulupa, what's there to hide from him? I am sure he knows every bit and has already noticed that Prosanto isn't around.'

Dorongi-aaita had come out of the kitchen to the dining room where we all sat on mats and short stools according to hierarchy and ate. We, all the men. Mukut-khura's stool was the tallest and the broadest. On it, you could cross your legs and sit in a meditating position if you wished to. Mridul and I sat on smaller ones, meant for younger men like us. Prosanto-da's even-smaller stool was near the golden-coloured brass pot: unused.

'Okoni was here this afternoon. She was furious. She blamed us. She said if Prosanto could speak his heart out to Jitendro's mother and not to the women of this house, it is apparent that there is something wrong with us—the women of this house—because Jitendro's mother is his sister-in-law too, just like Lahori and me. Now that she has started blaming Lahori and me, the whole village would soon join in. She was really very furious,' Onima-borma said.

'When is Okoni-bai *not furious* about anything?' Mukut-khura drank an entire glass of water from his steel glass, producing soft *kot-kot-kot* sounds. 'Wasn't she furious when Mai was sick this morning? Didn't she blame me for not treating her mother well?' Mukut-khura started making loud noises when he sucked the bones. I didn't know if it was deliberate.

'Please don't speak like that! We must go deep into Prosanto's matter. Why is Prosanto staying in Jitendro's house? Okoni has raised a valid question. Why isn't he eating here, but taking his meals in Jitendro's house? He left that day halfway through his meal when Mai was telling him that she couldn't ever allow Onulupa to be her daughter-in-law. He threw the stool away from the place he was sitting. Something must be lacking in our family because of which he lives in Jitendro's house and expresses his sorrows to Jitendro's mother, not to any of us here. Though it puts the blame on us, Okoni is right, and I was embarrassed when I was reminded of the situation—I should have been able to counsel him, if not anyone else. After all, he is like my son—so young he was when I got married and Mridul's father had told me I should take special care of him. That man may be no more, but isn't his wife still around? I feel so worthless.'

Onima-borma was speaking in a low voice. It seemed that the conversation had been all planned among the women as they cut vegetables, pulled off the feathers from the hens and roosters, washed the golden *kanh* dishes with ash and lemon. It seemed everyone had entrusted Onima-borma with the responsibility of broaching the subject to Mukut-khura, the head of the family. Meenu-jethai, Dorongi-aaita, Sunjira-jethai were outsiders in a way. They must have decided amongst themselves that one of the men from the house must inform Prosanto-da. To inform Prosanto-da, they would at least have to take Mukut-khura's permission, because informing him would mean that they were waving the white flag. That he could marry Onulupa.

'Something has to be done,' Onima-borma said. 'We can't take big decisions; the men of the house have to take the initiative. But at first, he should be brought back home. His self-imposed exile should end. If someone from the house goes and informs him, it wouldn't mean that he can marry that girl. But we will have to solve it through dialogue. The entire village is talking about the matter and we aren't. We are sitting at home like koels who think the storm will go away if we keep our eyes shut.'

Mukut-khura washed his hands on the dish hastily—as if he was annoyed and he was expressing his anger on the little food that he hadn't finished. Onima-borma looked at his plate. The water collected in a pool and a curry leaf and bits of chewed bone floated in it.

'What can we do? He is a man with a modern outlook and doesn't care about all those things that Mai and you are worried about.' He laid stress on 'modern outlook'. 'Mai isn't allowing this marriage, nor am I allowing such a thing to happen in this house, and he has been waiting for the last four years for her permission. I don't know where this is leading. If he thinks not eating meals in his own house and living elsewhere would make us give our consent, he is not being wise.'

Oholya-jethai tried to say something but Mukut-khura dared to cut in for once, 'Bai, please don't ask me to go and bring him home. Please!'

Oholya-jethai reacted like a wounded cobra. 'What did you say? *Ha?* What did you say? We should let him stay elsewhere and let the whole village talk and make fun of us?'

Anil-da rushed towards her with the movement of a kite, leaving his meal where it was, and held her finger that was pointing at Mukut-khura. 'Jethai! Jethai! There are too many guests outside and if Aaita gets to know, she won't be able to bear this and will not survive the wedding. Everything will be ruined then.'

But she continued in hushed yet angry tones. 'What did you say, Mukut? If you don't take responsibility, the women of the house will have to go discuss those shameless things with him. Fine! I will go tomorrow to Jitendro's house and announce while I walk through the village that the men in this house are all gelded!'

Dorongi-aaita covered her ears with her palms. Onima-borma slapped her forehead saying she regretted ever bringing the matter up. I think Anil-da wanted everyone to know what had happened in the kitchen. He wanted the guests who had come from faraway places to know and discuss and rip apart the matter to a million tiny shreds, enjoy the smallest morsels of it till it had vanished, till only the memory of its bitter taste remained.

I think he wanted Aaita to know every detail of it as well. And, if possible, every exaggerated detail so that she would have died of a broken heart before the wedding and the Brahmin would tell us that we couldn't have an auspicious occasion in the house for another year. Before leaving, Mukut-khura threw the stool outside the kitchen. It landed on a dog and it ran away, barking. The people outside must have wondered what had happened to the dog. Curious men and women, or curious children among the guests, must have walked to the back of the house leaving the warmth of the bonfire to find out if the dog was seriously injured. Aaita, who was lying on the bed almost like a dead body, waiting for Oholya-jethai to bring her food, must have wondered if a robber was trying to break into the house and harm the family that she tried to keep together without crumbling.

When the stool flew out, it brushed against the mud wall and a small chunk of mud fell on the ground, revealing the bamboo frame beneath it. Nobody seemed to notice it.

~

Since Aaita's condition wasn't good at all, the rest of the day was filled with anxiety. It was a long and tedious day. Aaita could manage to say just a few words with great effort. But she didn't ask where Prosanto-da was. Maybe she knew he wasn't around. She had understood the futility of asking for her youngest son. Her favourite son or, as Onima-borma said, 'The son who locked her womb'.

We waited for that son to arrive—the son who locked Binapani Bishoya's womb. I hoped he would honour my request. The people in the family hoped too that he would get the news and come. But how, they didn't seem to know. As if he would get the news of his dying mother in his dream, during his morning walk, while bathing.

But at last he came. And he came with Onulupa.

Onulupa stepped into the compound of the house, gently pushing open the bamboo gate on the day after the owls hooted. The night-jasmine tree that leaned against the gate was in full bloom that day. But the foxtail orchid that grew from one of its branches was dry and withered, pining for spring to arrive as soon as possible. Aaita was so sick that everyone was sure she wouldn't make it to the wedding. Yet a faint hope forced people to continue working for it. The women continued to separate the rice from the husk, pick pebbles from the lentils and complain, winnow bag after bag of flattened rice, and debate how much would be enough. The men continued to cut firewood, trim shrubs and trees, and build the wedding tent. They would use the most beautifully patterned tent over the courtyard and it'd be done at last.

A little before Onulupa's entry into the house, Okoni-pehi had wept in front of Onima-borma while she cut cauliflowers and cabbages for the night's meal. 'I really don't want this wedding to be postponed but . . .' She had bit her lips and said, 'If Mai *leaves* us, the Brahmin won't allow us to conduct the marriage rituals for another year. We are from the bride's family; anything could happen to us in a day. And one year means many days, many weeks.'

Onima-borma had consoled her, 'Don't worry; God will ensure justice. I have promised to keep Thursday fasts and sacrifice a black male goat to Goddess Kamakhya. I believe everything will be fine.'

'Moina is petrified. She is trying hard to remain calm. You know, being the youngest daughter, she is like our baby. I mean, I was quite old when she was born and Oholya-bai was already a woman, having an affair with that doctor. She is our baby and since she always has been a little chicken, we took extra care of her. She gets scared easily, she won't even go out alone in the night to pee. Now all these bad omens have shrunk her like a dry fruit. Years of bad luck have turned her superstitious.'

Both of them sighed. Okoni-pehi continued, 'After we finished lunch this morning, I was sitting beside Mai for nearly an hour. While feeding her milk with a spoon, I kept telling her, "Mai, you can't *leave* us, you will have to *see* this wedding; you will have to wait till you bless your son-in-law. This is your last daughter and then you are free to *go*." I don't know if anything went into her ears. She was staring at the ceiling, gulping down each drop of milk. Much later, she just said she won't, God won't be so cruel. At least, she has gained back her consciousness. I was very

scared when she couldn't breathe last night. Another dose of
mokordhwoj did the trick.'

The previous night, the sound of the conches had rung through
the house, its courtyard, and we all had chanted aloud God's
name again and again.

So Onulupa came on an auspicious day.

A suddenly auspicious day.

That was the day I saw her properly for the first time. I was
disappointed. She didn't look like the heroine of a legendary
love story, fit to be canonized and made part of a Bihu song.
I wondered what was so great about her. She looked perfectly
ordinary. What was so special about her that had turned Prosanto-
da into a moth drawn to a flame? Where was the fire in her?

I was mean, like most others in the house—we all believed
Prosanto-da was too handsome for such an ugly bride (bony,
dark, with a protruding jaw).

Together, they would never look like characters, or rather
like a couple, from a legendary love story, even though their
story had all the elements of one. In photographs, they'd look
incongruous; an elephant and a fly, a white stork marrying a
night-black crow. His four long years of waiting had turned
him into a romantic hero among young boys like us. And now,
standing at the gate, next to Onulupa, he seemed to have fallen
in everyone's estimation.

Prosanto-da went straight to Aaita's room with Onulupa and
shut the door. I turned to find Oholya-jethai's shocked face, as she
realized that something had happened in the house without her
permission, that the girl she hated so much—perhaps without
ever thinking why—had gone inside Aaita's room to partake of
a privacy that many in that house were not entitled to. She did
not even wait to seek the permission of the one member of this

family who dictated who should be around Aaita, who should marry whom, who would sleep where, who would clean the house at what time and who was responsible for finding a match for Moina-pehi.

She ran towards Onima-borma. 'Did you see that, Onima? Did you see that?' she said, her voice rising menacingly.

Onima-borma looked perplexed as well. 'Bai, look at the way she went in! She didn't even acknowledge our presence—let alone mine, but she ignored you too! And this is the woman who would come to live with us? I won't be able to live in this house even for a moment. She is definitely going to brainwash Mai. You have to do something.'

'What can I do?' Oholya-jethai's voice was louder. Then she said in a lower voice, 'What can I do? I am helpless. I guess we will have to accept our destiny!'

'Oh, I so wish my son's father hadn't died so early. He would have never let this happen, I know.'

'My brother was not just a brother; he was a precious gem that brought good luck to this house. Since he has gone, all sorts of evil influences have gradually eroded the very foundations of this house. Sometimes, evil planets come in the guise of women who were already married once!'

Inside, in a muffled voice, Moina-pehi was telling me, 'Eeeh, this witch has eaten up my younger brother's brains! She is not even beautiful. Thin as a stick! Look at him, any girl would die for him. You know, apparently they have been in love since college. She studied with him in Guwahati. Both BA and MA. She was always after him. She stands in all the photographs just beside him. Pressing her body against his. Eeeh, even we had boyfriends! But we were never like that.'

Anamika laughed out. 'Tell us! Who was it?' She left the clothes she was folding and joined Moina-pehi on the bed. Her body grazed against mine.

Moina-pehi pretended to get angry. 'You have become too mischievous. It's time to teach you a lesson!'

But when the door opened several hours later, everyone in the house got to know that Aaita had placed her hand on Onulupa's head in a symbolic gesture of accepting her into the family. Outside, Anil-da speculated if the two had already got married, but Oholya-jethai confirmed to Anil-da and Onima-borma that she hadn't seen any sindoor on Onulupa's forehead.

There were angry faces all around. Later that evening, the women sat dicing vegetables for dinner and grumbled about how Onulupa had bewitched Aaita at last and how she had tried to bewitch the whole family one by one by touching the feet of Mukut-khura, Dorongi-aaita, Onima-borma and Oholya-jethai. The last two had moved away when Onulupa had bent to take their blessings, saying, 'You may not touch my feet. There will be more opportunities.'

Onima-borma wasn't taking part in the conversation. Slowly she peeled the potatoes and threw them into a large pot filled with water, brown with the soil from the immersed potatoes. She bowed her head like a drooping stalk of grain in the paddy fields.

Mridul looked bored. Or was he tense? After all, he was setting the scene for another storm to blow over the house.

Onima-borma told Oholya-jethai, 'Bai, you must never go near that witch. You never know, she might enchant you and you will end up liking her more than me! Then I wouldn't have any option but to tie a steel pot around my neck and jump into the river.'

Oholya-jethai hissed like an angry cobra. 'Who would put a charm on me? She doesn't know me yet. I will talk to Mai and see to it that this wedding doesn't take place. I always knew Prosanto was extremely shameless. Do you remember the way he dared write letters to Bolen? My tiger-like brother who everyone in the family as well as the village was scared of! He went in to talk about his own marriage with his own old, dying mother? How shameless! Onima, don't worry, this Onulupa won't be able to put a spell on me. She doesn't know Oholya Bishoya yet! I will charm her fourteen generations and tether all of them in my cowshed with Ronga.'

She stressed that Onulupa was not even from Mayong, so, unlike most women and men in Mayong, she would not know any black magic.

But that evening, when people in the family heard that Prosanto-da was returning home, everyone was happy. Their faces ashened when they heard that he would be marrying Onulupa, finally.

Oholya-jethai let loose words as sharp as arrows at her ailing mother as soon as the feet-touching session was over, and Onulupa and Prosanto-da had left the house with bright smiles on their faces. Aaita was helped out of her room and she was sitting on the veranda now. Mukut-khura joked that she had feigned sickness to get back her youngest son, her dearest son, the son who had locked her womb. Anamika murmured that love was powerful—just Prosanto-da's return could cause such a change in Aaita's condition.

But Oholya-jethai was cruel. She didn't bother about how weak Aaita was. She went to her and said, 'Do you know why he came home at last, Mai? Because you are dying! He thinks you will die and he will never get your permission. Don't be blind with love for your son.' She used the word 'putrosneh'. Love for one's son. It lent her sentence a biting, satirical edge. 'Think about us too. We'll have to stay together. She has already slept with that army officer and aborted his child. Will you be able to eat food served and cooked by her hands? You have maintained rituals for so long, now you want to go to hell?'

Aaita chided Oholya-jethai very slowly in a low voice, 'Why are you burning so much?' Her voice was weak. Like trapped winds in an ancient mahal. 'He won't listen to me. Bolen had spoiled him. If Bolen were alive, he'd have agreed to this marriage.'

Onima-borma wiped off the inevitable tears triggered by memories kindled by their conversation—the memory of something lost four years ago. Mridul looked at his mother. I looked down, made circles on the ground with my toe.

Aaita said, slowly, leaning against the pillar in a resigned way, 'You know how generous he was. Bolen had spoiled his youngest brother. He loved him like a son, brought him up like his son. Bolen was eighteen years older than Prosanto. He carried him on his back everywhere when he was a baby. Okoni cleaned him always. Bolen bathed him. Dressed him. Taught him O, Aa, and those Engrazee ABCD. He slept on the same bed as Bolen till his voice was husky . . . And what's there to worry about eating what she cooks? I won't allow her into the kitchen anyway. And how many mouths do I have? You don't need ten women to cook for a single mouth. One is enough. *Tohoti nukhuwaleu moi jiyai thakim.* Anyway, I know I will die soon. I'm just waiting to see my youngest daughter married off.'

Oholya-jethai turned her face towards Onima-borma. She knew she had lost an ally. She stood up in rage and said before leaving the stage, 'At least you could have done something *good* before your death.'

But no, Aaita lived much longer. She not only saw her daughter's wedding, but also the preparations for her youngest son's wedding five years later and passed away just an hour before her youngest son was about to step out of his house to go to the bride's family in Tezpur. They married around one and a half years later, in the autumn of 2008. Aaita was around when her daughter Moina drank phenyl the night before her wedding after hearing what Anil-da had to say about the groom's family.

~

Mridul had stayed home all day since anything could happen any time.

After dinner, I asked him what was keeping him so busy that he had been staying out of the house so much. But once again, he gave me an evasive reply. He said I had enough company in the house, that he was sure I wasn't bored. I didn't want to get into a long conversation with him. I felt he was referring sarcastically to Anamika when he spoke of me having 'enough company'.

I waited for him to mention her, about our walk on that sun-smeared morning. But he didn't. He was once again lost in his thoughts. I was convinced something was brewing. But I had no idea what it was.

Mridul was changing, I thought. He would have told me everything a few years ago. But now he inhabited worlds that I had no access to. He occupied a secret chamber I had no keys to.

I left him that way. I went looking for Anamika. She must be done with cleaning the dishes. When I crossed the courtyard, where around fifty people were sitting under the open sky, I heard someone complaining that there was no fun in the wedding, that people should have fun, sing, dance; old men and women agreed that it'd cheer up Aaita and she would feel better. 'We must dance.' One of my aunts egged a little girl clad in a pink frock to dance. She stood up, but bowed her head in shame and sprinted back to the place where she was sitting. 'Why doesn't someone play a song?' Mukut-khura said loudly. 'How much shall we mourn? Mai is feeling better. Play a song!' Playing songs was Mridul's department. But since he was in another world, his sister went inside and played some old Assamese film songs. The little girl stood up and shook her hands sheepishly. The crowd clapped and cheered her along. 'Only now, we are finally getting the wedding feeling!' they said.

I was in the backyard now. Anamika was nowhere to be seen. Like a fish, she had vanished into the pond. From the backyard, I could hear the sounds of claps, jeers, laughter and the Bihu song that was playing now. A woman's voice was singing she could do anything for her lover. She could turn into a dove and sit on the roof of his house; she could turn into a duck and swim in his pond. The guy replied that he would turn into beads of sweat and trickle down her body; he would turn himself into a fly to plant a kiss on her red cheeks.

I felt light-hearted. This is how a wedding should be. After all, a wedding was taking place in the house after such a long time. This would make Moina-pehi feel good, assure her that things would be fine. She looked sad and worn out. The termites called worry and fear had entered her body and were eating her up from inside. The songs, the jeers, the claps, would make her feel better. Her three childhood friends would be coming the next day, or the day after. Oholya-jethai said that would lift her spirits further.

No, Anamika was nowhere to be seen.

Should I go and read?

Nah, I would rather hang around in the courtyard. People would tease me if I sat in a corner with a book.

I started walking back when I found Anamika coming towards the house with a brass pot filled with water. She asked me where

I'd been. I said that I wanted to ask her the same. She said she was older, more important; she had work to do. I knew she was teasing me. I said men have more important things than women to do. She said 'Ehehehe!' in a mocking tone.

She placed the pot on the ground and said, pointing to the dog that was still sniffing around for some morsels around the place where the dishes had been washed, 'This dog would soon lay eggs.'

'What?'

'Yes, it's time this dog laid some eggs,' she said seriously.

'You have gone mad.'

'What are you talking about? Maybe the dogs in the city don't lay eggs, but village dogs do. Ask your father.'

'I am never going to believe that nor will I ask him. He will send me to Tezpur Mental Hospital if I did.'

'No, he won't. I can prove it.'

'Prove it?'

'What proof do you need? Just look at the back of that dog properly. You will see two large black eggs.'

My cheeks burned, my ears became hot, my spine tingled. 'What?' I gulped.

She started giggling.

'What a sick girl you are!'

I couldn't hide the smile on my face. I couldn't believe what she had just said. I couldn't believe I even took part in that conversation. I sat on a wooden stool there, just beside the foot loom that was covered like a corpse with a white bed sheet. It was Oholya-jethai's foot loom, where she wove gamusas and clothes for herself. Every year, the ceaseless clatter of that loom announced to the people in the house that the first day of the Assamese calendar wasn't too far away, the day elders gave gamusas and blessings with betel nuts to the younger ones, the day when the younger ones gave loom-woven gamusas to their elders and sought their forgiveness, blessings, advice.

The people in the courtyard were laughing. Someone must have been cracking jokes. Old women, who had breasts like the nests of weaver birds, often cracked dirty jokes, jokes Mridul used to tell me when we were younger. Standing there, I recalled Mridul's joke about Ms Slutty Hen, who would never scream when fucked. Tiger fucked her and roared when he had orgasm; Buffalo fucked her with his penis and horns thrusting so hard that the earth shook; Dog with his lipstick-like penis fucked her until he lay flat, panting like a puppy; Horse gave it to her with his monstrous weapon—but still she wouldn't scream. She could take on anyone, without the slightest sound coming out of her mouth. Then Fox hired her for a night. The denizens of the forest who'd done it to her before and couldn't make her scream had challenged Fox to do so. Just a few minutes after he had entered her 'house', the entire forest echoed with the scream of Ms Slutty Hen. 'What happened?' they asked sweating Fox once he came out of her house. 'What would happen?' He remarked triumphantly, 'None of you know how to do it. I entered her only after I'd stripped her naked.'

I didn't want to go back to the courtyard. Anamika held me in place where I was standing. The smell of her wet clothes, the cheap perfume she wore, overwhelmed my senses. Suddenly, I changed my expression into one of anger and walked away. 'I don't want to talk to you,' I said sternly. I walked back to the courtyard, leaving a surprised Anamika staring after me.

About half an hour later, she accosted me near Prosanto-da's room.

'Are you still angry with me?' she asked with a touch of mischief in her voice.

I had spent the last half an hour among people in the courtyard who were sharing jokes, talking about other weddings. As I had guessed, an old woman told the sickest jokes and everyone laughed thunderously. If Mom were around she would have sat there and, later, told me censored versions of those jokes. I wished Papa and Mom hadn't cancelled their plans to attend the wedding. Though she had grown up in a city, she always loved spending time in the village, unlike most of her colleagues, unlike most of her friends who asked her how she could stay for so long in the village where the toilets were still old-fashioned, inconvenient, smelly and without flowing water.

A few others were still taking a walk. With toothpicks, they were cleaning their teeth, rubbing them with toothpaste and charcoal. Around the large iron cauldron, where a fire was lit, they sat and talked. No one wanted to go in. No one wanted to hit the sack.

I wasn't angry with Anamika.

But I didn't want to answer her question directly as well.

I said, 'How does it matter? You still think I am a kid, don't you? I don't think you'd care to know the plight of kids.'

'Ah, kids say big-big things these days! Great! Stay in your own world. I was only asking if you are still offended because of that small thing.'

She walked back into the house swiftly, leaving me there. I felt defeated and amused, tickled and challenged. I wanted to tell her something that would shut the lid with the right kind of cork. I wanted to do something that would make her feel angry and defeated, challenged and amused. I followed her, but she walked too fast, so I lost her in the large house of many rooms, seventeen windows and no ventilators.

Briskly, I walked to the part of the house she had gone into. It was the new, extended part of the house where Mukut-khura and Lahori-khuri lived with their children. No, she wasn't in the room where the guests were seated, where bamboo flower vases of fake flowers were carefully placed, where greetings cards given to Mukut-khura by his students in the high school were stapled together into a garland and hung on the wall. There were no sofas, only a few wooden chairs with cushions thrown on them.

She wasn't in the next room as well, where Mukut-khura's two daughters slept, where the walls were covered with posters of actors from Assamese and Hindi films, with calendars, with timetables of schools and exams, where Assamese and English primers languished on the beds.

The bedroom door was ajar.

Should I go in?

I could smell the burning sandalwood incense. Someone must have burned it in the evening—the time when Goddess Lakshmi arrives, sitting on a white owl.

Where had she vanished?

She was in the last room in this part of the house. She was sharing the room with Moon-baideo. It was an extra room that Mukut-khura had built for guests, for weddings and funerals.

When I saw her from a distance, her back was turned to me just like that first day when I had seen her after reaching Mayong. She didn't notice me coming towards her with the quietness of cat's paws and when I hugged her waist from behind, she didn't scream, she didn't protest. But for a few seconds she stood still, breathing fast, without turning back. In those seconds, I felt her waist; I pressed myself against her, and then turned her around and kissed her on the lips. She was still looking at me in disbelief when I let her go. I was smiling. She blushed.

'What did you just do?' She gasped.

'When you are left alone in a wedding house, this is what happens.'

I must have raised one of my eyebrows. She kept looking at me for a few seconds and then moved forward towards me. We kissed, until we heard footsteps. That was my first kiss. I must have raised one of my eyebrows, to create that triumphant look. I must have. A few months later, when I would hear more about Anamika, what happened to her after our short-lived, meaningless, lust story (not love story) from Mridul, I couldn't remember if I did. But I must have. I must have raised my eyebrow just a bit.

~

I went to Prosanto-da's room when the sound of crickets thickened the night.

I didn't want to sleep. Mridul had vanished again.

Once again, I felt that ache in my heart. The ache of betrayal. The kind I used to feel when my best friend Probal sat next to someone else in the class. The kind Probal used to feel when I shared my tiffin with someone else. He would avoid me then. And later, the kind of ache I had felt when I had heard from another person in the class that Probal had said 'I love you' to Nirmali. When that had happened, I hadn't spoken to him for several days, for not telling me, for pushing me into the ignominy of hearing *his secrets* from other people.

Would I hear Mridul's secret, which he was nurturing like a

marigold sapling in winter, from Brikodar?

Did Brikodar know what Mridul was up to?

Why was he staying out, especially in those crucial days when he was needed the most around the house?

Once in a while, Oholya-jethai or Onima-borma would grumble, noting his absence. But soon, their grumbles, their complaints, their creased foreheads, would be drowned, evened out, by the chatter of the guests, by the many hands that shook their fingers at them and unleashed a flood of questions and remarks at them.

It was the same ache that had stopped me from asking Mridul what he was up to. But I had sensed it had something to do with Manju Mahatu. Perhaps that was why he had smiled mysteriously when I had asked him at the riverbank if he would bring in a wing-clipped fairy to the house. Perhaps that was why he didn't want to tell me anything, rather, he'd reveal his intentions to me by bringing her home. I shuddered at the thought. What if they were planning to elope? I saw him folding some of his clothes last morning and putting them into his red duffel bag. He should have taken the clothes out, not put them back, after returning from Guwahati. How would the house withstand this new storm?

The sound of crickets had turned the night mysterious. Most people were asleep or were preparing to go to bed after ensuring that the kerosene lamp wasn't too far away, the torch was under the pillow, the overnight cream had been massaged well into the skin and warm coconut oil had been applied on long tresses thoroughly. Anil-da, Roton and two other guys were standing in the middle of the courtyard, playing carrom. A few women were still sitting around the fire. Who were the other two guys? 'Montu and all', I assumed.

I walked past them. Anil-da asked me why I wasn't asleep. I said

I wanted to talk to Prosanto-da. In his room, he was arranging his books. He asked the same question that Anil-da had asked moments ago. I told him I wasn't used to sleeping so early and he asked me when I usually went to bed.

'Late, pretty late,' I said.

I didn't tell him about the landline phone I had in my room. Suddenly, I was ashamed of my privilege. I could have told him that it was my time to make calls, discuss homework, crib about teachers we hated and gossip about the love lives of people in our batch. Who kissed whom? Who got drunk and made out with the wrong person at which party? I could have told Prosanto-da how I decreased the room temperature in the air conditioner in the peak of summer after my parents were asleep, who were of the opinion that though we had an air conditioner, we shouldn't get used to it. I was suddenly ashamed of having a phone, an AC, a better bookshelf, branded plastic chairs and softer, buoyant mattresses where I imagined having bouncy sex with girls who had crushes on me, though they didn't.

I sat down on the cane chair. Prosanto-da became busy. 'Let me look around for the cushion.'

'I will be fine,' I said. 'I can sit on the chair without a cushion. Are you looking for a specific book?'

'No, I am just arranging them. I had taken quite a few books with me. Now I have to put them where they belong so that I will be able to find them easily before class.'

'So even you have returned to where you *belong*,' I said, looking around.

'Ha?' He stared at me for some time. 'So little you were when I had gone to Guwahati to take admission in college. You didn't even come out of your room to speak to me.'

'That little boy has grown up, Prosanto-da.'

'I see! And he talks big-big these days. Wise and pedantic—even to his uncle.'

He sat on the bed and patted my right cheek with his rough hand. As rough as a cow's tongue. I wondered why it was so rough. Perhaps it was rough because he also worked in the fields sometimes and chopped firewood with an axe. The money from the college wasn't enough, and yet he wouldn't move out of the village and get a better job. Mom said Prosanto-da was a 'different type of guy'. He wouldn't leave his place even if he got a better job. That was partly because they had so much land, but also because he wanted to do something for his own region, his own village, his own people.

'I don't like calling you uncle. You are too young to be an "uncle".'

'That's why I never get the respect. You treat me like a classmate.' He laughed. Silently. His eyes danced, his body shook and his lips changed shape into a naughty curl.

'Prosanto-da?'

'Hmm?'

'Why is Oholya-jethai so mean?'

He looked at me for a while. Then he looked down and remained silent. Since he didn't answer immediately, I started feeling guilty for asking the question. I had started apologizing when he said, 'She isn't mean, Pablo. You don't know anything about her, that's why you can't forgive her. When you know her history, you will forgive her.'

I was filled with embarrassment though I didn't agree with him. I still thought she was mean, and since I couldn't agree with him, I felt even worse.

Outside, Mukut-khura was telling 'Montu and all' and Anil-da, 'We have to finish digging the holes around the courtyard before we go to sleep. We can't keep digging late into the night, people wouldn't like the noise.'

Prosanto-da said, 'Pablo, an unmarried, unemployed woman has no respect, no ground beneath her feet in our society. The only way somebody can hold her head high is by adhering strictly to what society expects from her. By becoming a jealous guardian of the rules and regulations, she buys acceptance and respect, carves a place for herself.'

I couldn't understand him. She was one of the elderly members of the house. Why wouldn't anyone respect her? Why would someone respect her less if she were pleasant, more generous? So all these years, she was just struggling to find the ground beneath her feet with her meanness? I looked at his face in anticipation, hoping to hear more. When he didn't speak, I asked.

'Why didn't she marry?'

'Don't you know already?'

'I just know that she had become the subject of a big gossip and no one married her.'

'In those days, when you fell in love, you automatically ensured that you would become the subject of a big gossip, especially if you were a woman. She was in love with a government doctor who was posted here. He had come to examine our father, when he met her. I was too young—a baby. But that's what I have heard from people. She even went to his house in his Standard car—they were rich. Stayed over at his place for several nights after the ring ceremony. That hadn't gone down well with the villagers. Mai asked her not to go, but she wouldn't listen. You know how headstrong she is. She went; the villagers were furious. They said they wouldn't come for her wedding and our family would be excommunicated. Everyone talked about it. In the early seventies, things were different. The panchayat is strong

now, but was even stronger in those days. Then something so
unexpected happened that it just shook the ground beneath her
feet.' He sighed and paused.

'What happened? The wedding didn't take place?'

Of course the wedding didn't take place. Otherwise, why
would she be hanging around here? Why would she turn into
this acerbic person? I felt silly for asking such a stupid question.

From where we were sitting, we could see the courtyard clearly.
The four men who were playing carrom seemed reluctant to leave
their game in the middle. Mukut-khura said that they needed to
dig at least four deep post holes for the bholuka-bamboo pillars
that would be brought early the next morning. He said that more
guests would arrive the next day and would prefer to sit around
most of the time in the courtyard, so it was necessary to have the
shade ready if the weather became hot suddenly during noon.
He took up one of the four long, rust-coated iron hole diggers
that were leaning against the wall of the storeroom and started
digging the courtyard with it. After a few stabs, he stopped to
ask Roton if he was digging at the right spot.

Prosanto-da cleared his throat. He left the bed and kept the
last stacks of books from his satchel on the shelf one by one,
swiftly, and told me, 'The doctor cancelled the wedding. His
family had issues. They were too rich, owners of a Standard car,
and we were too poor. When he had come to tell her this, she
had thrown a chair at him in rage. "I don't need your gold ring."
She had thrown it at him from this same veranda. He waited in
the courtyard for a long time, with bowed head. He couldn't go
against his parents' wishes. He couldn't live without marrying
her. Mai says it was raining and he stood there for a long time
but Oholya-bai didn't come out of the house. She wasn't even
crying. Fuming with anger, she kept standing like a statue in her

room, while Mai consoled her. They never met again. His family applied for transfer on his behalf, and he was posted in Guwahati.'

Prosanto-da stopped when he saw Oholya-jethai and Moina-pehi stepping on to the courtyard. They were perhaps returning from the well, their hands and faces dripping water. Moina-pehi didn't stop; she went straight to her room. Prosanto-da looked at her, his neck turning as she moved further; perhaps, he was trying to attract her attention, to sit with her and chat, or at least to smile at her. He had been away for a while and now wanted to be normal, to catch up with people. When Oholya-jethai stopped there, Roton, who was digging the earth, stood transfixed under her sharp gaze. Prosanto-da concentrated on arranging the books, but soon her loud and sharp voice reached us. 'What are you all doing digging around after dinner? At night?'

'Digging to set up the tent,' Mukut-khura said, scraping out soil with his palm.

'That I can see! But have you lost your mind, Mukut?'

Startled, the rest of the guys paused. Anil-da said loudly, 'I was just about to say that we shouldn't use sharp tools at night. It's a bad omen. It invites bad luck, but no one listens to me.'

Mukut-khura gave him a stern look. But I knew he wouldn't scold Anil-da. Anil-da's nature was to keep speaking when he wasn't expected to, keep poking his nose into matters where he shouldn't. Sometimes he got a hearing. Sometimes he didn't.

'You are right, Anil. As if we didn't have enough of bad omens,' Oholya-jethai said with a nod of approval.

Hearing her angry voice, a few others started coming out of the house to see what was up. Prosanto-da left his bookshelf and walked out. Anamika came out, wearing her yellow nightdress, a gamusa covering her shapely breasts that were jutting out under her dress. Onima-borma, who must have been getting ready to sleep, walked out of her room, holding a pillow. She gave it to one of the guests and said that it was the only extra one she had lying in her room. Okoni-pehi stood on the veranda, doing her hair with a bamboo comb and trying to tame her unruly curls.

Mukut-khura looked at everyone and said, 'The bamboos that would be used as pillars will be delivered early in the morning. We can't let them lie around like that. We have to keep the holes ready so that as soon as they reach . . .'

'But you shouldn't be using sharp tools at night. Also, anything might come out from the ground. It's winter and who knows you might end up waking up a hibernating snake or stirring other poisonous insects.' Oholya-jethai's voice grew louder. Mukut-khura had scraped out some more soil from the deep hole he had dug. Holding the moist soil on his palm, he started looking for something in it.

'Are you listening to me? Dig the holes tomorrow.'

'There's enough light, Oholya-bai,' Prosanto-da said.

'Did I ask you anything?' She turned towards him and paused, as if to increase the blow of that insult. 'Where were you all these weeks, leaving the entire weight of the wedding on my ageing back?'

Prosanto-da was hurt. He walked back into his room and shut the door with a loud thud. Oholya-jethai kept looking at the shut door. Then she started unleashing her fury at Mukut-khura—the anger that the thud had sparked off.

'Are you going to listen to me or will you . . . ?'

But Oholya-jethai couldn't finish her sentence. Mukut-khura looked up at her and said in a voice that had all the sadness of the world. He called out to her. 'Bai, please come here, please.'

At first, everyone looked alarmed. They must have thought, just like me, that *something* had happened. There must have been a poisonous insect in the soil and it must have bitten him, stung him, spreading the venom into his well-built, tall body. And perhaps that had made him call out to his elder sister, with such helplessness, such eagerness. But no, nothing like that had happened. He was perfectly fine. When Oholya-jethai reached him, people also closed in, squeezed in like evening ducks gathering around a plate of rice husk. In the bright light of the electric bulbs, we saw the glitter of a ring he had found buried in the earth.

'Oholya-bai, this ring . . .'

'This ring?' Oholya-jethai said—the helplessness of Mukut-khura now in her tone too. What was the poisonous insect that both had been stung by? What was in that ring? Another bad omen? Another bad news? Or a story I didn't know?

I could hear Okoni-pehi gasp. 'It must be the same ring,' she said and stopped. Moina-pehi had come out of her room. 'What is it?' she asked the crowd that had gathered. There were so many people and yet there was absolute silence. Amidst that silence, amidst that flood of lights in which the golden ring glittered, after Mukut-khura cleaned it, polished it with the tip of his vest, we heard a sound.

That sound was coming from Oholya-jethai's throat. She was weeping. 'This ring!' she said again, staring at it. As if a poem was written on the small, slim wedding ring that she was looking at with tender eyes. As if she were a goldsmith who was finding it hard to decide the value of the ring. 'This ring!' She held it against the light. It sparkled, though some of it was still muddy. In the bright light, we could see the ring. It had a bluish stone set in it. But most of it was golden. 'Real gold from yesteryears!' I heard a female voice gasp. Oholya-jethai looked as if she were in pain. As if someone had stabbed her. As if her entire body was riddled with a sharp ache. As if an arrow had pierced into her heart.

Slowly Moina-pehi walked up to her. Slowly Onima-borma went and stood near her. She didn't fall on Moina-pehi's shoulders. She didn't lean against Onima-borma's body. But she slouched. Oholya-jethai, the tallest woman in the village, slouched like a tall betel-nut tree bending in a strong gust of wind. Okoni-pehi came and stood near her and it was her body Oholya-jethai fell on, weeping softly. I could see her moist eyes. Eyes that had thick eyelashes even at this age. A murmur started moving across the courtyard like a bad smell, like a damp breeze, like bees over a yellow bed of flowering mustard plants. Gradually, Oholya-jethai started to move towards her room. After a few moments, we heard another thud. She had locked herself in. Okoni-pehi stared at it for a long time and exclaimed, 'Oh God!'

'Why did it have to appear after so many years?' She looked at Onima-borma and asked. Both of them stood facing each other and wiped the tears away from the corner of their eyes. 'Why did it have to appear after so many years? We have had so many weddings, so many funerals since that day.'

The crowd started talking.

'The hopes of a spinster have remained trapped in that ring. Something must be done to release it.'

'Didn't the doctor die after three years? Had he never married?'

'Yes, yes. He did. How could you forget what happened after that? Do you remember how Oholya kept writing letters to him even after he was dead?'

'Why would she do something like that?'

'Eh, no, she didn't know he was dead. She kept writing to him for around two years after his death, and one day his brother came here with thirty-two unopened letters. She fainted. I was here that day! She lost consciousness—I am telling you—and I ran into the kitchen though I hadn't bathed that day, got some water and sprinkled it on her face.'

'Writing letters to a dead man for more than a year after his death? Ah, that's called a tragedy.'

The discussions became louder. Oholya-jethai didn't come out of her room. In the morning, Okoni-pehi knocked for a long time on her door before she opened it. She had food in her room. After a while, Okoni-pehi went to her room to collect the plates. Suddenly, Oholya-jethai vanished from the wedding. Though she was in the house, she was in another world. Just like Mridul, she started inhabiting a world that she didn't give anyone else any access to. Sometime towards the evening that day, she opened her door and walked out, took a bath, wore fresh clothes, had some food and again went back to her room. I noticed her bun had come loose. Her hair hung behind her, over her nape, loosely knotted, like a weaver bird's broken nest.

What was she doing inside her room? Some people thought the blow would kill Oholya-jethai. That she'd wither away like roses that are plucked too early to keep in vases. That she would gradually vanish like camphor exposed to air. Memories were stinging her like angry homeless bees.

~

Along with the many other guests, Moina-pehi's three childhood friends also arrived that evening, a little after Oholya-jethai had locked herself in her room again. That cheered Moina-pehi up a little. Her friends with whom she had sat and shared sour fruits, sprinkled with rock salt, garnished with chopped onions or green chillies, when they were young unmarried girls. They looked older than her, with their broader faces.

There were three of them—Lereli, Gedepi and Aaijoni—and all of them had brought their children with them. Lereli-baideo had a ten-year-old son and he was her second child. Moina-pehi told me in the evening that she had married very early. She had eloped with her lover since her family didn't allow the marriage. We spoke about rats. I didn't want to bring up the topic. It seemed that the hooting of the owls had left a scar in her mind that refused to heal. So she told her friends about the owls again. And they said there was nothing to worry about. But I saw lines forming on their foreheads. Moina-pehi looked at me and said, 'Our Pablo says they came looking for rats.'

I liked the way she said 'our Pablo'. So I responded immediately, 'Poor hungry souls. They must have come with the hope of a sumptuous meal and we scared them out of their wits.'

Gedepi-baideo laughed showing her yellow teeth, the black dot on her chin too prominent. 'Why are you all so worried? You've got such a large backyard with too many big trees and a hill with thick forests right outside the house. If *owls* don't come to your house, would crocodiles come? Not only owls, you will have honeybees and tigers too.'

The conversation soon moved on to tigers. Mridul listened quietly, while Suruj narrated an incident when a tiger had tried to enter the cowshed and take away a newborn calf. It was tempted by the soft meat of the newborn calf that was yet to learn how to stand. Everyone listened attentively.

Mridul cut in. 'Soft must be the meat of fat rats too. We should include them on the wedding menu.'

Moina-pehi shrieked like a little girl, 'Eeeeh! Chee-chee! I won't be able to eat a morsel today if you say such things!'

But she was laughing. One of her childhood friends patted her butt hard and laughed, saying she should actually roast a few rats and take them along with her to feed her mother-in-law if she turned out to be a nasty old woman. The other friends joined in the laughter, and so did Moina-pehi. Somehow Suruj, Gedepi, Lereli, Aaijoni, Moina-pehi, Mridul and I started laughing hysterically until someone pointed out it was such a poor joke. Then we laughed some more until Okoni-pehi came in and asked what was wrong, with a smile on her face, which all of us found so funny that I punched Mridul's back and broke into peals of laughter. Moina-pehi slapped her friend's back and laughed as well. Our laughter was infectious. Soon Okoni-pehi joined in too.

After the retreat of the stern Oholya-jethai, Okoni-pehi had gradually filled up that void left by her older sister. All of the past week, she would come home early in the morning and work till everyone went to bed. Only then did she go back to her house. Her husband was home these days, so she preferred not to stay over. Though she didn't mention anything, she could sense the storm that was raging through Oholya-jethai's mind. Before leaving, Okoni-pehi even ensured that the children had gone to bed. That they weren't running around screaming 'train-train'.

How soon things got replaced. How soon the grass grew back on the ground. How soon the yellow sun-denied grass became green once the brick was removed from it. How soon life moved on.

Okoni-pehi lacked the air of self-reliance that Oholya-jethai carried about her.

She was attached to Mridul since it was she who had looked after him when he was a baby. It was she who had suggested he be called 'Mridul' and Onima-borma had liked it.

When Mridul didn't listen to her, she screamed at him, telling him that he had forgotten that he had soiled her clothes once upon a time. Onima-borma never denied it. Like all mothers in joint families, she asserted she faced no problem in bringing up any of her children because she always found someone to babysit them, to bathe them, to change their clothes, to carry them around. Now as she took charge of the bulk of the wedding-related work, the childless Okoni-pehi, who was often referred to as 'a barren plot of land' behind her back by women in the village, wanted the support of the child whom she had reared as a baby. She expected Mridul, the man whose penis she had powdered when he was a baby, to listen to her. She wanted to boast about that.

Mridul, the eldest son of her eldest brother, obeyed her as much as he obeyed his mother. She'd often say that the new generation was not ungrateful: they remembered who changed their diapers and who washed their crap-smeared buttocks.

Often she'd sit down with Onima-borma and discuss random matters: for instance, the wedding menu—which variety of fish ought to be served; should the mutton be cooked with less spice or more spice—and about the hired cooks, who must be clean and good-looking; which Brahmin (he should wear underwear under his dhoti so that 'nothing would be visible' when he sat cross-legged for conducting the rituals) was the best in the business; how the maids weren't working properly. Onima-borma always had the same reply to everything.

'Yes, yes. You are right. The cook from Bordubi is the best one. I remember going to Nirola's wedding and couldn't help asking who the cook was. Nirola's family didn't want to tell me at first! But they did tell me eventually. I mean, you can't hide such things! I extracted it from them!'

'Oh, don't tell me about Nirola's family. What a bunch of compulsive liars! What a selfish family! When Nirola's first periods started, the family was broke. They didn't even have a single gamusa to carry on the rituals.' Okoni-pehi's voice would rise higher. 'I opened my wooden chest and gave them six gamusas with wide flower patterns on them, woven with my own hands! Six!' She held up six fingers to emphasize the point. 'I wove them in the loom with these hands! Not Nirola, nor her great-grandmother could weave such gamusas. I didn't accept any money. I said, "Don't thank me, what are friends for at times of crisis? We live in the same village; we should be helping each other out." But when I went to them next year for some cotton, they refused! I was so shocked. This is what happens nowadays when you help people.'

'No, Okoni, the Nirolas are made of a different metal altogether. I have never seen bigger misers than them.'

Onima-borma would chop a betel nut, wrap it in a betel leaf, put a small piece of aromatic root in it, give it to Okoni-pehi and add, 'But Mukut did a good thing by booking Yogendra Narain Sharma. He conducted the rituals at Mukut's wedding as well, and what a lovely baritone he has! He chants all the montros. Doesn't leave out even a single stanza. And it's very essential for a successful conjugal life of the couple to listen to the montros well.'

'Yes.' Okoni-pehi would agree in a disagreeable, reluctant tone, stretching her 'yes' a little longer, and add, 'But he is a little greedy. Anyway, we want a peaceful life for the groom and the bride. So such exceptions can be made.'

'As if I don't know, Okoni! He had come last month to our house to meet Mukut. I went inside to heat a cup of tea and bring some chopped betel nuts but he wasn't sitting on the veranda by the time I came out!'

'Where was he then?'

'He was roaming around in our garden. Came to me and said, "Your gourds are lovely." Well, what else to do? I had to offer him one and he didn't even refuse! I have seen many greedy Brahmins, but not like Yogen Sharma!'

'All Brahmins are greedy!'

As they chewed their betel nuts red, and felt warmer, Okoni-pehi would often say, shedding the forever-furious, schoolmarmish air that she had acquired as a teacher at the primary school near Hatimura, 'Soon there will be another wedding in this house.'

Mridul would be embarrassed and fidget if he sat near them. Somehow Okoni-pehi always brought up that matter in his presence. In my presence, she loved it more since I would not let him go. I'd pull him back to his chair and let him see how his mother laughed finding him blush like a nubile bride. It was one of Onima-borma's happy, pleasant moods. 'God knows if there would be another. Who knows if our young men have already decided who they would marry and soon, one day, we will find that his clothes have vanished from the house, and so has the man himself.'

And it was so true. Nobody in that house knew it better than me how true her statements were and I wanted to go and tell them to stop building castles in the air. I wanted to ask them to shut the wooden chest and stop counting the number of silk dresses Onima-borma had preserved for her daughter-in-law. For a long time, they would talk about various things. Sometimes I hung around. Sometimes I didn't. Okoni-pehi would list what she did all day and Onima-borma would do the same.

~

I was late when I entered the kitchen for breakfast. Only Aaita and Oholya-jethai were in the kitchen. I was stunned to see

Oholya-jethai. In just two nights, her appearance had changed. She looked tired and worn out.

She surveyed me with weary eyes, asked me to sit down and served me flattened rice, curd and light-brown date-jaggery. I asked Aaita how she was feeling and she said she was alive somehow and thanked God that He had given her a few more days. 'A few more days are what I want to have Moina married off.' I wanted to talk to Oholya-jethai but I wasn't feeling comfortable because she looked distant, as if she were living in another world.

Oholya-jethai wasn't the kind to sit in the kitchen and serve meals. If she were in a better mood, she would have been roaming around, supervising everything—who should dig holes for the tent and when, how large the hearth should be, where exactly the firewood must be stored and who should bathe how many times. I ate my food slowly. She brought out a tin of rosogollas and gave me two with her hand, putting them on my palm. At home, I wouldn't eat if someone had touched my food like that.

Ignoring my presence, Aaita said slowly in her husky voice, 'I haven't greyed my hair in vain, Oholya. I have seen how the past comes back and each time I realize that nothing changes. It's the same thing that happens again and again. In the last thousand years have we changed? Human beings? Our mentality has remained the same. We all behave the same way. Like stories. Only the scenes and settings change—but stories of love, longing, loss, desire, all remain the same. What are you going to do with the ring now? The ring you had thrown away, returned to him, actually never reached him. He loved you, but he was not brave.'

Oholya-jethai replied angrily, 'Will you please keep quiet? I don't want to talk about it. The past is the past, and it's my past, I will deal with it.'

'That doesn't answer my question. It's a gold ring and the

desires of the man who gifted it to you must be still inside it, attached to it. We must be careful what we do with it. I can't remember the chants and rituals that should be followed when such a ring or any other item turns up after so many years. But someone in this village would know. Yes, the past is the past and you have always dealt with everything yourself, without listening to me. You didn't listen to me when you went with him to meet his parents on the pretext that he was a man with *modern thought*, but look what happened? When you got off in this village from that white Standard car, the whole village was waiting in our courtyard. Your father had to listen to so much. They didn't burn you alive only because your father was a freedom fighter. He was respected by everyone.' Her words were slow, clear and sharp.

Oholya-jethai stood up. 'I will throw the ring into the Brahmaputra River. I hope that answers your question and stops you from speaking nonsense. This conversation is over.'

Aaita ignored her. 'Gold that comes back must be sent back too. We must be careful what we do with it. Don't take a hasty decision. It will destroy the house, each and every one in the family.'

For the next two days, we only had short glimpses of Oholya-jethai, like streaks of lightening across a night sky. Whenever she stepped out of her room, we noticed how quickly she had aged in two days. It was as if she had crawled upwards in time by twenty more years in those few hours. She was no more the tallest woman in the village. She looked small. She had developed a hunch along with the silence she wore around her like a shawl. Unruly strands of hair covered her forehead and changed the way she looked. She didn't look scary, only tired and weary and timid with her unkempt hair, with her reddish eyes. She preferred to stay indoors, and didn't bother if any of the guests were sleeping on unchanged sheets and who was responsible for such a lapse. Didn't care if someone had not lit the lamp in the prayer room in the evening. Scolded no one when children chased one another till late into the night and screamed for no reason. She ate her food, did whatever little she could.

One evening, I heard Mukut-khura grumbling. His words were not directed at Oholya-jethai, but at her pet bull Ronga. He was distinct, yet soft. Soft like the fat that hung loose around his waist. It made me wonder how such a soft voice could be produced by such a large, tall man. As tall as Oholya-jethai. Oholya-jethai had set the benchmark for everything in that house.

Following Mukut-khura's grumbling, Dangor-bhonti had gone and asked him what the matter was and it was then I got to know how much he loved flowers. He had not planted the varieties of hibiscus in the garden near the bamboo gate. But still, he loved them. Even before anyone woke up, he put cow dung around their roots every morning, dug the soil around them with a spade, and weeded the garden. They were blooming beautifully, until an hour ago. A bed of blooming marigold flowers were planted around each of the hibiscus plants. We chased his grumbling, only to find a garden devastated by Oholya-jethai's pet Ronga.

I felt that I was looking at a war-ravaged place. The naked, brown branches of the hibiscus plants stood there like mournful saints standing with their hands stretched towards the sky. As if they were waiting for flowers to fall, for rains to drench them, confirming that their penance was over. It annoyed Mukut-khura and elicited varied responses from the people. The flowers had greeted the guests with a cheerful, colourful radiance. Some said it would take a long time for the flowers to bloom again. I thought there was no point in saying such a thing. Of course, first the tender leaves would come, then the sprigs, the buds and finally the flowers. And before that, the rains would have to descend. The garden looked like a graveyard. It sent out 'bad signs' to the guests. Later, when Roton, along with Brikodar, Montu and several other men from the village, was setting up the wedding tent, Anil-da hid the ravaged garden skilfully under thick, green cloths brought on rent from the tent house.

Oholya-jethai walked outdoors much later. She had a banana leaf on her hand, with a fistful of salt. Seeing the white of it, or seeing the tall figure of Oholya-jethai, now shorter, Ronga came to her like a dog to his master. He rubbed his head against her body. Hid his face under her *aansol*. Pulled her sador, chewed it. He refused to lick the salt she had brought. 'I'm sorry, I'm sorry, I got delayed today. Please have this.' She pleaded with the bull. It was then that I realized that if Oholya-jethai was married and had a son, she would be talking to him exactly this way. That scene broke my heart.

But there were enough people in the house during those days to keep one occupied. That was why Mridul's absence wasn't boring me. That was why, though people asked about Oholya-jethai, they didn't bother too much about her. Everyone knew her past. They sucked their teeth, talked about it and drank tea. They rubbed their heels with bits of broken pottery near the pond instead of pumice stones, wondered if the wedding would take place and ate bakery biscuits with their tea. They thanked God that Aaita was feeling better, recovering, that the drama she was 'showing' was gradually closing down and didn't drink the remaining, sediment-filled tea at the bottom of the glasses but poured it on the ground and watched it get soaked into the soil. Oholya-jethai and Aaita and a frightened bride kept the women busy. The elderly men, middle-aged men, remained preoccupied with the wedding preparations: who would carry the bags of vegetables, who would look after the fourteen goats that were tethered behind the house for the feast. Occasionally, the goats bleated and the children stared at them. When the dancing little girl in the pink frock heard that the goats would be killed and skinned and cooked, she sprawled on the ground and cried, spoiling her new frock. Anamika kept the young men busy. It was fun to argue with her, to provoke her more to argue. To meddle with her razor-sharp wit. When she went around distributing tea in dwarfish steel glasses, it was evident that she had befriended everyone, and compliments came her way from the men as well as the women. She was like one of those women without whom a wedding can't be called a wedding in the truest sense. You need someone around in any wedding to keep that thread of laughter between the men and the women. So when she dance-walked, when a man complimented her that she was looking better that day, than the previous day, giggles would be presented to that man. Another man would comment, 'Why are you talking only to Gubindo, Anamika? Is he going to take you to see a Hindi film in a Guwahati theatre? I will take you to Dilli. Talk to unfortunate souls like us at this side as well!' And the girl who everyone thought was eager to go to 'Dilli' would say, 'Cinema? Every day there is a new drama in this wedding house. Oholya-jethai is the heroine and—don't tell anyone—even my sister-in-law, Moon-baideo, is quite adept at creating dramatic scenes. So, wait for a while, we might see two great actresses performing. So, for the time being, I have no plans to watch films. I'm enjoying the wedding! And I'm talking to everyone equally. After all, I'm in charge of the tea-and-snacks department! I can't be partial to anyone. Won't the bride get curses then?'

Everyone loved Anamika; they were attracted to her. She was the soft light, melodious song, the soothing wind and the lightning across the sky in that wedding. Her long hair hung braided down her back. She wore the mekhela-sador in such a way that I never thought anyone could look so sexy in our traditional dress. It clung tightly to her body, but nobody could say that she was not supposed to wear it that way. Perhaps only Oholya-jethai could; but she was busy battling ghosts from her past, busy deciding if she should throw the gold ring into the tempestuous waters of the Brahmaputra that constantly threatened to engulf the village out of a mad love. The only face that disapproved everything of Anamika was that of Moon-baideo. Her unsmiling face became stern when she talked to her. It was as if she didn't like her popularity. The women remarked what a cheerful, cute, adorable sister-in-law Moon had, that Anamika took care of everyone, asked them if they needed another cup of tea, unlike others who thought their work was over after handing out the first cup. At times, she sat with the old women and helped them pound betel nuts in the mortar. Then I'd observe her from afar. She sat among the young girls, newly married girls and cracked jokes that they loved and hated; loved because they too wanted to crack such jokes, but couldn't gather the courage to talk about men's genitals so openly, and hated because they had to act as if they hated these jokes and slap each others' backs as they rolled in laughter. Young girls pretended they were embarrassed. They looked away, smiling, shutting their eyes, pretending to lean-and-fall and fall-and-lean against one another's bodies, like bent stalks of paddy in the wind; and the newly married women asked the young girls to leave. Sometimes one of the men—either Mridul, or Anil, or I—landed up there, and their laughter became even more bawdy, almost threatening to blow away the tin and hay roofs of the house.

Anamika didn't crack those jokes with the men. She spoke to each of them in such a way that each thought she liked him the most. And somehow I knew the secret to her popularity. I felt she knew I knew her secret. When a man would ask her if she would like to go out with him for a film, she would tilt her head in such a way before refusing that he would believe that she had given his proposal a serious consideration before refusing. If someone asked if she would mind bringing him a glass of water, she would immediately agree with such an expression on her face, looking into his eyes, that he would think, *he* was doing her a favour by asking her for a glass of water; the thirsty man would immediately become conscious of how he looked, how he was dressed, how he should have been dressed. Each of the men thought she cared for him the most and hated the others. Each of them thought she had a deep, soft corner for him and only pretended to like the others.

Anamika was like that: who walked on paths that she shouldn't have.

She had walked over that part of the road in the village market where the mutilated body had fallen years ago, the part Mridul resolutely avoided.

Perhaps, that was why she had to *leave*.

Yes. Anamika had to *leave* very soon.

I heard about it from Mridul a year later. When I had returned to Guwahati to spend my summer vacations after an academic year in Delhi.

Leave.

Not leave.

One day after that evening when the hibiscus plants had turned into saints praying with their hands stretched towards the sky, Anamika and I were sitting on the broken bed in the storeroom where curd was stored in the earthen pots; where books were kept in rows like soldiers in a battlefield inside creaky wooden shelves. A few pots of curd were already taken away from there on the day of the juron. Moon-baideo scooped up the topmost, yellowish layer from one of the pots and distributed a spoonful among the children. Okoni-pehi who was always furious at something or the other grumbled that Moon-baideo wanted to have the topmost layer, hence the facade of giving the children some bits of it. 'She was always like that, age has not changed her bad habits,' she complained in front of Oholya-jethai and Onima-borma. Oholya-jethai shook her head in anger and disapproval and irritation. Onima-borma condemned it vehemently, saying women should be able to restrain greed. Oholya-jethai kept quiet.

To save myself from Okoni-pehi's fury, I escaped to that room. The room where the thousand novels, the disintegrating almirah and the termites lived. I hadn't expected Anamika to be there. We sat down on the bed for a few moments and then I got up to look at the books. So many memories were stored in the pages of those books.

'So kids like you also read books?'

She placed her hand on my shoulder and turned me towards her.

I remained silent. I didn't do anything and I thought she wanted me to do something. She opened the almirah, brushing her shoulders against mine, deliberately (or so I thought). The almirah moaned like a rheumatic patient crying out in pain. Chunks of red soil slid off the hinges and fell on her feet.

'Let us see what kind of books kids read. Are they about moms?' she said, browsing through the dust.

I walked closer and smelled the cheap, strong perfume that hung around her body. It had blended with the smell of Liril lime soap with which she must have bathed some time ago. Does a woman always smell like this? I said slowly, 'This collection was built by Mridul's father. Did you ever meet him?'

'No. This is my first visit to this house. Your Moon-baideo's husband, my suspicious brother, thinks your Moon-baideo would sleep with other men so I have been sent as a watchman with her.' She said 'suspicious brother' in such a way that I wanted to laugh out loud. 'Not that he trusts me either. I am sure his emissaries are around who are watching me. I was just sitting at home after my BA final exams. I thought the wedding would be a good place to have a break.' She raised one of her eyebrows and said, 'I wanted to meet men, but I can only see kids around.'

'Really?' I pushed her against the wooden almirah, brought my mouth close to hers and said, 'You want to know what some kids are capable of?'

'You are hurting me.' She was now breathing faster, looking straight into my eyes.

'I can hurt a lot more. If you want pleasure, you will have to accept some pain as well.' My voice was a hoarse whisper.

'Then why are you waiting?'

She unbuttoned her blouse slowly.

'Then why are you waiting?' she said again, gently this time.

That was the first time I had seen the breasts of a woman so closely. They were as taut as I had imagined. Like tender green coconuts, just a few weeks left to mature, but they were the colour of bamboo shoots—fresh and bright and glowing.

'Why are you waiting, Prachurjya Medhi?'

The smell of her freshly bathed body lingered less on her clothes. Does a woman always smell like this? The smell of lemony Liril soap. I believed all women smelled like that. And then she was there. Looking at me. With her all-knowing smile. Lopsided. My nose had touched her breasts, and suddenly, she pulled away and quickly buttoned up her blouse.

She was staring and saying, 'I'm years older than you, little boy.' I hated her and loved her and wanted to kill her and tear off her clothes for saying that, for pulling away. I wanted to show her I could do so much, though I hadn't till then.

'That age card won't work any more. It's passé.'

Her mood had changed. The din of people working for the wedding, bits of sentences welcoming guests floated into the room in sharp, sporadic flashes. I knew she knew what I was thinking. And at that moment I didn't have any idea that it would be on her that I'd test my youth the night Moina-pehi drank phenyl.

Later, the next morning, on the day of the wedding, in Mridul's room when the rooster signalled the beginning of day and reminded the whole family to wake up and start working for the wedding, I was lying on the bed with the most unusual, pleasant feeling of exhaustion. I was also feeling guilty thinking what'd happen if anyone came to know of what I had done. How would I face my mother?

I didn't know Anamika would have to die for that little pleasure we shared with each other.

~

Oholya-jethai did notice the sudden increase of intimacy between us. While I smelled her perfume that day, standing beside her, it was Oholya-jethai who almost barged into the abandoned room and demanded what we were doing there *all alone*. She had just pulled away from me a few moments ago. I laughed saying we were not *alone* but with each other. In her dictionary of right and wrong, a young man and woman weren't supposed to hang out 'all alone' in a room.

She didn't say anything. Maybe she wanted to be careful. Oholya-jethai looked at her, but kept quite. She was a guest after all, how could she be rude to Anamika?

And I knew I could speak like that to Oholya-jethai that day. After all, she was a changed person by then. She raised her eyebrows. 'Pablo, you must leave. And Anamika, come along with me. I need to speak to you.'

'I have to go somewhere else, Jethai! See you later.' She didn't follow her.

But Oholya-jethai must have told Moon-baideo something. The morning after the wedding, Moon-baideo was grumbling something. Anamika looked angry.

I asked, 'Anamika, are you all leaving today?'

Moon-baideo looked at me sternly and didn't let Anamika speak. 'Isn't she older than you? Shouldn't you address her respectfully with a 'baideo' after her name?' Then she spoke to herself and occasionally looked at Anamika while she spoke, 'But what is your fault? People should be dignified enough to earn respect. People should learn from their past mistakes. People shouldn't be fickle.' She looked straight at my face again. 'You are a young boy, Pabloo. Stay away from distractions. Anything might happen. You never know. I'm your first cousin: your father and my father were born from the same womb. I am your well-wisher. You are at an age when most guys make mistakes.'

Oholya-jethai was looking at me. I knew that expression. 'I

will poison your tea.' The curl of her lips that looked like a bow.

Did she know something? *Something*. If not everything.

I moved away without even asking 'what are you talking about, Moon-ba? I don't even understand' because I knew what she was referring to.

I shuddered. I felt that I was walking naked like the foolish king, who thought he was wearing new clothes, and everybody was jeering at me. I remembered the feel of the rough, soft hay on my naked bottom last night, while Anamika lay beside me naked, and was frightened.

The wedding was over.

Moina-pehi was sent off to her in-laws the last night. Onima-borma accompanied her since she would need someone there to take out the right gift for each person at her in-laws, to check if the pleats of her dress were in order, to lend a shoulder to her if she wanted to cry.

The house was teeming with wedding-weary people.

In small and big groups they were talking about the clothes and jewellery that people wore. Gifts were unwrapped. The food including rosogollas was distributed. Girls who looked bigger reminded the elders once again how time fled. Some reminisced how the same girls were dribbling babies even a few years ago, when they had last visited on some other social occasion. They spoke about the groom's mother as well. Her unfriendly looks. Her calm hostility. The rude curl of her lips that looked like a bent bow, more unpleasant and annoying than Oholya-jethai's. Some remarked that it was unfortunate to marry off Moina-pehi to that old guy.

Some confessed how relieved they were that the wedding had gone well, except for the sudden sickness of the bride because of which she had fainted while performing the rites near the sacrificial fire. (And some of us heaved a sigh of relief that no one suspected that a lavage had been done on Moina-pehi behind closed doors the night before the wedding.) So many people: chattering, eating, laughing, unwrapping gifts. Children running around with sweets in their hands, the elders scolding them, worried lest they develop a stomach ache, workers unfolding the pleats, the designs of the tent, unmaking the wedding pandal, Mukut-khura giving instructions, Mridul sitting sullenly in one corner. I felt lonely. Singled out. Don't know by whom. The king walked out in the open naked, thinking he was wearing new clothes.

Later, when I was eating breakfast, Anamika looked straight into my eyes, closed them for a moment and shook her face gently on both her sides. 'No, don't worry . . .' I finished my meal of milk and flattened rice and walked out. When she left in the morning after the wedding, a few hours before the groom's family brought Moina-pehi's corpse to the village, I didn't meet her. Nor did she ask for me. And I was angry and hurt that she didn't ask to see me one last time. She didn't say 'where is Pabloo?' before leaving.

I never saw her again.

~

Perhaps I would have met her again, had she lived. Would have met her at another wedding, looked at her from a distance, and felt attracted to her again, taken in the lemony fragrance of her freshly bathed body.

But that never happened, because she *left* us six months later.

A few days after I had returned from Delhi for the summer, in 2003, Mridul had turned up at our house unexpectedly. Although Guwahati was burning, it was better than Delhi. The monsoons had arrived. The weather was so pleasant that we did not need the ceiling fans. Delhi was an oven, I would complain often to Mom. But in the upper parts of the state, the flood was playing havoc, sweeping away houses, trees, schools and people.

I preferred to stay home, reading books and watching horror films, supernatural thrillers. That was my ideal homecoming; that was my way of spending the vacations. In the evening, I'd get out of the house to take a walk on the Chandmari flyover— one of the most romantic spots in the city; go to eat momos at Momo Ghar near Rabindra Bhavan or sit for hours, looking at the Brahmaputra from the Kharghuli Hill, just a few metres away from Hotel Belle View and Governor's House.

It was afternoon and no one was home when Mridul came. I answered the door, welcomed him in and then poured him a glass of Fanta to drink. He walked straight into my room, holding the glass of orange liquid in his hand, taking slow sips. I asked him what had brought him to the city. I asked him how everyone was, especially Aaita and Oholya-jethai. He said he took a wild guess that I would be home for the summers. I didn't have a cell phone in Delhi. My parents called at the landline number that was at the end of the corridor in my hostel at a specific time and I didn't like to share that number with everyone because someone or the other would keep calling me if they had the number.

Lying down on my bed, he said, slowly, 'Do you remember Anamika?'

I was combing my hair. The humid weather had dampened my hair slightly and it was itching. Instead of scratching it, I loved running the teeth of the comb over my scalp.

I stopped.

What was he trying to say? Why did he ask me about Anamika? The last time he had asked me about her was during the wedding.

A sharp question, it was. Looking straight into my eyes, he had asked me if I was in love with Anamika.

But why now?

'Yes, I remember—that girl . . .'

'Whom you hung out with quite a bit? Moon-baideo's sister-in-law? You do remember her, don't you?'

He had interrupted me. There was a sense of triumph in his tone, a hint of sadness too. I thought why was he triumphant? That he could finally accuse me of falling in love with her? He knew I loved girls with long hair. Anamika had long hair. I was 'hanging out' too much with her during the wedding. He had all the reasons to believe that I was in love with her.

A little later, when he told me she died around six months after Moina-pehi's wedding, I had gone into the bathroom, taken off all my clothes and stood under the shower for a long time. I had looked at my thin, yet-to-be-man body and wondered if Anamika thought about it before dying. If she had been in love with me. I wanted to know if she had uttered my name when her brother had kicked her bulging stomach. Whose child was she carrying? She had died while trying to abort it. A local village woman had inserted a wild root through her vagina and pierced something inside, poured down a concoction and forced her to drink a strange brew of herbs. It was too late for an abortion. She had died in a pool of blood, after a long night of bleeding. No, no, no . . . I wanted to bang my head against the wall. Inside the bathroom, under the shower, I was one of those coconut trees that shook their heads 'no, no, no' in the wind when Mridul had come to invite us to Moina-pehi's wedding.

I had forgotten about Anamika. 'Everything ends with this wedding,' she had said that night. Now, this piece of information ensured I would never forget her. She will come back to me like migratory birds, flapping wings of accusation, dropping beads of dew-like memories on my eyelids that would burn and singe them.

Mom had returned from work by the time I came out of the bathroom and she scolded me for bathing repeatedly when I went to the dining room, rubbing my hair dry with the red towel. Mridul wasn't looking at my face. He knew something. He didn't ask me anything—just as I had been too offended to ask him anything when I had a sense during the wedding that he was planning to elope with Manju Mahatu and hadn't told me anything about it until he needed my help to cover for him. And later I found out, as I had suspected, that he had indeed planned to elope with Manju. He ate the meal served by Mom quietly.

No, he didn't look at my face. Had he looked at me, he would have seen the ash that had been smeared on my face. Only he would have seen through me, because he knew I liked girls with long hair.

Anamika, who I should have forgotten after Moina-pehi's wedding (because 'our story ends here'), never left my dreams after that day. She would perhaps live in my mind for the rest of my life because I would always wonder if the baby she died aborting was mine.

Nine

That morning after the wedding, a few hours after Anamika and Moon-baideo had left along with many other guests, the groom's family turned up unexpectedly. They fought with our family. Accused us of marrying off a 'sick bride' who suffered from mysterious ailments we had hidden from them. It was partly true. People in the house couldn't decide if they should fight back or cry over the dead bride.

Moina-pehi had drunk phenyl the night before the wedding. The village doctor was not called. The family thought it'd harm their reputation. Even most of the guests didn't know anything. Oholya-jethai, who had become a recluse, decided to go back to being her old self for a while and slapped the retching Moina-pehi. 'You want to become like me? You don't want to marry? Didn't I tell you this afternoon not to even think about it? My child, my baby, there's no respect for an old maid.'

'Better to die than get married into such a family,' she moaned. 'Let me die please, I don't want to suffer later, I don't want to be killed by unknown assassins! You can shoot me dead here, right here in my head—in this house!'

She dribbled, she retched and when she got those scary convulsions, even the bed shook.

I continued to wonder, for years afterwards, how much horror must one feel in order to take such a step, based on some gossip that had reached the house a day before the wedding? Based on what someone like Anil-da had said?

Rumours inevitably destroy all happiness in weddings. But with the *girip-garap* sounds of boots, with the fratricidal violence in the state, I guess such rumours became verdicts, alternative realities, faceless voices turned real. Some of those faces had scars. And you could count the number of stitches on them.

I knew Oholya-jethai had crumbled like the house. The termites called memory and loneliness and insecurity had eaten her up like an almirah, a pillar and a door in an abandoned house. Made her as hollow as a widow's life though she wasn't one. Though she wove multicoloured dresses in her foot loom, she had become colourless, white, from inside.

That night, after the juron, Aaita, Mridul, Oholya-jethai, Mukut-khura and Onima-borma were in the room where Moina-pehi had gone in and drank phenyl. Outside, the guests wondered what had happened. Moon-baideo knew. But after all, Moina-pehi was her aunt: her father's mother's brother's daughter. So she must have tried to placate the rising levels of suspicion. She must have said that some matters regarding the groom's family were being discussed. And they must have believed her. After all, everyone knew by that time what Anil-da had brought into the house along with sheaves of coloured papers that morning.

Onima-borma forced glass after glass of saline water into Moina-pehi's mouth to induce a lavage. The water was charmed by Aaita. At first Moina-pehi had refused, in spite of her convulsions. Aaita's weak pleadings, coupled with a quivering voice and quivering mouth and a quivering hand on her head, finally made her relent, or perhaps she had lost the will to resist.

Perhaps the exhaustion brought on by the repeated vomiting made her long to live. Told her how difficult it was to die. How long it could take to die. How tired one could get while trying to die. But it was difficult to live as well. How much she had to retch. How much salt water she was forced to drink. How much fear she had to negotiate with.

She didn't die. She looked weak, but everyone thought she was fine, she'd get better. Thought that she was no longer concerned if the groom's brother was an ULFA member. If she would be raped during combing operations by army men, whom she feared more than death, more than the taste of phenyl. The signs of which she had seen on the bodies of women in the village. One of them was, of course, Brikodar's sister Mamoni who had screamed and fainted, leaving behind a pale yellow trail, when she had heard the sounds of boots marching girip-garap. When she saw the jeeps, when she saw khaki dresses, when she heard the men in uniform speaking in Hindi.

Near the sacrificial fire, Moina-pehi fainted during the rites. Mukut-khura sprinkled water on her face. He was sitting beside her and performing *kanyaadaan* rites. He was almost crying. It was a heart-rending ritual. You must cut off a blade of kush grass into two and swear in front of the fire that the bride would no more be related to you. That, when she died, you'd no longer follow any mourning rituals, would continue to consume garlic, onion, oil, meat and fish. He must have been thinking it was nice that his sister was married off to Khetri. When he'd go to his father-in-law's house, there would be another place from now on to go and chat, have a meal, share news, be loved, be welcomed with sweet words. He must have even thought about her children. He was almost crying. Something so incongruous to happen with that pillar-like man—who had kept the house in order after Bolen-bortta's death.

Oholya-jethai came with the speed of a kite to its prey to hold her in her arms. Onima-borma too sprinkled water over her face, eyes, and said, trying to cover up, looking left, looking right, like an alert hen with sharp, mean, suspicious eyes, 'Oh, these cruel wedding rituals!' She raised her voice. 'Fasting and all! The bride is not used to this.'

The groom's mother was wiping off the sweat from her forehead with a white handkerchief. She had stood up shocked when Moina-pehi had fainted and as she had seen Oholya-jethai rushing to her, she had sat down assured. She now fanned herself fast with the handkerchief and snarled, 'What do you mean, my dear?'

I didn't like her tone. Mridul was not around. Last night, things had changed between us after he had gone out of the house with that red duffel bag of clothes and had returned the next morning. A little before leaving, he had sought my help, asking me to cover up for him. He had told me what was brewing, proving my suspicions true. After Moina-pehi had regained consciousness, he had left the house to find a waiting Manju Mahatu in a secret location, from where they would leave for another village. But sometime near dawn, he had returned like an owl—defeated, dejected, pensive and brooding.

When Moina-pehi fainted near the ritual fire, he must have been somewhere inside the house, sitting alone or playing songs on the sound system. Otherwise who else would be playing so many songs, all by Zubeen Garg? And the song that was playing when Moina-pehi had fainted was one of our favourite songs, where the male voice asks the bride to leave aside the rajanigandha garlands on the night of their consummation because they might get crushed. The couple is bathed in moonlight peering through the window.

Mridul was not around, only the songs he played wafted in the air. So I didn't have eyes to look at for support, to silently show my displeasure at the groom's mother's remarks.

'Which woman is used to fasting during the wedding?' She said, 'You are saying as if she is the first girl in the world who is fasting! Aha! Only characterless and unfortunate women yearn and dare to go through these gruelling rituals more than once. Nobody learns them in the womb. You learn as you follow them . . .'

But Okoni-pehi couldn't keep quiet. She said politely but firmly, 'Oh, what are you saying? These two eyes have seen hundreds of weddings till date.' She smiled and pulled the sador towards her chest and added calmly, 'And let me tell you, fainting brides due to excessive fasting is nothing new in Assamese weddings. We women are so weak. God has only created us like that. Nature is unjust. If *we* don't understand the plight of women, who will? Even you are a woman, I'm sure you do understand.'

Okoni-pehi's statement only increased the tension. Mukut-khura had stood up. And the groom's mother stared at her for some time. She didn't keep quiet. She couldn't have. She was the groom's mother after all. She must have the last word. She added in a deadpan tone, 'If the bride's elder sister speaks so much, I wonder how much the bride would argue. It seems I'm going to have a bad time with my daughter-in-law. Well, even I was sickly, but I never fainted.'

We kept quiet; we were after all the bride's family. There were creases on Mukut-khura's forehead on the anticipated verbal war. He couldn't do anything. He had to keep quiet. One word of caution, one gesture of warning from him, could add fuel to the fire.

Dorongi-aaita knew how to ease tense situations and I wished Mom were present too, to do the same. I wished that they had not cancelled the plan of attending the wedding at the last moment.

'Ha ha,' she laughed out loud and said playfully, 'the groom's mother has a good sense of humour. If our daughter answers back, just let me know. I will come and teach her a lesson. I have five daughters-in-law back home. With these hands I have taught them how to keep a house in order, without letting it crumble.'

The groom's mother gave her an expression of clear disagreement. Moina-pehi had come back to her senses by then and was feverishly apologizing. Mukut-khura sat down, and again it seemed as if he was about to cry.

~

But the next afternoon, when the groom's family brought in Moina-pehi's corpse, like a log of wood, like garbage, like a dustbin, he couldn't cry.

The groom's mother was still wearing the silk dress she had worn the night before and there was no sign of sadness in her face. She looked annoyed. The winter sun was unusually hot over our heads. She was grumbling. Onima-borma who was sent with Moina-pehi looked exhausted and tired. She must have finished her quota of crying, howling incessantly. Or she must have already been stung by the hostility of Moina-pehi's mother-in-law.

We never got to know what happened to her, though all of us wanted to ask if the groom's household had a bottle of phenyl stored in some corner of the room. It was such an odd-sounding question that no one dared to ask it.

Actually, we couldn't have asked them. The groom's family was polite, but looked hostile. They accused us of hiding some secret disease that the bride had. Threatened us with 'dire consequences'. It was too noisy. There were too many people crying. Another mourning had begun. Though, according to the rituals, Mridul and his family didn't have to follow any, but since the groom refused to light the pyre, the family would have to follow the rituals meticulously. Mukut-khura had fallen down on the groom's feet to stay back for the *mukhagni* ritual since the soul reaches heaven only if a husband or son or son-in-law lights the pyre by burning the face of the corpse first. He refused. Who knows why. They were too polite. Too calmly hostile. Something you couldn't break, cross, invade, decipher. The Brahmin said it was *'opaghat mrityu'*—an accidental death—so there was no need to follow any rituals. So Moina-pehi was not mourned for twenty-one or eleven days as Bolen-bortta was.

In the evening, when Onima-borma had stopped wailing, she said that she didn't know what had happened. 'They came and woke me up in the morning in the room I was sleeping. All of them looked worried. Her mother-in-law was weeping. I found her dead in the bedroom on the bed of flowers.' She lowered her head and added, 'She had no clothes on. I fought for one and a half hour to get her clad. They didn't have the heart to help me. She was dead long ago; her body was cold and stiff like a piece of log.' Her sentence was followed by a new wave of weeping. Someone said it was difficult to clad a corpse and only people with special training could do so.

Soon many others joined in. Weeping kept breaking the silence for the next two days like claps of thunder on a sunny day: startling. Some people, who had left, returned to mourn. Some didn't come back. They must have been bewildered. Papa and Mom couldn't come to the wedding. But they came rushing down. This time, I didn't stay back.

On the third day after the wedding, I left.

I was hoping that Anamika would return. But she didn't. Moon-baideo came, howling from a kilometre away. With her husband. Anamika's brother. A tall, fat, bearded man.

Moina-pehi's story ended there. Her story could have many different names. 'The Old Maid Who Didn't Want to Marry Since She Didn't Want to Be Raped During Search Raids' or 'The Bride Who Died under Mysterious Circumstances'.

Etc.

It is difficult to explain how scared she was—like many other women in Hatimura Village—of khaki dresses. After all, till this day, mothers in Hatimura scold their children saying, 'Don't cry, or else the army will get you.' After all, they are always more scared of the government than the insurgents. Actually, they are rarely scared of the insurgents. At least the insurgents speak their own language and address women as baideo, pehi, khuri and borma, with great respect.

Since no one knew what actually happened to her, Moina-pehi's story haunted us for many years. Somehow the small, insignificant woman who was forced to marry a forty-five-year-old man (since old maids seldom have much choice) became the source of a great story which seems to have ended—but actually hasn't.

Anamika and my story that oppressed me for many years to come was also akin to Moina-pehi's saga. Though both Anamika and I knew it ended with the wedding, we knew, in our heart of hearts, that it hadn't actually ended. When I would be alone for a long time, I would pause and think what would happen next, what could be the next episode, the next chapter in our story, though she had made it clear that night, as she had disengaged herself from me, 'It ends with this wedding.'

Actually, we didn't even know when our story had started.

After all, our story was not based on love. It was simply the human desire for knowledge. To discover. To learn skin secrets, smell secrets, sweat secrets.

So one could begin by saying it had started behind the house, in the backyard.

We had gone to the *meji*, the large heap of hay stored for the rest of the year for cows to feed on, for mattresses to be made by stuffing it inside gunny bags. It was post-harvest fresh hay. It had the smell of sun and as we made love, sinking our bodies into it, covering ourselves with it, we unearthed the sun stored in its creases and in its million layers. In the white, cold moon, they looked golden. I didn't tell anyone about it. Not Mridul. Not Probal. No one. Nothing. Not even about the deep impression our bodies left on the heap of hay, absorbing our secret lovemaking. There was no love in it. No heart. Only skin. Only smell. Only sweat. Only touch. But how does that matter?

What mattered was that it happened.

~

On the afternoon of the juron, I left the wedding house to walk on the white road that looked like the unfortunate white middle parting across a Hindu widow's head, deprived of the colour of passion.

Even before I started moving, there was something else moving inside me, stirring and churning. It was a strange wind. It had the rage of imprisoned winds that eroded me from within. I didn't want to crumble in front of fifty different people. Propelled by the alien movement inside me, which I thought could only lead to despair, I plunged myself into the silence of the village afternoon on the white, dusty road. It was the windy month of Phagun, the red rebelliousness of the silk-cotton tree two houses away from ours reminded me. I looked at the flowers lying on the ground—lonely, tragic, unloved, dust coated. They also told me that it was the month of blood-red rebellions.

Afternoons in a village can be eerily silent, like the atmosphere of a house that has just mourned the death of a family member; where everyone has taken to bed in exhaustion after prolonged crying. But that day, I felt I was prepared for it, since such a stillness—when you could even hear the drone of bees, wasps and dragonflies around the house, accompanied by a silence spread by the afternoon songs of crickets and the cooing of bright-eyed doves—had already descended over the wedding house, from where I wanted to escape.

I wanted some sound and knew I could find it in a place which was larger than that house, larger than life itself. I could even go to the harvested paddy fields behind the house, dry and parched, cracked, waiting for the rains to seep in, the coming spring. Lie down on it, my face towards the sky. I could see how far away the birds flew; or how long it took a bird to cross the slice of the sky visible to me from the ground on which I lay, where ants carried grains from one place to another and tiny dry roots of short grass lay upturned after an invasion by the cows. But I wanted something else. It was more than warm, though not hot, there. I wanted warmth and coolness, I wanted silence and sound. I wanted something that was free as well as cosy.

It took me a long time to walk up to the banks of the Brahmaputra. If it were another day, someone would have stopped me. If not anyone else, Mridul would have told me not to venture out on my own, with his innocent possessiveness, his elder-brotherly affection towards me. But things had changed.

He saw me leaving the house, sliding open the bamboo gate.

He didn't ask me where I was going. Perhaps he thought he had lost the right to ask me anything. He must have assumed that if he asked, I wouldn't reply, shaking up his self-respect, leaving him chiding himself for trying to begin a conversation. That would take him back to the embarrassing moment when he had asked me if I were in love with Anamika.

Embarrassing?

I had made him feel that way. Without answering his question ('Are you in love with Anamika?'), I had left the room wearing a disgusted look, and even years later I had marvelled at my ingenious reaction and felt ashamed by my pretention.

Just to revisit the matter properly, one more time: I was innocent. I could have shouted at Mridul and told him I was not in love with Anamika since I was *not* in love with her. I could have pushed him away and snapped at him. How he could ask me such a question when he knew me so well. How he could be so petty and parochial. Couldn't he accept an intimacy between a young man and a young girl (a few years older than the young man) without clouding it with suspicion? I could touch the holy shrine in the house and swear to him that I was not in love with her—and indeed I was *not* in love with her.

But at that point, I thought the best way to react would be to leave the room. It told him, without a single word from me, how parochial his mind was.

It pointed a finger towards his so-called modern thoughts without a verbal war between us.

I presumed it had left him unsettled, wondering, for the rest of his life, if he had asked me something so insulting that it threatened to end our friendship.

But did he leave me alone?

He was eager to find an answer to that question. Perhaps he was feeling the same ache. The ache of betrayal.

A few hours later, he had accosted me once again. This time, he stood casually, blocking the door. As if he wasn't blocking it, just standing there by chance. The black, wooden door was open. The latch on it was dark brown, rusted over years. I wondered how strong the latch was, how strong the door was.

'Tell me the truth.'

'What truth?'

'What's going on between you and Anamika . . .' His lips curled. It was a playful curl, but not an honest one. He wanted to ease the situation with that curl, that playful, naughty, mysterious curl that friends present to each other before sharing forbidden stories.

'Nothing—but why should I tell you the truth? Have you been telling me what you have been up to? After the day I arrived, you haven't sat down with me for a moment and spoken to me. I don't know what you are up to. But I have seen your packed bag. I have seen how you have kept your shirts ironed and the broken earthen piggy bank. You think I haven't noticed anything, Mridul?'

He shut the door, latched it, sat down on the bed.

'I didn't know how to tell you. I thought you'd judge me.'

'Of course I'd judge you, Mridul. You are thinking about yourself when your help is needed here, in this wedding. You think I am a fool? I wouldn't understand anything?'

That day, he finally told me his plan to elope with Manju Mahatu and sought help from me. That, if people asked where he was, I should say he had to suddenly go to Maloybari Village, two hours away from there, half an hour away from Teteliguri Village on the banks of the Tamulidobha River. That would give him enough time to elope with her. He was going through a tough time. Manju's mother was sending her to Arunachal Pradesh, where her uncle worked as a daily wage earner so that she could be married off to some guy out there. He ought to do something soon. They were planning to elope the night before the wedding because on the day of the wedding her uncle would come to take her. They would elope to Maloybari Village—where one of his closest friends lived, where farmers grew the largest pumpkins in the country. He had planned to return after a month.

'They won't be able to separate us if we reach Maloybari. I'm sorry I won't be able to stay back for Moina-pehi's wedding. We are eloping on the night of the wedding. People will be busy. They won't notice my absence until the next day. And by that time, I would have also accomplished my mission. If I'm not seen around, they would think I might be taking a nap somewhere or hanging around in the village. But when they ask, if there's any panic, you will have to cover for me. Tell them, I had to leave for Maloybari suddenly. Going to Maloybari isn't unusual.'

I was shocked.

'So both of you are finally eloping? I see—that has kept you out of the house all these days. Is that what you've been planning?'

'Yes. I have been making rounds to the bank in Kolongpar and withdrawing money in instalments. If I withdraw too much, the employees will tell Mukut-khura.'

'And? What else have you been doing?'

'We will go to Dhubri after staying in Maloybari for a few days. It's not safe to remain in a single place for too long. One of her friends lives there. I went to Nagaon twice in the past few days to meet one of my friends to borrow some money . . .'

'Amazing . . .' I looked at him with disbelief. 'I am not surprised by what you are going to do. I am surprised by the fact that you will be eloping with her on the night of the juron—have you any idea what might happen? You will be putting the wedding at risk, Mridul! The groom's family might just leave if news spreads that you have eloped with a Nepali girl! You know how people are!'

'Why? What's so strange about it? You are being so narrow-minded.'

'Fine, I am the most parochial person on earth. But what about the villagers? I am leaving the day after the wedding; think about your family and postpone this plan at least for a week or so.'

'Don't advise me—you have no idea what I am going through,' he snapped.

I was offended.

Not because he was leaving the night before the wedding, not because he was asking me to cover up, not because he had snapped at me, but because he was being so selfish, that he was telling me everything so late. I felt that ache of betrayal in my throat. Perhaps my Adam's apple was moving up and down too.

'So much has been planned, Mridul, and I don't even know about it. You didn't bother to tell me even a bit?'

'I'm sorry. It's been so hectic organizing all this. I have been too preoccupied. And when have we got time to speak, Pabloo? Not even Brikodar knows about it. I haven't told anyone.'

'We haven't got any time to speak because you don't get back home on time as you used to. Don't think people are not noticing. At least Okoni-pehi is. She asks me every day if I have seen you.

'Mridul, don't think it's all that simple. Your decision to leave the night before the wedding could lead to unimaginable disaster. It may have any number of consequences—one of it being what I just said: the wedding. Anyway, since you don't want to tell me anything, tell me what I should tell the family when they ask me about you,' I said sarcastically.

He looked at me for some time. Then looked away. 'Tell them

you don't know anything . . .' And then he accused me suddenly: 'Pabloo, even you are hiding a lot of things from me.'

'What do you mean?'

'You know what I mean.'

He looked straight into my eyes with quiet conviction. 'Isn't that also the reason we are not getting enough time to speak to each other? I wanted you to meet Manju one of these days. But when do you have the time? For the last few days even when I am here you are busy . . .'

'What? For the last few days, what?'

'Are you in love with Anamika? You are not telling me many things nowadays.'

'I am not going to dignify that question with an answer. Don't you dare ask me that again.'

I stormed out of the room.

~

On the day of the oil-smearing ritual, when Anil-da brought the story in, the wedding house was dressed in flowers. Flowers hung from every nook and corner. Long marigold garlands at the entrance. Rajanigandha stalks with flowers blooming on them pinned to pillars that held the pandal. From flower vases kept on small tables, lilies wept with long faces. The groom's family not only brought gifts (clothes, lipsticks and bras with and without laces) for the bride but also a large borali fish, different kinds of milky sweets in separate coloured boxes. The women who came from the groom's house were dressed in silver-white pat-silk, creamy pat-silk and yellow pat-silk mekhela-sadors with flowers woven on them in many intricate patterns.

Since our conversation, Mridul had the look of an apologetic convict in his eyes—a convict taken to the gallows who wanted to confess his guilt to the world before dying but couldn't, since his pride was too much. I felt a thrill as his apologetic eyes followed me everywhere.

Once, when the women, men and children from the groom's family were eating in the dining place, where Anil-da was distributing the food, along with Roton, Jethpeha and Suruj, I went to Mridul's room to lie down for some time in the bed. I was tired of everything. I had met Anamika on the way and she had said there wasn't a single handsome man in the groom's group, nor was the groom's youngest brother (who was supposedly as old as Mridul) good-looking.

Meeting her brightened me up; for a while I shunned away thoughts that bothered me, incidents that made me wonder in anger why people were so parochial. I told her, laughing, with fake disappointment on my face, that I was disappointed too for not finding a single hot girl in the wedding. She rolled her eyes and asked me what I meant by the phrase 'a single hot girl in the wedding'. I said I meant what she understood it to mean. It included even the girls from the bride's side. She chased me. I ran. She didn't chase me fast. She didn't mean to. I didn't run fast. I didn't mean to.

I was slightly exhausted after serving the food, carrying the large aluminium bucket of dal or mutton curry (all the goats had been slaughtered), or huge steel jugs of water. In each batch around fifty people ate. I served till the fourth batch. Prosanto-da came and I asked him if I could leave for a few minutes. He took the aluminium bucket of mutton from me.

Moon-baideo exclaimed, chewing betel nut, standing beside me, 'If there are so many people just for the juron, I wonder how many would come for the wedding.' She wore a densely embroidered muga-silk mekhela-sador and golden *junbiri*, *golpota*, around her neck, her lips red with the incessant chewing of betel nuts. 'This is really strange.' She spoke like an old woman. 'In our times, only women used to come for jurons. These are women's affairs. I wonder why those young men sporting tight jeans and shades are roaming around! I wonder what's so great about showing off shapely buttocks, and those too which are so tiny. With girls it's different; they need large childbearing hips, otherwise who will marry them? But why are the guys showing off their butts?'

'Moon-ba!' I cut in, starting to leave the dining place. 'The times have changed. No one wants to miss even a little bit of fun. So they are here.' I placed the jug of water on the table where the vessels of cooked food were kept and refused to comment on buttocks, or extend the discussion in that direction.

'What's the fun in coming here and staring at the women decking up the bride?'

'Do you think they are looking at the bride? They are checking out the other girls in the wedding house. They are also of marriageable age, aren't they? God knows the seeds of how many more marriages will be sown in this wedding!'

'Yes! Yes!' She started her sentence in a mocking tone: 'And God only knows how many more storms such beginnings will bring to different homes, how many more mothers and fathers would die of grief and how many more mountains will be brought down on the heads of people from respectable families! True, true, the times have changed. You have to take permission from the cooking pan before heating it nowadays, but in our times, pans used to remain silent. Our parents decided matches for us and neither the girls nor the guys used to utter a yes or a no! *Hai Hori*, what an age has come upon me.' She left before I could, very annoyed with the new rules. But how old was she? Thirty-eight? What was wrong with her? What was she trying to prove by speaking like old, forever-righteous women who only know how to create more problems than solve any? I had no idea.

The conversation exhausted me and I think that the strange wind started to blow then; for a second, I thought that its speed would increase, blow away the wedding tent, the rajanigandha flowers, the houses in the village, the trees in the forest near the house from where the tigers came to take away newborn wobbly legged calves. I looked at Prosanto-da for a while who was serving food to the guests. He had been working too hard, perhaps to compensate for his long absence before he returned to the house with Onulupa. Oholya-jethai could be seen here and there, but she was mostly quiet. We almost hadn't heard her voice for the last few days. Onima-borma was inside, taking care of the bride's presents, her clothes, her handkerchiefs, the keys that would hang from her waist.

The strange wind brought dust with it that got inside me. Dust that should have smarted my eyes. I should have rushed out of the place to grab a mug of cold water to wash my eyes but it was my heart that felt heavy. I tried in vain to find the reason behind it. Sometimes both Papa and Mom came back late from parties, very late. During those days, I would feel such heaviness, such anonymous pain, wondering what would happen if they didn't come back. The storm inside me always came with that weird ferocity and left me shattered, but also took very long to shatter me completely. It stayed on for a long time, wreaking havoc slowly. Leaving the place—though Moon-ba had already left, stabbing me with her words, boring a hole for more wind to enter my soul—was a way of escaping that lunacy.

So I loved it when Anamika chased me. I wanted to run behind her. Grasp her waist with my hands and lift her up in the air and laugh till I cried. I was so ashamed of myself for having those feelings. I didn't want to think about them any more. I refused to think if they were wrong or right. In terms of should and should not. I didn't want to think like Oholya-jethai. I wanted to think about chasing Anamika, about taking a walk with her, sliding down her clothes, unbuttoning her blouse. The smell of Liril lime-fresh soap on her body.

Inside the room, while staring at Mridul, I wondered if he was ashamed of himself. I looked at his eyes and he looked away.

He knew that if he wasn't seen around in the wedding, people would ask questions. News travels fast in a village. News of the disappearance of Manju Mahatu with her clothes, money and whatever little jewellery she had would travel as fast as a dust storm. The drooping, bare trees caressed by the dusty winter winds would speak. The sleeping birds would wake up fluttering their wings to testify. Fireflies would light the way to Mridul's room, reveal the room shorn of his clothes, his shoes, his piggy bank, the red duffel bag he used only for long journeys, and soon everyone would come to know about the recent journey Mridul would have embarked on with someone special in his life. All laughter would vanish. The groom's family might refuse to carry on with the wedding. A hum in the wedding house could tell them that someone from the house was missing and another hum could tell them about a red duffel bag and a wine brewer's daughter. Things would fall apart. He knew, my eyes said the same thing, but the eyes of the escaped convict were too heavy. So he kept quiet, holding on obstinately to the bag. For love.

That afternoon, I left the room without speaking to him but much later, after Anil-da had brought in the story, I asked him once again what he had decided, when I saw his hand clutching the duffel bag with the same obstinacy on that weary afternoon.

He wanted to leave behind inspiration for 'future lovers' (or 'future rebels'). So many things could crumble because of that.

When he came back with the same duffel bag the next morning, even before the rooster had given out its wake-up call, it was I who had wanted to talk to him, but he hid his eyes from me.

I couldn't even assess if those were still the eyes of a convict.

The next day, after Moina-pehi was sent away with Onima-borma, he told me that Manju had changed her mind at the last moment and had not told him.

In his soft-hunched back, his gentle tone, I sensed defeat.

On the morning of the wedding, the night after I had made love to Anamika, the night after Moina-pehi had drunk phenyl, Okoni-pehi had to pester Mridul just to get him to shave, to change into the new clothes that Mukut-khura had bought in Sonapur. So I didn't ask him anything further. I didn't want to open the doors to another story. I didn't want to know if it was out of the fear of doing something wrong that Manju had refused to come, and left him waiting all night in the cold under the peepul tree with roots hanging like the braids of witches. Or if it was her last-minute realization that he was too young to take responsibility for her, too young to even think about life, too young to be so swayed by the realization of love that he could never realize that love alone would never ensure food, new clothes, the rent for a house, the cost of mustard oil to fry fishes or even the money needed to buy the fish, money needed to travel to the market if it were far away.

She didn't come.

I didn't press him for further details.

The truth behind stories mercilessly ensured that certain things should remain unsaid between us forever.

Period.

~

But the wind didn't stop blowing. Somewhere in the deepest chambers of my mind it was shattering furniture, eroding walls. Flakes of plaster fell off like dried bark and were strewn across the floor like glass.

The juron party from the groom's house had left, leaving their gifts, claiming with songs, with vermilion powder, with new clothes on the bride's body that she was no more *ours*. But someone who was washing dishes with songs on her lips kept the memory of the juron alive. 'Rukmini, leave your mother's ornaments. Ram has brought new ones for you.' Someone else joined her (perhaps Phulam), like one dove joining another's cooing.

A song, with a refrain of meaningless words, began to take shape:

Siju biju biju bon,
blooms at Vrindabon.
Siju biju biju bon,
her groom's name is Probahon.
Siju biju biju bon
the rich businessman's son.

The bride has gold ornaments on.
He is the rich businessman's only son.
Siju biju biju bon,
blooms at Vrindabon.

There couldn't be any delay; the work must go on. Onimaborma looked at the sun and said, 'I guess I can bring the puthi fishes to the courtyard. Cayamoni, let's cut the borali fish for dinner. It's pretty large, so it will be sufficient.'

Okoni-pehi had already started to scream, when I noticed Anil-da getting down from the cycle, 'Aai! Phulam! Junti! Where are you? I had swept the courtyard long back, right after the groom's family left. Didn't I ask both of you to come and mop it up with cow dung immediately? People are not ashamed to take up to four helpings at meals, but when it comes to real work . . .'

Anil-da's face was sullen. As if someone had humiliated him publicly.

There are so many ways of telling the same story. It really depends on what you want to leave the listener with. If Mukut-khura would have heard from somebody in the market that the groom's younger brother didn't live and work in Delhi, as we had been told, but had joined the banned ULFA, with a vengeance, long back in the late eighties after he was tortured by the army, he would have moved straight to the backyard leaving the coloured papers either on a table in the veranda or carried them along in a trance to talk to his sister-in-law Onima. Both of them would have discussed it between themselves to arrive at a final decision of not sharing this news with the rest of the family. And if they decided to share, they would have decided to even the tone in which they would present it so that people would go on scaling borali fish, disembowelling puthi fish and mopping the courtyard—and there would be no interruption in the wedding. Aaita would have said, 'This is nothing new. Rumours reach all weddings. During my wedding, somebody came and told my parents that the groom already had another wife. But I still got married. For many years, when he used to come home late, I used to think he had gone to visit his first wife.' And Moon-baideo couldn't have cried out, 'Oh dear Anil-kai! What did you say! Why did I have to live to hear this news! It's better to cut our Moina into pieces and throw her body into the Brahmaputra than marry her off to a groom whose younger brother is a rebel!'

So many other people joined her. Some said families of all rebels and surrendered rebels were unfortunate. (So surprising. A decade ago, the same people showed off to others that they had ULFA members in their family. 'My grandmother's first cousin's son's grandson's friend's brother is an ULFA and I know him very well . . .') One day—they stressed *one day*—one day there will be no ULFA, SULFA, Bodo rebels or Karbi rebels. And along with them their families would also be wiped off the map of Assam by the army and the police. But they were not sure how many families would be killed and how many women the army would strip during search raids, during secret killing operations by masked gunmen who shot mothers, fathers, brothers, sisters-in-law, brothers-in-law, uncles of ULFA members who had not surrendered before that blessed day arrived.

If Onima-borma had got to know, she would have shared this news only with Aaita and Oholya-jethai who, in turn, would have suppressed the news, since they knew well that there was no respect for an old maid. By the time Anil-da was adding fuel into the fire by saying how Diganta Sharma, a home guard who worked in Guwahati, who had eight daughters, was dragged out from his bedroom and shot in front of his howling daughters, since his wife was the cousin of one of the ULFA members, by some masked gunmen, everybody in the house was crying and Oholya-jethai was back in her furious mode. Craning her neck, she asked Anil-da, 'Why wouldn't you tell us what you have heard?' Her default mode was suddenly back and soon after she heard from him what the matter was, she started scolding the walls, the air and the dust for getting such a match for her youngest sister. 'Who was the one who brought news of the match?'

Everyone knew that Dorongi-aaita had brought it.

All of us knew the ways of Oholya-jethai. Or maybe because all of us wanted her to get back to her venom-spewing state, we kept quiet. But though some of us kept quiet, some didn't. Eventually, everyone started speaking. Women came out, sat on the freshly mopped-up front yard and contributed similar tales. They spoke of how marriages were called off even an hour before the groom came, or even two minutes before the groom streaked the girl's forehead and middle parting with the red vermilion powder. They discussed what happened to such girls in villages. 'Nobody marries such girls. They stay on like ghosts in their parents' houses.' Unfulfilled dreams and wishes settle around their eyes to turn them into bespectacled, brooding owls.

'There is no point living like that.' A little away Onima-borma wept, failing to find the best match for her sister-in-law, that it was her mother who had brought in the news of a prospective groom a few months ago, that she couldn't perform the unfinished duty of her late husband. Perhaps that made her feel even guiltier.

'God knows why people took revenge on us this way, and for what.' Oholya-jethai's voice was becoming louder as she was becoming more and more irrational; once again she was becoming the hated one, and yet the revered one. 'Folks kept on saying—he is a good boy from a good family.' She mimicked someone, or was it Dorongi-aaita she was aiming her verbal arrows at? '*Boy?* When he came I saw he was a man! Old enough to be our bride's father. But beggars cannot be choosers! Who else will marry her now? My sister deserves much better but all men want is soft flesh, all of them want soft bodies. But our bride is so beautiful that he couldn't even take his eyes off her. And we saw he is wealthy, he would be able to feed her, clad her, but oh dear! What are we hearing now! Folks didn't even investigate properly before making the decision. Now her bad luck has settled around her head like a dark cloud!'

It didn't take her long to get back to her original self. The bitter Oholya-jethai. And when Moina-pehi rushed indoors weeping and declaring she didn't want to get married, Oholya-jethai ran after her.

'Do you want to become like me?' she hollered. She wept. All the guests, all the neighbours who had gathered, looked at the angry, broken Oholya and spoke amongst themselves. 'Poor Oholya. How much pain she has held within for so long!'

At that time, I wanted to speak out as Mridul had four years ago, saying how happy all the people were to see the Oholya who was crying. I wanted to hug her and plead with her not to cry. Not to create a scene that would be so enjoyed by the people around her. I sprinted indoors and, before more people could come in, shut the door.

I saw Anamika trying to come in, but I didn't wait for her. If I had let her come in, I would have had to let another ten women come in, eager to console Oholya, to tell her they knew how difficult it was for her to remain unmarried all her life. How happy they were. How they savoured each moment of her misery. How they enjoyed seeing the bride who refused to get married.

It was late January. The dogs were yet to stop sleeping on the warm ash of the extinguished fires, after people had fallen asleep, or on heaps of hay in the cowshed among the warmth of ruminating cows. And people still slept under blankets, if not under quilts stuffed with silk cotton. During the day, whenever the cold wind blew over the warm skins of people, they tightened their arms around themselves. Men and women who wore shawls pulled them closer. Men who wore sweaters folded their arms as they walked or stood staring at nothing with a slight hunch.

Inside, it was becoming hotter with the anxious breaths of so many women and elderly men. One of the women complained how stuffy it was and asked aloud why the door had been suddenly shut. But her query was drowned in the clamour of voices rising around us. I pushed my way in. The armpits of some people smelled like coconut water. Like clothes worn in summer for long without a wash. People were pushing, jostling. With Mridul, I followed the muffled sounds that came from the corner of the next room, which could be reached only through the room where many people were already gathered. Mukut-khura joined his hands and pleaded, 'Will you all please wait outside, if you don't mind?' It started as a small hum, like ripples left by a pebble thrown into a pond. I heard a woman grumble, 'Of course we do mind. We thought we would come and console the bride. Fine! Manage *women's matters* on your own!' It was soft but sharp like glass. I opened my mouth to say there were enough women in that room, they should leave and not worry. But before I could say something, Mukut-khura patted my shoulder. 'Don't say anything, Pablo.' Mridul pushed me into the other room. And there she was, taking off her new ornaments, wiping off the blood-red sindoor from her forehead and the straight middle parting of her hair made by her mother-in-law. 'I won't get married. Why can't I stay in this house forever?' Meenu-jethai and Onima-borma had become even more hysterical than her. They held her hand, pushed her on to the bed and let her cry there. 'You shouldn't do this! You shouldn't do this!' Mridul said there was nothing to worry and Anil-da repeated after him, adding that rumours always managed to sneak into a wedding house. Mukut-khura said, 'My daughter, my youngest sister, please don't behave like this, my child. Don't get scared by such things. There is government in this country. There is law and order in this country. No one can kill anyone so easily. The papers report only the bad news, don't worry, everything will be fine.' But she was not listening.

Perhaps too many people were saying the same thing at the same time in different ways, and so she continued to cry, louder and louder her screams became, and once I wondered if she was in some sort of acute physical pain and couldn't explain it to us.

There is government. Such rumours come to all wedding houses. My parents heard my future husband had already taken a wife. There is law and order in this country. My child, please don't behave like this. Do you want to remain an old maid like me? There is law and order in this country this is just a small rumour. Please don't cry. There is government suchrumours come to all wedding houses myparents heard the groom already hadawife there is law and order mychild, please don't behave likethis do you want to remain an old maid likeme there is lawandorder inthiscountry this is just a smallrumo urplease don'tcrysuchru mourco met oallwedd ingsm yparent she ard-al readyhadawifethereislawoldmaidlikemecountrythisisjustasmall rumourplease . . .

And then, it was at that moment, I knew I really needed some air.

~

Without a second thought, I left the room with some unknown desire to scream and cry but there were so many people that I couldn't, and since I couldn't scream, lie down on the ground, bury my face in the ground and weep, I feared I would die, lose my breath. With the force of a squall, I pushed open the door, stepped on to the courtyard where the borali-fish scales and the disembowelled puthi fish were still lying on a banana leaf and Anamika was sitting there, chasing flies. I looked away when she looked at me, rushed right into Mridul's room and lay myself down on the bed where I slept at night. I got up after a few minutes. Restless. Wild. Not knowing what to do. I tried to tell myself, I shouldn't care. It was all a lost cause. Nobody cared for Moina-pehi. All everyone cared for was another mouth to feed, another old maid, what people would think if the wedding was called off. Nothing to be done. Nothing could be done. What will happen to us. Our community. Our people. Our state.

I wanted to think of something else, but the image of Moina-pehi howling in pain, the white of Mamoni's eyes, loomed over me like the charred remains of electrocuted bats from electric poles. Suddenly I felt something heavy on my right shoulder. The tears that I was longing to get out of my system were showering upon my shoulder, shaking me, taking shelter in me.

I turned around, shrugging off the throbbing, sobbing, shaking face from my shoulder and stared at Mridul for some time. 'Deuta always wanted Moina-pehi's wedding to be the best wedding in the whole village.' He could hardly speak. 'What will happen now?'

'It's a rumour, Mridul. Relax.'

'No, it's not! Anil-da has heard it from Lokhimai-pehi. Her son's marriage was fixed with a girl who lives in the same village. It can't be a rumour. Pehi heard it yesterday when they went to fix the date of the wedding.'

Even before we realized we were speaking to each other again, the storm twisting my insides pushed me out of his room. Walking across the eerily silent village path, I knew I would have to scream my lungs out that day, otherwise I would die. I sat on

the banks of the Brahmaputra for a long time. I couldn't scream.
I wanted to jump into it. Really.

~

That night, Mridul left with his duffel bag. The red duffel bag he
used for long journeys. For special journeys.

He was chasing dreams. His ambition to be a daring example
for 'future lovers'—not rebels.

When he got to know that Moina-pehi was moaning again,
breathing normally once again, had retched out all the fear she
had in her mind since her body was unable to absorb them, he
left. He walked slowly out of the house, after everyone had
fallen asleep. Even after Phulam, Junti and Dangor-bhonti had
dozed off—who usually went to bed after everyone else would
be in the middle of their first dream. Dorongi-aaita went to bed,
after sprinkling a palmful of water into the hearth and shutting
the bamboo door of the kitchen. Following her usual routine,
Onima-borma checked if each and every door and window of
the house was latched and then retired for the day.

In those days of the wedding, people stayed up till late,
working, peeling vegetables, decorating the pandal, chatting,
cracking jokes, cleaning, folding clothes, soaking clothes to be
washed the next day, arranging the upturned, disorderly chairs.
Children played train-train, guys playfully stalked girls, girls
enjoyed being playfully stalked. Mridul didn't look into my eyes as
he walked out into the stillness of the night, the empty courtyard
ready to greet the groom's family and the guests the next day
with flowers, the green chairs, flower-patterned bamboo mats and
the cool shade of the green, blue, red tent waiting for the guests.

I looked at his back. It was not straight. It was the back of a person who had the guilty expression of a convict in his eyes and, this time, I knew he was not searching for at least another pair of eyes where he could plant some of his guilt.

I wanted to scream out loud and ask him how he had the heart to go. All for love? I couldn't approve of such love, love that makes you so thoughtlessly selfish. Love that blossoms in a graveyard of fear. Underneath it, black, lonely fear multiplies like worms, eating away at the root of such love.

The storm started churning within me again, reminding me that I was yet to scream it out of my system, urging me to weep my sorrows out.

I wondered what was making me so restless. So wild that I thought I would faint if I stood still staring at the darkness which had absorbed the yellow-shirt-clad figure of Mridul. I walked up to the gate, stood under the arch from where yellow marigold garlands hung. Why did he go? How could he be so selfish? He should have stood by his family at this time. The next day, Anil-da would work for many hours with Jethpeha and Roton and create a beautiful design. It would greet the guests, the groom's family and friends. Someone would sing, breaking the silence, eyes would look for the groom's brother with the hope that he had come back from Delhi—that's the lie the groom's family had told us when Mukut-khura had asked where he lived and what he did—to attend his brother's wedding and would be disappointed.

Inside, Onima-borma would weep, murmuring, 'I think what Anil said is true.'

She would cry in front of Meenu-jethai and Meenu-jethai would tell Mridul, who would move away without speaking. She would ask me what was wrong with Mridul and I would say, 'I don't know. I don't know, Borma.' Outside, scores of people would laugh, singing bawdy wedding songs:

Ripe tomatoes,
    Ripe tomatoes;
Girl-greedy groom,
    You reached too soon.

And someone from the groom's side would sing in reply to the girl who had sung those lines:

Mahogany tree's wooden plank,
    Mahogany tree's wooden plank;
The mouth of the girl who sings
    Opens and shuts with a noisy clank.

The fragrance of rajanigandha flowers floated in the air. Rajanigandha. The flower that smells at night. The flower that rules the night, attracts snakes as screw-pine flowers do. Its long, slender stalks smooth like a baby's cheeks. The smell that could make anyone forlorn. I had to go out and tell someone I wanted to weep, and also add that I didn't know why I wanted to weep. I wanted to go back. I wanted to call Mom and say, 'Send the car tomorrow, I want to leave,' but I didn't want to walk all the way to the market where I could access a phone.

I walked back to the courtyard. From the courtyard, I walked back to the entrance. I kept pacing like that for some time.

Sometimes you don't need to say a thing. You know the person standing in front of you understands, wants to hold you, and you just move ahead, without any invitation, suggestion, beckoning, knowing that shoulder is yours, those soft breasts are yours. My hands were around her waist and my face digging into her breasts so fast, that I didn't have time to think, or even ask, why she was there, what was she doing there, if a strange wind was also destroying her from inside.

Turning back from the arched marigold-flower gate, I had seen her and I had known she was asking me with those eyes what was wrong. Language was inadequate to express that feeling. Only by embracing her waist, only by pressing my face to her soft breasts could I let her know what was raging inside me. It was then that I knew I needed her.

We walked to the backyard. We saw the heap of ash and sand next to a large bucket of water for washing dishes. We walked ahead. We heard the chirping of birds. The sounds of their wings flapping, questioning each other who that couple was that walked below. From their nests, they observed our movements till we reached the large heap of fresh, warm hay. Even the cold wind didn't urge us to search for warmth in the heap of hay, search for the sun which had left us many hours ago. We didn't even know when. When she sat down, her black-bordered, bright-yellow dotted sador had already slipped from her body. She was trying to read a story in my eyes even in that dark, in my restless behaviour of an explorer as she opened her blouse, her bra, and introduced me to herself. Bit by bit. With my right hand, I pushed up her black homespun-cotton mekhela with orange and yellow flowers blooming on it, and she moved my hand away, stood, unfastened its knot, stood naked in front of my eyes, sat down again, waiting for my hands to make a move. She extended her hands to unzip, unbutton my ridiculously expensive Lee Cooper jeans, the white cotton shirt I wore that was rumpled like waste paper, and kissed my chest. With her teeth, she held my skin and pulled at it. With her fingers she pulled at the hair on my chest. With her nails, she pinched my right nipple. It made me laugh. She giggled. She laughed too. Softly.

I slid myself out of her mouth and wanted to ask her where

she had learnt this since this was something I had only seen in the forbidden films I had watched with Probal. I didn't have time to wonder if I would tell Probal about this episode in my life. It was a different part of my life, distinct from the life I led in the city and remained unsaid, hidden from Probal, with whom I shared all my secrets. Perhaps, it was too fragile a secret to be shared. And it was too transient to be told to another person. Yet it cost one of us much too dearly.

So we just told each other how much we were enjoying ourselves. Without words. Silently. With the rhythmic movement of our bodies, with our impatient hands, our nails digging into each other's bodies. With urgency. The readiness of our hands, the kisses, the tongues, told us there was nothing wrong with what we were doing.

So she pulled me to her. Squeezed me into the path that I explored for warmth, since there was not enough warmth left in the hay any more.

In our initial movements, we had let that warmth in the mound of hay escape like dust in a mattress spread in sunlight, like camphor in a container left open. And we realized that the warmth of our bodies was something more reassuring than the sun stored in the yellow hay that shone like gold under the white moon.

I was nervous.

She was not.

Or was she?

Later, I tried to reconstruct that moment many times in my mind, in Guwahati, in Delhi. Before my pre-boards. After my boards and after I started working in Delhi.

Many times, even after years.

I liked to think that she was nervous, like me.

I liked to think, she too thought that every part of me was like a new alphabet.

But actually she did not. She was the one who undressed me. Touched me where no one had touched me before. Kissed in places that no one had seen before. Caressed me between my legs with her warm palms, making me shudder from my spine to the deepest cores of my brain, my heart.

She looked down below, laughed and then asked me if it was all for her and I smiled, saying yes, it was indeed for her, for her stories, for the way she held fireflies in her palms, for her long braid that could tether a goat.

She was the teacher. Introducing me to the letters, naming them for me and I followed, learnt the curves, the expressions, where my tongue should touch as I spoke out each of them.

And when the explosion of sentences came, gushing out, chattering, I hated it. I hated the wet feeling between my legs, the spread away of her once-upon-a-time-taut breasts, the cool feeling on my quickly drying skin, the itch on my inner thighs because of the hay. I disliked that moment of feeling spent so much that I would have loved it to restart. I loved that moment of feeling spent so much that I would have loved to go back to where we started.

But I didn't know what to do. She was lying there, with a smile on her face. Her eyes, half-opened like a child sleeping.

We started to cry. She cried, then laughed a little, saying that she couldn't understand what I murmured but told me distinctly that she didn't want to go back home and live with her brother. I asked her to keep quiet, and when she didn't, I pressed my lips on to hers, felt hers, hungry, on mine. And when we parted, she said that she would have loved to go and live with me, but it all ended with that wedding; it was impractical, and it was sad that our lives would continue as they were. When I said that I loved her, she said that she knew I was lying but didn't mind hearing it again and again since it made her happy. I wept and said again and again that I loved her and she laughed.

A little later, I thought about the fireflies and the people who had come for the wedding.

She moved away, her back and bottom to me, her sweat glistening in the moonlight.

A few strands of hay stuck on her back. There were some more on her bottom.

I brushed the hay off her body. The ant that crawled on her skin. In the cold, I shivered, and my sweat dried fast.

She sat up, her breasts hanging slightly, like weaver birds' nests.

How she laughed then. I couldn't believe she was crying just some time ago.

She teased me.

She said I looked scared.

I said I was not.

She laughed and I knew she had guessed it.

Suddenly I was shy.

It was a different kind of shyness. Not like that of the naked king who thinks he is wearing new clothes.

A shyness that was aroused by the cold air that suddenly ran between my legs since her palm was not there any more, making me aware of the limpness, of my jeans that had slid down to my ankles.

In the same teasing tone, she asked me if I planned to spend all night there. Hurriedly, I pulled up my white underwear and my jeans, and zipped up. 'No. I will go in a while,' I replied.

Smiling brightly, she announced she was leaving; it was too late, and someone might be looking for her. She bent down and kissed my mouth. She used her tongue. Her teeth. Her hands slid down and scratched my belly.

She left.

Like a dream.

Confident. With a straight back. Happy. Unaware that six months later, she would *leave* us. I will never know why.

What was she thinking when she was dying, with blood streaming out from between her legs? She loved going for long walks. Holding fireflies that floated like dreams, shining in the air, blinking at night like flickering wishes. People say fireflies are souls of people with unfulfilled wishes, souls of people who died when they shouldn't have.

She left. Like a dream.

As she walked away on the soil, she wrote our story on it with the depressions made by her feet.

A story that looked like a foot.

With five toes.

A story that moved in five more directions.

So confident she was. So happy.

'Our story ends here,' she had said, before leaving, before leaving imprints of the same story on the soil, as she walked away, crushing the dry leaves.

Branching out into five different directions, they were actually the prologues to another series of stories.

Acknowledgements

Dipti Dutta Das and Surjya Das for giving me the values, for teaching me the importance of dignity and humility, for telling me early on that life must rest on ideals. Krishanu Kashyap, Mini-baideo, the late Rajani Dutta: for their trust and love. Jhulan Krishna Mahanta, Nabish Alam, Pallab Lungthulu: best friends, who decided to become my fans way back in their early teens without reading anything I wrote. The late Indira Goswami: the most important person in my life after my parents; I can never speak enough about your positive influence in my life.

Dipanwita Shome, Kuhu Tanvir, Sharbani Chattoraj: special thanks for reading and critiquing the first draft, for your perennial support. The late Ashish Roy, Rajeev Nair, Smita Gandotra: for being the kind of teachers every student dreams of having. Ashmi Ahluwalia, Anannya Barua, Isawanda Laloo, Ribhu Borphukon, Pranav Prakash, Priyasha Mukhopadhyay, Saumya Premchander, Shreya Chakraborti: dearest friends, for understanding when emails and calls went unanswered, for bearing with me all these years, for making me sure when I am unsure, for reading shitty first drafts. Aditya Sudarshan, Kanishka Gupta, Nii Ayikwei Parkes, Rahul Soni, Sumana Roy, Vaibhav Vats: for beating my drum, always; for listening, when things looked too dark. It is rare to find friends like you.

Namita Gokhale: for your tremendous support, for your friendship, for screaming at me occasionally, for always telling me the harsh truths. David Godwin: for believing, for responding to the foolish query letter of a college student and taking on the hard task of representing me on the basis of that messy first draft. Anand Prakash, Mridula Koshy, Rana Dasgupta, Shivam Vij, Vivek Narayanan: for your early encouragement, for your razor-sharp, honest feedback on my unripe writing. Ravi Singh: for ushering in the manuscript to Penguin India. Somak Ghoshal: for changing the fate of this book with your Midas touch, for editing 'our book' so wisely, thoughtfully. Thank you, I am indebted for life. Chiki Sarkar: for making me feel safe, for your generous help, for being such an amazing person to work with. Shruti Narain: for carefully, thoughtfully copy-editing the book. Paloma Dutta: for reading the proofs meticulously.

Amit Rahul Baishya, Arup Kumar Nath, Anuradha Sharma Pujari, Dhruba Jyoti Borah, Diganta Oza, Geetali Borah, Homen Borgohain, Jahnavi Barua, Jayanta Saikia, Mitra Phukan, Manoram Gogoi, Preeti Gill, Russell C. Leong, Sanjib Baruah, Sanjib Pol Deka, Shelley Fisher Fishkin, Uddipana Goswami: I am grateful for your generous, unconditional support, guidance and friendship—always admired you for the kind of work you have done.